FLASH

MALORIE VERDANT

For my mom,
The redhead in my life who taught me the
value of hard work, honesty and compassion.

Human life is as evanescent as the morning dew or a flash of lightning.
Samuel Butler

Who steals my purse steals trash.
William Shakespeare

PROLOGUE

COOPER

Two Years Ago

I'VE ALWAYS HATED the word family.

I've also hated home.

Safe.

Love.

Because their definitions never reflected the truths I witnessed. Shit like betrayal, indifference, pain, and cruelty were concealed within those words. They were like fucking Trojan horses: deceptively harmless while patiently waiting to destroy everything and everyone they touched.

But I kept my opinions to myself. I listened to the cop tell me, "Look, usually we can't release a minor into anyone but his *family's* custody, because we need to think of the boy's *safety*—" and then showed him the money.

Money always cut through the bullshit.

"Okay then." The officer slipped the crisp note in his pocket before handing over the paperwork for me to sign. Since it wasn't the first time I'd done this, nor would it be the last, I kept the pleasantries to a minimum. I signed my name, grabbed the keys I left on the counter, and gestured with my head for Jake to make a move toward the exit.

The moment we stepped out of the concrete money pit, I tried to do the sane thing. I attempted to convince Jake to stop this shit.

"You can't keep doing this," I muttered as we walked toward my car.

"Lay off," he grunted before power walking ahead of me. Pissed off at the world as usual.

I watched in frustration as he swaggered like a wannabe gangsta, completely unaware that he didn't look cool or tough. His exaggerated shoulder drop just emphasized that he was an eleven-year-old with more brashness than brains.

I watched from a distance as the little twerp climbed into the passenger seat of my fully restored Mustang and slammed the door closed. He knew that would piss me off. The car was the only gift I'd ever received in my seventeen years. Apart from my closest friends, it was the one thing I gave two shits about. I exhaled, raked a hand through my still bed-messy brown hair, and walked slowly to the driver side door.

He's just a kid. Even if he's trying to convince everyone and their dog that he's the next Jesse James, he's still one of mine.

It didn't make me any calmer.

"You think Mitch and Doreen are going to keep watching you?" I gritted out when I climbed into the driver seat and turned to meet his sullen gray eyes. My hand rested on the keys I put in the ignition. "You think if they find out you've been picked up by the cops at 4:00 a.m. three times in the last two weeks that they aren't going to send you back to the group home?" I asked as I started the engine, trying to keep my voice level. "You think their lazy asses are gonna be okay with coming to pick you up from the station the next time I can't make it? Or there's a different cop in charge of bookings?"

"What the fuck do I care? Ain't nothing I'm not used to," he barked before turning to glare out the car window. He watched as we traveled away from the nicest part of town with its fancy Penmore College football signs in every window and people wandering the streets in college jerseys holding fancy cups of hot coffee.

It didn't take long before we'd passed all the manicured lawns and headed to where we belonged. The place where rubbish filled the gutters and no one cared about mowing their nature strips or buying soy lattes. Looking at us now, in our secondhand ripped jeans and grease-stained white cotton shirts, no one would know that even this neighborhood was a step up from where we came from.

"Eli still runs group," I sighed, losing some of the anger in my voice thinking about where we came from. "I can't be there anymore. You know I had to get Lizzie out. You go back, I'm not there to protect you. Social services won't let us take you. Not until we both turn eighteen. We also need an income that'll support all of us."

When he looked at me with his eyes filled with fear, I coolly reminded him, "Look, you aren't going back. I won't let that happen. I won't tell Doreen or Mitch about the shit you've been pulling. But you need to start realizing that you've got a good thing going at the moment. I need you to not fuck it up. It's only going to be a little longer before we can all live together."

"Whatever. I don't even care. And quit with the lectures already. I get that you think you're my boss or whatever, but you're not," he told me before he raked his hands through his surfer blonde locks and stared out the window again, hiding his fear with false bravado. "We're not family."

Fuck, I hate that word.

I exhaled and softly murmured, "We all know that word means shit. You, Lizzie, Beth, and I, we're always going to be there for one another. That's why you called me. Always there, no matter what. But listen, Jake, you need to help me. You need to stop this crap. You're only eleven. You've got a longer juvie record than birthdays, and you've still managed to get a pretty sweet setup. You fighting with cops, tagging buildings, and painting trains has to end. You're good. You got skills, man. Give me a month and I'll have enough put aside from working with Al to pay for some art classes. Keep you busy till we've got everything sorted. But you need to promise me that you'll quit doing stupid shit that requires the cops to arrest you."

"Like I need some pussy art classes to learn to paint fucking flowers," Jake muttered, rolling his eyes.

"You don't want them, fine. The cash is yours either way. Do what you want with it. You can start saving for your own car and spray the shit out of that. I just need you to stop this crap you're pulling."

"I should've called Lizzie," he whined, reminding me of how young he was.

"Dude, we've talked about this. We don't want her known as the girl constantly going to different police stations to bail out friends. We've got twelve months before we can talk to child services about getting Beth back. We need to finish school. They won't even lift a finger if they think we're a bad influence. Don't fuck this up, Jake."

"But you've found Beth? You know where she is now?"

"Not yet. We think she might be staying in a foster house near the train tracks. We won't stop looking though."

"You think she'll end up back in group? Without us?"

"Let's not think about it."

"You'll tell me, right? If you find her?"

"Of course. We're in this together. How about breakfast before I have to take you back to the Walters'?"

"Bagels?"

"Fuck yeah."

———

JAKE INHALED HIS second bagel while talking excitedly about some other street kid he met in lockup. Little punk could make friends with a cockroach if he spent long enough time with it in a cell.

I think he was telling me about the kid's facial tattoo or his pet lizard, but I wasn't paying much attention.

I kept looking over Jake's head, ignoring his hand gestures and staring at a fucking princess.

She was straight out of that old storybook Lizzie used to make me read to Beth, the mermaid one. The only damn kid's book I knew back to front because it used to stop Beth from crying during her first weeks at the home. I even pretended to see the red-haired princess in every sand pit or community swimming pool to make Beth smile.

I would've been certain that the girl sitting in the corner was a figment of my imagination if it weren't for the black smudges under her sparkling blue eyes and the to-go coffee cup in her delicate hand.

I was about to look away, focus on Jake's story, when she started laughing. I wasn't even sure I could actually hear her across the crowded coffee shop, but I *felt* her.

"I'm done," Jake yelled, inches away from my face, causing me to flinch and turn toward him.

"Fuck, you're a dick sometimes," I told him, wiping away the spit he got on my cheek. He burst out laughing and shifted in his seat to gaze at the redhead.

"She's hot," he said, looking at me with an all-knowing grin plastered on his boyish face.

I rolled my eyes. "Already noted."

"Then why aren't we walking over there?" His eyebrows rose. "You're not terrible-looking, even with that stupid beard you're trying to grow. And sure, girls love blonds more, but she's too old for me. I could maybe offer to draw her if you need an excuse? Give you a fighting chance to try and impress her. I'll even let you buy the sketch and give it to her as a gift and shit. I'll give you a *sweet* deal."

"Okay, for the record, girls like brunettes way more than blonds. When you get old enough, you'll be dying it every Friday night trying to look as good as me," I chuckled. "And kid, you're thinking about that library book again and forgetting this town ain't Paris. No one just walks up to strangers and offers to draw them here. It's creepy. Now here, take my keys. I'll pay, and then we should probably take you home before Mitch and Doreen start to worry."

"They won't worry," he muttered quietly before getting this far-off look in his eyes. "When I'm your age, I'm going to offer to draw every girl, and I bet it works for me *every* time."

"Buddy, you do that when you're my age and it works, I'll buy us beers and toast to your skills," I replied, laughing at the smile that twitched at his lips.

"Sweet," Jake murmured before reaching for my keys. "But seriously, Coop, you aren't even going to go over there?"

"Jake, look what her friend is wearing," I said to him softly. "That's a Penmore sweatshirt. Probably both college chicks. Those girls aren't interested in guys like us."

"Guys like us?" he parroted, his eyebrows pulling together.

"Yeah. Badass motherfuckers," I told him, putting him in a headlock until he pulled himself out, laughing like the victor seconds before scrambling toward the café's door and my car. I couldn't help but grin at the fact that in his mad dash to remain victorious, he looked less like a wannabe gangsta and more like the kid I wanted him to be.

After I paid, I took one last look at the princess.

Only in a fairy tale could someone like me get to talk to someone like her. As I pushed open the door, I shook my head to rid myself of the stupid ideas filling my brain.

I knew things had seemed to be looking up recently, but my life was no fucking fairy tale.

ONE

MILLIE

Present Day

I WAS NOT going to cry. He didn't deserve it.

That fuckhead with his "I can't wait to take you out" and "You choose, babe, no matter the expense, and I'll pay." I should've known this was how my evening would go.

It was thirty minutes past the time he was meant to arrive and I was still sitting there alone, my perfectly painted red nails tapping faster and faster on the white tablecloth. I took one final glance at the garlic bread balls sitting in the middle of the table—which I had been so excited about tasting when he arrived—before I accepted that all I would be stomaching that evening was bitterness.

He didn't hurt my heart. Hell no. I was not that girl anymore.

My pride, however, had taken a serious knock. It was way past the time that I should've left.

Leaving money on the table to cover my diet Cokes, I finally stood up, tried desperately not to wobble on my icepick heels, and headed toward the exit. I was careful not to make eye contact with anyone.

I decided that had to be the moment. It wasn't just about a douchebag with greased black hair conning me. I needed to give dating the "I'm done."

Trying to perfect my mascara and squeeze into controlled briefs. The hours spent shaving, plucking and concealing. It wasn't right. I should've been at home eating fried chicken and wearing a kiwi face mask while I watched the latest episode of *Keeping up with the Kardashians*.

Dating wasn't worth the hassle.

I might've told myself that if I were getting my life back together, I needed to start putting myself out there again. But now I knew that was wrong. As I weaved my way through the tables, I noticed all of the girls who weren't stood up that evening staring at their partner devotedly. Even with my head down, I couldn't help but think it was *nauseating*. I didn't need that in my life.

I never wanted to lose myself in someone else. Not again.

Granted, I hoped that everyone in the room stayed pretty oblivious, too engrossed with each other's perfect teeth to cause me further mortification. Having carefully pinned up my red curls, my face was exposed. Anyone looking could see the furrowed brow and pursed lips. I could only imagine that my face was somewhere between a pissed-off Jim Mora at a press conference and a Britney Spears circa 2007 breakdown. With one glance, patrons would most likely see that I was pissed about wasting my evening—and teetering on the edge of poor choices. Their chairs would make that scratching noise against the floorboards as they pulled away from my direction.

Thankfully no matter how hard they stared at me, they wouldn't know what a fool I'd been.

How I'd been bowled over by a pretty face.

Excited for the possibilities to come.

Too busy dreaming of a happily ever after to see the reality in front of me.

Damn, I'm an idiot.

As I slid into my cheap pickup truck, I couldn't help but wonder if this entire evening was some sort of punishment for overlooking the fact that my beautiful epilogue had already been written.

I might not be living a fairy-tale ending. I might not have a prince charming. I might not even have someone willing to pay for a twenty-dollar steak and sit opposite a damn restaurant table from me. But I had my baby. I had a little girl, who at that very moment was probably already asleep in her cot, sucking her little thumb between her precious pink lips. I just needed to focus on ways to improve her life.

I loved the hell out of my little girl.

I did whatever was needed to ensure that she was safe, without ruining my mascara.

I didn't need more than that.

—

IT WAS DARK when I unlocked the door to our dilapidated three-bedroom home. The blue light of the television illuminated the wooden coffee table and brown leather armchairs in the lounge room. The rest of the house was shrouded in darkness.

I noticed Tahnee was asleep on the couch, her thin glasses still perched on her nose. She must've returned home early and relieved the babysitter. She was always saving me money, always helping me out.

The embarrassment of the evening intensified.

I shouldn't be putting her in this position anymore. I should be capable of handling things on my own by now.

I took a look at the television and saw an old episode of *Outlander* still playing on the screen. The show's soundtrack seeping softly from our television's speakers—the blending of flutes, drums, and the sound of dancing feet—soothed the sharp edges of my annoyance and self-pity.

I decided to wake Tahnee later. She could continue watching her favorite episode in the morning and be able to enjoy Jamie Fraser much more with daylight helping to illuminate his abdominal muscles.

I just needed to see to one thing first.

She was always the first thing I saw to when I stepped through our slightly tattered front door. Before I slipped off my heels, dropped my handbag, or even thought about sitting on our old porch swing and staring forlornly at the decaying front porch slats.

I went to my baby before everything.

Moving down our thin hallway silently, I approached the brightest white door—the only door we bothered giving a fresh coat of paint when we first bought the place—and carefully turned the handle.

When I poked my head into the light pink room, I could already see Jessie fast asleep between the cracks in the cot. Her dark brown hair curled around her ears, her fists tightly clenched, fighting off invisible demons just like her mama.

I should've closed the door.

I definitely shouldn't have walked in and wasted another evening staring at her, but I couldn't help myself. I stepped inside the room to get a close-up look at her beautiful long black lashes. To stare at her rosy pink cheeks pressed against soft gray sheets covered in white elephants. Breathe in her sweet scent: a combination of lavender baby powder and innocence. I knew one day soon she'd need a big-girl bed.

I brushed my finger across her soft cheek. As I took in her chestnut locks and the shape of her eyebrows, I couldn't help but see her dad. If her eyes were open, they too would reveal where she came from, the bright green sparkling like his used to.

There wasn't a trace of me across her delicate features. Nosy people on the street who stopped us on the corner, wanting to play with a smiling baby, have always made the same stupid comment: "Shame she didn't get your red curls." They didn't know what they were talking about.

She was perfect.

I leaned over the cot so I could feel Jessie's chest rise and fall. It wasn't too big a risk; nothing ever woke her up. For the first month after bringing her home, I was scared shitless by how deep she slept. I was constantly afraid that she wasn't breathing, listing in my mind all the things I could've done wrong. Eventually I got over the fact that she wasn't like every baby on TV. There would be no crying and screaming and keeping her parents up all night; instead I had an angel in bed at night and a devil in the day.

I lightly ran my fingers through her soft curls one last time before using all my willpower to leave her sleeping and return to Tahnee.

I switched off the TV, then encouraged Tahnee to go to bed and let me clean up the mess. I told her I would go into detail about my nonexistent date the following morning over breakfast. I then cleaned up her evening snacks and headed to my own bedroom.

When I lived with my parents, my room used to be various shades of pink. There were hot pink silk flowers and sparkling trinkets I'd collected from local garage sales on display. But when Tahnee sold her one-bedroom colonial home so the homeless girl who had a one-time fling with her son, and her future granddaughter could live with her in a small three-bedroom home, I decided to reinvent myself.

I lived life efficiently here. Practically. I surrounded myself in chocolate browns, grays, and blacks, furniture and fabric that wouldn't show Jessie's fascination with emptying my makeup bag or squishing liquids into carpet threads with her fingers. My bedroom also had minimal decoration—fewer objects to be swallowed or knocked over. I thought I would prove my parents wrong in interior decorating alone; I could and would be grown up enough to handle my own baby.

When I finally pulled off my heels and slid out of my tight black dress, I went straight to my bed. It wasn't the first time that I scolded myself internally for not taking off my makeup, but I was too tired to spend another second on my feet.

I made a silent prayer as I climbed under the covers. Then I tried to envision myself happily sipping a Mai Tai in Maui. I pictured the floral dress I would wear and the little purple flower that would rest on the glass, tried to imagine the sounds of waves crashing against the ocean.

But as I fell asleep, the picture I planned faded. The dream turned into a nightmare. I was trapped in the past—in purgatory.

Where I see him.

Feel him.

Lose him.

All over again.

"You're hogging all the covers," Nate chuckled as he walked into the room, placing the glass of water on the bedside table.

"Well after what you just did to my body, it needs as much comfort as it can get," I told him smugly, hugging the blankets tighter to my body.

"Are you complaining?" He leaned over to kiss my shoulder before quickly

pulling all the sheets off my body with one sharp tug.

Fuck, it was cold.

"No," I muttered before reaching behind me and grasping a corner of the sheets, tugging the corner in an attempt to cover myself. Unfortunately, that action turned into war. It was ludicrous. I was exhausted and yet I was naked on my knees in the middle of his queen-size bed, playing tug of war with sheets. The sound of my laughter filled his small bedroom. Seconds before I could declare victory, Nate pulled the covers completely out of my reach and above his head. As a result, I was looking up at the stunning man, freezing cold in the middle of the bed, captured in his vivid green eyes. And that smirk. Damn, he was good-looking.

"I win. Now move over, Pamela, before you freeze, and if you're nice, maybe I'll share some of my covers," he ordered before climbing onto the bed. With one arm, he managed to pull me backward until we were both snuggling in the middle of the mattress.

"Stop calling me Pamela," I chuckled, pulling the sheets up above my chest, which Nate had conveniently left uncovered after spreading the duvet over our bodies.

"Nope, no can do. Parky will get angry at me, and this way I can admit to nothing."

"You can admit to nothing?"

"Millie? Who? What? I'm pretty sure she went to bed straight after the Halloween party. Nope, that wasn't me. I was with someone else."

"So, you don't plan on ever using my name?"

"Maybe, when I have her permission and call you tomorrow."

I couldn't help but snort. "You? You're going to call me?"

"Hey, I can call."

"Babe, you have a guest robe hanging on the back of your bedroom door. As in you have so many guests over who are naked and can't find their clothes that you need to provide them with a spare robe. I also don't even live here. I just flew in, remember?"

"Don't be hating on the robe. I'm just really hospitable. Not that it matters now, of course. Maybe I'll get your name stitched into the spare one. You're also totally going to move now that you've had a taste of me. Lock me down before some floozy tries to trap me."

"Is that right?"

"Yep. We'll wait a couple of months after you've moved here before we start living together, of course. Otherwise we might get called crazy. But straight after that we'll move in together, have two kids—twins, of course. I vote we call them both Jessie and save on that normal 'my parents forget my name' business. Although we might get a dog first. You'll want to practice your parenting skills, and I wouldn't mind the kids growing up with a trained dog."

Before I can come up with a comeback, my heart stuck in my throat, he starts singing.

What the fuck?

"Are you really singing the lyrics to the Laverne *and* Shirley *theme song right now? How do you even know that?" I asked, focusing on the absurdity of the situation rather than my racing heart.*

"Yep. Mom had a thing for old TV shows when I was growing up, and I'm just that awesome. Get used to it, Mil—Pam. We're a couple now. How do you feel about Labradoodles?"

"And when I don't hear from you in the morning?" I laughed.

"Babe, I'm a guy. You've got to give me at least a month to freak out. Then I'll come crawling back. It's a rite of passage."

I chuckled against his throat as he wrapped his arms around me, cocooning our bodies together underneath the covers.

"Fine, fine, I'll see you in a month. Now go to sleep," I murmured, smiling.

Even in my sleep, the memory of his heart beating beneath mine, his soft chuckle filling the air, and the romantic notion of a fairy-tale future we might have together squeezed at my heart, crushing it until tears seeped from my closed eyes. I couldn't remember the last time I woke up without puffy eyes. The following day would be no different.

I kept working toward a new life, but if life didn't destroy me during the day, it always defeated me in the dark. Night after night.

TWO

COOPER

"VISITORS MUST STAY behind the yellow line," the guard announced sternly to all the people waiting outside the prison gates.

Surprisingly, it needed to be said.

Some people were going crazy. They were clamoring to see their loved ones, holding up fucking balloons and pets in the air. At least three of them were snapping photos with their cell phones like it was Christmas day.

I didn't get it.

I was holding a brown cardboard box, had fifty dollars in my pocket and a cage behind me. The last thing I wanted was to immortalize that shit and stare at it for years to come.

As soon as the gates opened, I planned on getting a taxi to take me far away from this place as fast as possible. No big reunion or fucking celebratory cake. Definitely no selfie sticks. As I stepped outside the prison wire, I couldn't help but think, *Who the fuck even thinks to bring a selfie stick?*

When I spotted Lizzie weaving through the crowd—her pixie blonde hair, shaved partially on one side, and big emerald eyes making her stand out amongst the masses—my body went rigid.

"Told you not to come," I grunted when she planted herself in front of me.

"And when have I ever listened to you?" she replied, raising one eyebrow. Even in her black combat boots, Lizzie barely reached my shoulders. I was certain she thought her punk rock outfit—which included a bedazzled tutu—made her look hardcore, but all it did was make her look like a purple flower. She didn't belong there.

"Was hoping this would be the first," I gritted out before frowning at her boots standing on that damn yellow line.

The more I thought about the consequences of her being there, the angrier I got. My jaw clenched. I wanted to hurt something. I had so much pain coursing through my body with no way to fix it. Her presence couldn't have come at a worse time. I was the last person she should be around.

"What about Beth?" I asked, hating how this one visit might affect them.

"Coop, relax. She's at school. No one knows I'm here. Just get into my car and let me give you a ride. Your stupid letter said you don't have to go to the halfway house, but failed to mention where you're staying. So I'm here to find out."

"If you're here to try and change my mind, don't start," I told her, not moving an inch.

"Dude, just get in my car. I'll drop you wherever the hell you want to stay, and then you can do whatever the fuck you want to do," she groaned, completely oblivious to my anger, my concern, and the scene she was causing.

"Okay," I agreed, my lips twitching at the way her entire face became red. When Lizzie got angry, her ghost-white complexion turned tomato red. As kids, I was always trying to stir her up enough to see the color change. Now it reminded me of all the things I had missed when I was locked up.

As we walked toward her car, she started talking to me as she stared straight ahead. "Now that you've stopped acting like a toddler, you want to tell me how you are?"

"I'm good."

"You look different," she said quietly, taking a quick side glance at the tattoo sleeve that now ran up the length of my left arm, the way my muscles bulged against my T-shirt, and the beard that had grown some since my last day in court before she diverted her gaze.

I knew I looked five years older than my age. I wasn't sorry about it. It did no one any good looking like a nineteen-year-old kid in prison.

"I had a lot of free time on the inside," I replied nonchalantly. "Decided to work out."

I knew it wasn't the answer she wanted to hear or the question she was really asking. I could see it in her eyes. If prison transformed me so dramatically on the outside, she was scared how much it'd changed me on the inside. The concern in her body language and her tone still managed to yank at my buried emotions. I wished I could tell her I was the same guy she'd said goodbye to. Or at least a reformed man.

For her, I'd lie. But we both knew it wasn't the case.

I wasn't ever coming back from the person I became the moment that judge—a dickhead who smelled of stale coffee and liked combing his blond hair over—played executioner to my childhood. A man who decided to use my case to set a precedent for youth crimes against cops, making a short stint in juvie a pipe dream and an adult conviction my reality.

"As long as you're okay," she replied before meeting my eyes firmly. "Now, the hair salon doesn't expect me back until two. You sure you don't want to grab lunch?"

"I could do lunch."

"Anywhere in particular? To be honest, nothing's really changed in the last two years."

"Don't care where we eat, Lizzie. Wouldn't mind a burger though."

"How about the diner on Clarence Street?"

"Sounds good."

"Okay then." She paused for a beat. "Coop?"

"Yeah."

"I'm glad you're out."

"Me too."

WE FINISHED LUNCH with barely a few words said between us. I could see the anguish across her face as I gave her the directions to my new place. I was slightly concerned that she'd drive me straight to her house, then tell me to go fuck myself when I asked her to turn around—Lizzie wasn't one to mince words—but thankfully she parked out front of the apartment complex.

When she looked around the run-down building, she grimaced and asked with disdain, "This is where you're going to stay?"

I just nodded and got out of the car.

Her expression became worse as we climbed the stairs and approached my new front door. The moment the door swung open, just before we walked through the archway, a mouse scurried out. I ignored Lizzie's arched brow and began examining the one-bedroom apartment.

It didn't have any walls. Everything was open-plan, because the construction crew clearly didn't want to waste money on this shithole. I briefly took in the sketchy queen-size mattress, small dining room with plastic crates for stools, a dated kitchen, and pink-tiled bathroom from the doorway. The visible water damage and evidence of animal infestation highlighted the very minimal maintenance that had occurred in the last fifteen years. The smell of spoiled meat that drifted through my kitchen window from the back of the butcher's shop was also making the place smell like a sewer.

Lizzie's wide eyes, pursed lips, and total silence let me know she was mortified staring at the pseudo-furniture around the rooms.

I was just grateful. I knew it could be worse.

Housing for an ex-con just released from prison didn't include many options. There was a reason every halfway house in the state was over-crowded—no one wanted to rent to a convicted felon, let alone give him a place two blocks from the college. I knew this wasn't a gift to take for granted. It wasn't the best neighborhood—frat houses weren't likely to pop up anytime soon near the butcher's back alley—but the longer I could avoid having discussions like "I just got out of prison" or "What did you do, bro?" the better.

I still felt like I needed to explain. "A friend on the inside knows the owner. They've offered the apartment to me rent-free until I can get on my feet. Electricity and water has been paid for the first two months." I raked a hand through my hair and looked into her eyes. "Lizzie, I'm definitely not complaining. There isn't really anywhere else for me to go."

"Al didn't want you back?" she asked, eyes wide. "He didn't try to get in contact?"

"He tried, but Al's been taking care of my messes for long enough," I replied dismissively. "I didn't want to bother him this time. I can do this on my own."

"Bother him? Really? He wouldn't think of it that way and you know it."

"He's a mechanic, Lizzie, who felt sorry for me after he found me in the back of a rusted Mustang in his car yard with a broken arm and bloody nose at the age of six. If my bitch of a social worker didn't have stiff fucking rules, he might've had a fighting chance of adopting me, but he didn't. He shouldn't be stuck constantly dealing with my shit just because he wanted to save a little kid."

"Your shit? You won't approach him to handle *your* problems, but when I turned fifteen and started getting too much attention from those fucked-up social workers, you had no issues going to him then. Seconds after Jake and Beth went into decent foster homes, you made us run to him. And you were right. He gave us clothes, after-school jobs, and let us stay in the small apartment above the garage."

"Protecting kids from the system is different than protecting a felon, Lizzie. I just did time. That's different."

"He served time in the same prison you just left, Coop! You forgetting that? You think he'd judge you? The fact that his ties with that motorcycle club on the outskirts of Nevada might put him back in a cell any day makes your comments ridiculous."

I said nothing. She wasn't wrong, but I still wouldn't be asking for any favors. The only forms of generosity I accepted now were ugly, smelling of old meat and dead rats. Things I wouldn't miss when pulled from my bare hands or required acts of retribution.

If things seemed too good, I avoided them. Even the smallest gestures of kindness I treated like embers floating off a dying fire. Best avoided. Sure they were pretty, but if they hit anything, they could cause more pain. Start a fire I wouldn't survive.

"It's about the car, right?" she asked softly. "He knew you needed the money for court fees, Coop. He didn't restore the car he found you in only for it to be the reason you never talk to him again. He knew selling that car hurt you as much as it hurt him, but he would want to help you again."

"Just leave it alone, Lizzie. I'm not going back there yet," I told her firmly.

Lizzie clearly wasn't happy about my response and wanted to ask more questions, but she kept her mouth closed. She'd learned after trying to ask questions during lunch that the moment I decided I didn't want to talk about something, she could ask all the questions in the world and it wouldn't get her very far. I just wouldn't answer.

"Jake would hate this." She poked an old newspaper in the corner of the room with her foot, checking if a dead animal was hiding underneath. "He would've blamed himself for this."

"Good thing we both know that's not true," I muttered, ignoring the plea in her eyes to change my mind. To pretend like the last two years never happened. "Look, Lizzie, you know I've never needed a lot of belongings to survive. After watching numerous foster parents flush their dollars down the drain for random shit, I don't need a fancy dinner table or expensive TV."

"Coop, this isn't just living minimally—it's living with *nothing*."

"More than I had in prison. Plus it's a pretty good location. One of the best colleges in the state is just around the corner. I'm thinking of taking some classes."

"Coop, you know I love you, but you've got to be realistic. Getting accepted at Penmore, is that really going to happen? How the hell would you even begin to afford tuition or meet their admission requirements? And spring classes will have started already. Coop, please, just come home with me. We'll work something out."

"I'm not going to risk the life you've built. I'll hang around here, settle in, apply for the fall semester once I've got everything sorted. Don't worry about how I pay for classes or entry. Apparently the dean saw me play in a high school game and will do pretty much anything for his precious Herons to be the best. He visited me a couple of times, spoke to some of my guidance counselors about my grades, and went to the parole hearing. He kept telling me that his friends on the school board knew about my 'extenuating circumstances' and were willing to organize financial aid. I don't give a shit if he's trying to pretend like his star wide receiver and running back weren't just drafted and he ain't doing all this for a trophy in his cabinet. All I care about is that my record is now being overlooked, I've got my GED, and I've got money coming in to pay for tuition. Coach Hardy will even let me try out for one of the walk-on positions in a couple of weeks. Of course, the dean mentioned it was basically a done deal, but still."

She didn't say anything.

Once upon a time, she would've laughed or squealed at the idea of me being a part of the Herons. When I was fifteen and was put on the varsity team of my latest school, we had dreamed about me making it to a Division I school and the NFL. We talked for hours about the way football could help drag all of us out of the pit we were living in. Then I got a new foster house, new school. No varsity football program.

It's been a long time since we were foolish enough to dream. Now we were skeptics. Weary of even the most transparent situations, hurt by everything that we couldn't control.

"I've got something for you," she whispered, letting go of her concerns. "It's just a photo. I didn't think you'd have much from before, and well, we never did have many photos together. Anyway, the social worker took it the day I got approved as a foster mom and Beth finally came to stay with me. I thought—we thought you might want it here with you. I'll just leave it here near the mail."

Fuck. "You know I can't be around you guys and come for dinner without risking your ability to foster kids. But that doesn't mean I don't want to—"

"I know."

"My record now means—"

"I know, Coop," she said quietly before she stepped forward and hugged me. "Beth and I are just happy you're out. That you're here. Always, yeah?"

"Always."

"All right, I'm leaving you to this lovely aroma and heading to work. My number, my work, and Beth's cell are on the back of that photo. I know you won't call, but just in case, they're there."

"Bye, Lizzie."

"Bye, Coop."

When the door closed and her boots could be heard descending the stairs, I let out the breath I'd been holding.

I walked to the right of the door where my bed and pseudo-bedroom were erected and pried open one of the rusty fire escape windows. Climbing out, I sat on the ladder. I could feel the cool breeze through my hair and could hear the suburban melody. The buzzing of the shop's neon sign below, the distant rumble of passing cars, and the sound of feet hitting the pavement. It might not have been most people's idea of a relaxation mix tape, but compared to the sounds I had grown accustomed to over the past two years, it was exactly what I needed. Small reminders that I was out. The noise also helped fill the silence in my mind, occupying it temporarily, so I wasn't buried in memories and pain.

I was still numb. I knew it wouldn't last. I had eight months to get my shit together before school started. I thought about how I would need double that amount to stop hearing the sound of a skull hitting cement. Then I would start moving forward with my plans. All my actions and all my plans for the future were for one purpose: to distract myself from the pain I kept trying to bury. A pain that, without sound or stimulants, tried to smother me when I was alone.

THREE

MILLIE

"LOOK, YOU'RE NOT being very welcoming, and this is meant to be *welcome week!*" I hissed at the girl giving me nothing but shade. I wished I smoked cigarettes so I could blow smoke into her face. Instead I ended my statement with a big-ass smile, the 'stop being such a nasty person and start to give a damn about other people, you selfish prick' sort.

Usually I could control my inner bitch better, but after I tried talking reasonably with this girl for nearly an hour without success, my bitch was edging to the surface. I could feel her burning out my eyes, and I knew things were not going to end well. I already had a Taylor Swift anthem about bad blood playing in my head. I was prepared for some girl-on-girl hair-pulling, nail-scratching action. Getting nothing but foul looks and sass from this prissy blonde behind the counter was taking its toll. It was on.

"Ma'am, I can't change everyone's schedules to suit their work. You enrolled in the classes, and I've shown you your schedule. You already paid for your classes—I've checked the records. Unfortunately, you can't just come in a week before they start and expect to switch lecture times for one of our most popular time slots. Everything is full."

Did she just call me ma'am?

I was barely two years older than her. *Asshole.*

Deep breath.

Not worth my time.

Let's try this again.

"Look, I hate bringing this up. I hate it because it sounds like I'm making excuses, but I'm a single mom and I work nights. I may have been really tired when I filled in the silly online forms. Having a class this early in the morning, when my mother-in-law leaves before six and the only daycare place I can afford doesn't open until eight, makes drop-off extremely difficult. If I could just swap into the afternoon class, it would save me some serious stress."

"I thought you just said you were single? How do you have a mother-in-law? Look, lady, I don't have time for your bullshit. I get it that you don't want to wake up early. Your type never does. Cuts into doing your hair, I'm sure. Suck it up or drop out." She turned her seat, ignoring me.

"I just say mother-in-law because its eas—" I began to tell her before I realized she was already on her cell phone.

Well that's just great.

I took a few steps backward, watching the student behind me get served with a smile while I collapsed, exhausted, in one of the waiting chairs. Not sleeping properly for two and a half years, trying to improve my life inch by inch, and still getting handed shit made me want to cry. I was ready for a damn break. I was sick of everything costing more money than I had. More time than I could afford.

Or both.

I was clawing for my independence, and the only things I had to show for it were the dirt underneath my nails and a splitting headache.

I was tempted to give Gray a call. Everyone at this place worshiped my daughter's uncle. The star quarterback and local hero. I knew if he walked through those doors that the bitch's tongue would be hanging out of her mouth and she would be eager to give me any class I wanted. Hell, he'd been the one to ensure that the dean hadn't blinked at the idea of taking on a mature transfer student. He'd been the one to convince me that enrolling at Penmore was a better option than moving away from Jessie's only living relatives to go to a small community college.

I figured it had little to do with me. Him using every ounce of his stardom to help me get into this college had everything to do with how much he adored his niece.

If only I hadn't told myself that after Gray's help with admission, I was going to do this on my own. I was going to suck it up and deal with the dirt under my nails.

Before I left, I decided if I wasn't going to make the blonde bitch swallow her tongue by using my daughter's handsome uncle, I was at least going to put on a show. Pretend that the exhaustion I felt didn't go down to the bone. She wanted to think I was a Barbie who just did her hair, so I was walking out those doors like a freaking goddess.

I threw my handbag over my shoulder and did my best Beyoncé impersonation, complete with hair flick and sassy strut. *Millie-Fierce*. No matter what, I was *not* dropping out. I was going to be a college graduate. My life was going to be *awesome*. So I had to take an art class in the morning. A class I didn't really want to take, except it put me one step closer to becoming an elementary teacher. I was going to have a full-time job, work with kids, and have summers free to spend time with Jessie.

I just had to get through this year.

Hell, I was a fucking pro at dealing with setbacks by that point.

Nothing and no one was going to stand in my way.

———

COOPER

FROM THE BACK of the student services line, I saw her deal with the jealous chick behind the counter. I watched her fall into the big armchair looking defeated. When she threw her mane of red hair over her shoulder and strutted out the door like a model walking a runway, I couldn't help but chuckle.

She was beautiful.

Better than when I saw her last: a mirage sitting in a café, giggling with her friend, on the one day of my life I couldn't forget, no matter how hard I tried.

The events of that day started to replay in my mind. I remembered the boyish way Jake ran to my car. The joy I felt. I recall how *hours* later, everything went to shit.

Suddenly I was standing in the fucking college building once more, my jaw tightening as I clenched my teeth.

My life was like an acid spill, and she'd just reminded me that some lives go untouched by time. They were completely perfect.

If she was upset about an administration girl being a jealous bitch at a fancy college, she clearly hadn't experienced any real problems. Seeing her was a damn good reminder that I lived in a different world than those around me.

I stared at the chair she was sitting on and couldn't help but think that if life was a game of musical chairs, only the lucky got a seat. They found where they belonged without having to step in shit or be forced to stand alone.

I thought it was safe to say I was losing that game. I scrunched my fists and reminded myself that it was a good thing I liked to stand the fuck up anyway.

Besides, if I'd already lost, then I had nothing to lose.

I was about to turn my back and walk up to the counter, collect the student crap they told me I needed, and be on my way—forget about the princess, just like in the café—when the light shining through the office windows reflected off something in the chair. I told myself to ignore it, that nothing good could come from approaching where she was sitting.

Then the light fractured again.

Fuck it.

I spotted the gold charm hooked onto a tread of the armchair in seconds. It was smaller than a penny, a flat tiny house with a window and a door. I slipped it into my pocket, figuring if I saw her again, I'd just drop it into her palm. It was no big deal. I didn't notice that when I joined the line, my hand lightly felt and traced each ridge of the charm in my pocket. I didn't notice that the tiny gold charm had tamed my anger. Each stroke made me forget: forget that she was untouchable, that she was better off without me showing her what real problems looked like, that she lived in a completely different world, one without death, drugs, violence, and cruelty.

Playing with that damn charm, I almost failed to recall that I had a plan. I had my time here all mapped out. A goal and a reward were waiting for just the right moment.

When the service counter chick turned her attention to me, her eyes filled with interest, I remembered.

I couldn't allow distractions on campus.

The charm would remain in my pocket, because it was nothing. She was nothing. Just a memory from my past.

A flash of red hair in my rearview mirror.

FIVE HOURS LATER and I was no longer heated about the injustices of the world. I was not concerned about my focus. I was scanning the stands and the obvious groupies hanging around the field for any sign of that bright red hair.

I doubted she'd be close by—her attitude didn't really scream jersey chaser—but fuck, did I need a momentary diversion.

Watching the starters showing off their skills for all the coaches and reporters was doing my head in. Waiting on the sidelines, drinking water and ignoring the walk-ons was more painful than I could've imagined. Fuck, all the freshmen were trying to start small talk with one another to size up their competition. It was a damn joke. I found even applauding the senior douchebags who thought they were gods among men while they ran drills an idiot could perform was taxing.

At least when I was in prison, no guy was tapping me on the ass without expecting a fist to the face. And no one wanted the presidential treatment for handing me a fucking cup of water. It was starting to piss me off that I was being treated like a second-class citizen on this team because Coach Hardy had a stick up his ass about where I came from and how I got there.

When I had first tried out for the Herons in the spring, I'd barely strapped on my pads before the coach was in my face. "Dean Mathews thinks you're special, kid. Tells me Cooper Daniels has had a rough life, been dealt a shitty hand, but has lots of hidden talent. Thinks your prison sentence wasn't deserved and that you should be starting at running back when we play against Washington State in the fall," he informed me before pausing and staring me down. He seemed to be looking for something in the lift of my brow or the twitch of my lips. He got nothing.

We stood for a while, staring silently at one another, until I realized that he thought his words would inspire me to beg him. He was waiting for me to plead my case. I'd only done that once before, in a courtroom against police officers, and it had gotten me nowhere. I wouldn't do it on a damn football field.

"Happy to go wherever you want me, Coach," I told him during that first tryout. "Even if that's out the door."

"Good, because this team is mine and I choose our walk-ons, and no one on my team gets a starting position without earning it, tough life or not. The dean doesn't control my team. I also haven't seen anything yet that makes you so damn special, and you won't be moving up until I do. You hear me? You won't be starting in our first game, and you sure as hell won't start period until I say otherwise. You look like you're suffering withdrawals, boy, and we aren't a rehabilitation program or a charity case. You want that shit, there are teams in Mississippi that'll have you. And if you don't pass one drug test or I hear one word about you violating your parole, you can be damn certain that you won't just be off my team but out of this damn school."

"Don't want charity, sir," I gritted out. "I served my time, not looking to do it again. You can even ask my parole officer. I'm clean, I've got a job, a place to live, and I'm not associated with any of my old friends. I'm just here to work hard. My past is no secret, but that's what it is, the past."

When he dismissed me with a jerk of his head, I made it a mission to show him exactly why the dean had heard whispers about me. With his snide comments burning through my veins, I ran every drill, every play like my body was on fire. My muscles screamed and my mind blanked. I was good. Better than fucking good. I ran faster than people expected, and it took more than a couple of guys to take me down.

A talent I developed out of *necessity*.

At every school I was bounced into as a kid, it took less than a week training with their high school football team before I heard that I was good enough for an athletic scholarship. I was told if I practiced and played for them that in no time, scouts would've been knocking down my door. Unfortunately, I never stayed at one school long enough for scouts to come calling. Then it wasn't about scouts; not a lot of time for many varsity games and pep rallies when you're locked up. But now I'm at a Division I school as a walk-on.

Granted, I was stuck sitting on the bench or standing around on the sideline, waiting for Coach to finish his pissing contest with the dean and give in to my presence. Waiting for him to realize the scrawny kid everyone was paying attention to was crap, and I was better. It pissed me off, but I knew it wouldn't take much longer; then my plans could be put into motion.

"Daniels?" some boy standing to the right of me asked. "Hey, I'm Kyle, but everyone calls me Trick. I saw you at the tryouts. You were awesome dude."

As if watching from the sidelines wasn't shitty enough, now I was babysitting. He looked like he was fifteen, lean and narrow with short, curling blonde hair.

"Thanks, dude," I muttered. Alas, Trick didn't understand that if someone didn't ask you a question in return, they didn't want to talk to you. He just kept talking like I actually gave a damn.

"Coach Hardy has been my neighbor for like ever. He's sort of my mentor. He's totally just waiting, going to show the boys he doesn't have preferential treatment. But he isn't stupid. No way you aren't starting this season."

"If he's your mentor, why the fuck are you standing here with me and not talking to all the reporters?" I asked him.

"I'm a freshman. Going to be starting quarterback as soon as Gray gets signed or graduates, whatever comes first. Not too many of them notice me when Gray's around, but this is going to be *my* season. Coach promised that I'll be given a shot to shine in one of the bigger games. All I need is for people to see me out of Gray's shadow, and then there'll be plenty of time for the reporters wanting to interview me," he told me cheerfully.

We stood on the sidelines until all the reporters left the stadium. Trick didn't stop talking once.

"Daniels," Coach yelled at me. "Start training with Cunningham."

"Told ya," I heard Trick chuckle before I threw my helmet on. I took a second to ensure the small gold charm I'd put on a shoelace was tucked beneath my pads—so I didn't lose it, of course—and jogged out onto the field to take instruction from our offensive coordinator.

I was concentrating on proving myself, winning the coach's trust. I tried not to nod or show any acknowledgement of Trick's presence.

I didn't want to make friends while I was there.

I just wanted to stick to my plan.

I wanted to win.

FOUR

MILLIE

IT WAS THE first day of classes and I'd managed to get Jessie to the expensive daycare on time. I also got a parking space that didn't force me to walk across the entire quad in my nicest pair of kitten heels. I also managed to find the lecture hall early.

It was a freaking single mom miracle.

And now I had a new problem.

Instead of panicking about the course material or how I was going to find time to study, I was standing in the hall entrance worrying about fitting in. When I signed up to start at Penmore, I knew I was going to be older than nearly all the people in my classes, but staring at a sea of eighteen-year-olds was making me feel ancient. They all looked so fresh, like a new tube of lipstick yet to be dropped on the floor or put in the mouth of a toddler. Undamaged and unaware of the danger that lurked behind every corner.

Jessie was in a rare mood that morning. She actually let me put on my lipstick and mascara without interruption, happily played with her toy animals and allowed me to fix my hair without a catastrophe. Noticing the baggy sweaters and ripped jeans of my classmates, I realized I didn't need the extra time. I had overdone it with not only my makeup but my clothes as well. My outfit consisted of a figure-hugging gray pencil skirt, a pale pink sweater, and white peep-toe kitten heels.

I should've just worn sneakers. It would've been more comfortable and less attention-grabbing.

I couldn't help but scan the lecture hall for the seat where I would draw the least amount of attention to myself. I couldn't sit in the front row; it didn't matter how many years it had been since I'd sat in a classroom, I knew that would be a rookie mistake. My best friend Parker would've voted for the back of the hall. She always preferred to be silently observing the masses from the back. If she were there, I would consider it, but in the time it took me to have Jessie and save enough to start my first year, Parker had almost completed her sophomore year at Penmore and was on her way to becoming a pediatrician. Parky was now in classes about nutrition, pharmacology, and physics—not Art 101.

Finally, when groups of students walked in and around me, I decided to just follow the crowd. I figured if I couldn't work out where to go, I would let someone else choose for me. I ended up sitting in the very middle of the hall. It wasn't until I'd put my purse down and pulled out my notepad that I noticed the people on either side of me were all talking to each other.

I was the invisible woman. Two-way glass.

I should've just sat in the back.

I was about to pull out my cell phone and stare at cute photos of Jessie, distract myself from my pathetic social life, when I heard a "Hey, sweetheart." I looked up to find a good-looking guy sitting in the row in front of me, turned in his seat and smiling at me.

I couldn't help but internally bet myself fifty dollars that he was in a frat house. A frat house that kept score on how many girls they saw doing the walk of shame. His blue polo shirt, backward baseball cap, and shaggy blond hair screamed 'full-of-ourselves fraternity.' Thankfully, the beauty of his face rescued him from his obnoxious outfit. Olive skin, crystal blue eyes, and a small dimple in the middle of his chin charmed me. I might have blushed and seriously considered the open invitation in his eyes—forgetting all about my pact to no longer date—had he not opened his mouth.

"You're looking *fine* today. Seeing as you're just sitting there, and the professor isn't here yet, how about I sketch you?"

"I'm sorry, what?"

"A drawing. Not to boast or anything, but I'm pretty good. Art major. I've been told I'm great at capturing a woman's best features, if you know what I mean," he told me before leering at my chest. "Maybe if you like my drawing, we can go back to my place later? You could let me do a figure study."

His words and facial expressions made him more insufferable by the second.

"A figure study?" I repeated, my eyes narrowing.

"Babe, I'm willing to spend hours if needed *studying* your figure."

"Did you actually just say all that shit to me? Out loud? Do you honestly expect me to find those pickup lines endearing?" I managed to ask in complete bewilderment. I was honestly shocked. *Is this how college guys pick up chicks?*

"Damn, sorry I asked. No need to get prissy. It was just a suggestion," he said before turning back around to face the professor.

If I wasn't a mother and planning on telling my girl that violence never solves anything, I probably would've 'accidentally' hit him in the back of the head with my notebook. *Why couldn't I have wanted to study nutrition?* I saw the girls beside me giving me their sympathetic smiles and rolling their eyes at the boy. It was nice that they finally noticed me, but feeling their pity only made me wish I were invisible again.

I was still considering the likelihood of Jessie ever finding out if I decided to maybe tip the ink from my pen down the back of his shirt. Rationalizing that if I kept it a secret, no one would have to know that I liked violence—or petty revenge—under the right circumstances. Except chuckling behind me and the soft "Fuck, dude. You would've owed me like twelve drinks if you had failed that bad" distracted me.

I decided to turn around. I was done with being made to feel like a fool in this class. I was going to use my disapproving mother-knows-best tone—one I had perfected since Jessie started walking and reaching door handles—to tell the strangers laughing behind my back that it was *super rude to eavesdrop*. I schooled my features and prepared to make someone—on their first day of class—no less, feel like a naughty child.

When I turned in my seat, all I could do was gape, mouth fully open. I will neither confirm nor deny the presence of drool. There was just one guy sitting all by himself in the row.

A guy who was definitely *not* in a fraternity.

A gang maybe. Or a motorcycle club.

Hell, he could even be an actor—if he was playing an extra on the *Sons of Anarchy*. He was clearly over six feet, and his two hundred pounds of muscle made his lecture chair look like a doll's seat. I was pretty sure a polo shirt would melt on his body should it ever be stupid enough to touch his bronzed skin. Really, he was that delicious. A god in a room of frat boys.

Actually, scratch that. I'd bet twenty dollars that gods surely weren't allowed to have a tattoo sleeve. He was clearly more than likely Lucifer. A leather-bound, tattoo-covered, muscle-ridden devil. Or was Lucifer a fallen angel? I knew there were myths about fallen angels: men cast out of Heaven, impossibly good-looking with the ability to seduce mere mortal women with a glance. Which would also explain the crazy reaction my body was having to his. There were tingles and butterflies in places that hadn't experienced tingles *or* butterflies in a very, very long time.

After a second though, I barely even noticed the effect he was having on my body. I wasn't staring at his dark brown hair, cut short but with enough left over to run your fingers through the top. I wasn't desperate to feel the beard that covered his boxy jawline, trimmed close enough that I could still see and appreciate said jaw line. I wasn't even curious about the story behind his thin nose that angled a little to the left, clearly showing it had once been broken.

I was trapped in dark moss-covered eyes. Eyes that made me wonder if he was Scottish. If he spoke again, I wondered if I would hear a brogue that matched the dark valleys and roaming hills that swirled in his irises.

"Um . . . it's, um, rude," I managed to stammer before my brain became distracted by the smirk on his lips. *Wow. Those lips.*

"Staring at someone without forming a sentence? Yeah, babe, that is rude," his deep gravelly voice rumbled.

Fuck, that's better than a Scottish brogue. I had never thought any voice could be better than a Scottish accent.

Except suddenly his words registered, and instead of being turned on by the husky deep tones of his voice, I was angry.

"I meant eavesdropping," I scolded.

"Sorry, *Flash.*" He smirked.

Great. One minute, dickheads are hitting on me with bad lines, and the next they're giving me cheesy nicknames. College is wonderful. Why didn't I do this sooner?

—

HOURS LATER, I was sipping coffee in the cafeteria on campus with Parker. I had a few minutes before I needed to race off, grab Jessie from daycare, and deliver her to Tahnee before work. However, I wasn't thinking about time, too invested in sharing a play-by-play of my first class, hand gestures and wide eyes included. Parker hadn't spoken for fifteen minutes and I hadn't even noticed.

While I detailed each word spoken by the frat boy and my reaction, Parker sat opposite me with her brown hair up in a messy bun, her boy-friend's football jersey hanging off her shoulders, and a calmness that I'd never managed to project oozing from her posture. Granted, we'd always been different. Very different. Where I tried not to leave the house without a face full of makeup, Parker had only just realized tank tops weren't the devil in the last couple of years. But for as long as we'd been friends, our differences had never mattered. Parker loved how loud and dramatic I was even when she barely spoke. She loved it so much that when I stopped speaking about my potential love interests, stopped acting my age and decided I wasn't going to be a dreamer anymore, it hurt her more than it hurt me. When I decided I no longer needed another person, I never once thought about how that would hurt the only person who had always been there.

When I finally finished with the description of my badass self, walking out without looking back to see if the bearded god was appreciating my tight skirt, I noticed Parker's smile. A smile that was part humor at my exaggerations and part nostalgia over the days when I would lie across her bed complaining dramatically about my failing love life with the latest high school baseball star.

"So, he was good-looking?" Parker asked after swallowing a mouthful of her caramel latte and trying to hide her enthusiasm over the reappearance of boy-obsessed Millie.

"Fictional-motorcycle-club good-looking," I explained, still picturing those piercing green eyes. "He could be on TV or on the cover of one of those books you love. He's got that 'I'm sexy with a hint of danger' thing really going for him. I can't help but think he'd be the president of some group of outlaws. That is if he wasn't talking to himself. Can they be crazy and still be the leader of a gang?"

"That's right, you mentioned he was talking to himself." She started giggling. "That's really why you turned around, isn't it? You're trying to befriend all the crazies at Penmore, am I right? Find your people?"

"Ha-ha. What can I say? Hanging out with *you* has made everyone else seem boring if they appear normal. Stalk anyone else lately?" I joked, narrowly dodging the napkin Parker threw at me. "Anyway, you're missing the point. It's not like I'm looking to be his friend or date him. I've sworn off dating. I'm just appreciating the eye candy," I told her, trying to regain some of the composure I had perfected over the years.

"You know, if you want eye candy, Keeley didn't run off to New York with the only good-looking Heron football player. Gray's got a lot of teammates. . . ."

"Babe, thanks, but no thanks. You know I'm just teasing about the stalking. I love how happy you and Gray are together. I also adore that your wild roommate was able to run away from school like a Kirsten Dunst *Crazy/Beautiful* love story. But let's get real. That shit's for girls who dress in leopard-print tank tops—not for single mothers. I'm too old and have too much baggage to run away. These days I'm too busy to even date. You girls have been lucky in love, and I'm lucky in other ways. I have my girl, and I get to watch Gray and Tahnee dote on Jessie like she's the best thing since sliced bread. Honestly, I'm so grateful for everything he's done for me, but you know how I feel about going to the games. Looking at Gray from a distance for long periods of time, my brain and heart start to hurt. He looks so much like Nate and it's just . . . I'm not exactly ready."

"I know it's hard. It's okay, I'll leave it. However, you ever want to come check out the talent during practices, I wouldn't mind some company. I miss gossiping with you. I also don't think you need to act like an old lady all the time, but that could be the selfish part of me talking, considering the groupies I'm stuck standing with at practices have been driving me crazy lately. Last game I started a full conversation with them about the team's tight ends and all they could do was giggle and talk about which player's tail end they'd like to play with. But if you need more time before you come to the games, take as much as you need. Just know you're more than welcome whenever you're ready."

"Thanks, babe, but don't hold your breath. Now that I have my new classmate, I doubt I'd ever be desperate enough to put up with groupies just to check out some man candy." I smiles. "I also doubt I'll have time to sit around this year. As is, I'm impressed that I was able to manage squeeze in coffee."

"If you're pressed for time, you can rush off, but I want an update on the princess first." Parker grinned.

"She's perfect," I replied solemnly. "But she's evil."

"Aren't moms only meant to talk about how much they love their babies?" Parker asked, her lips twitching. She was used to—I would even go so far as to say enjoyed—my occasionally melodramatic interpretations of life with my daughter.

"Oh, I love her, but I can still think she's evil. Take for example that she only threw up on my favorite clothes when she was sick last week. And she's a chicken thief. Every time I have chicken in my salads, she cries until I let her have some. And by some, I mean every piece. The mastermind of passive-aggressive behavior is what she is." I rolled my eyes skyward. "Clearly she doesn't take after me at all, what with my dazzling, completely accommodating personality."

"Oh yes, nothing like you at all," she scoffed, swallowing her laughter. "But I'll remember to bring chicken next time I visit."

"Listen to you. 'I'll bring chicken.' She's suckering you in already and you aren't even eating a salad!"

"Well, I really like watching her eyes sparkle."

"That's how she manipulates everyone, the sparkle. She's going to rule the world soon. Sure, it starts with stealing chicken, but soon she'll take over nations. And everyone will be okay with it because of those damn eyes," I muttered.

"You're just jealous because you were always trying to manipulate me with your blue eyes in high school to get me to agree to a crazy road trip and it always failed."

"I still think we should go on a road trip."

"And I'll repeat the same thing I said when we were twelve. We are not Thelma and Louise. We are not buying cowboy hats, and we can't afford to rent a convertible. Now that I'm older, I can also remind you that the story didn't end too well for them, and even though we both now have our driver's licenses, I can't imagine it would go so much better with our sense of direction. Plus you have a kid now, and I have Gray. We'd need to do some serious planning to be able to get away for the weekend."

"Fine. I guess you're right. Jessie's nearly two, and while I think she could handle herself, Gray is definitely really needy. So we stay and my pursuit of finding a young Brad Pitt is yet again diminished. Gosh, your life choices really have limited our spontaneity."

"Yeah, um, I'm really sorry for that." Parker chuckled. "What time do you need to leave for your very nonspontaneous life?"

I glanced at my watch and nearly choked on my coffee. "Five minutes ago. I'm going to be late." The guilt started eating at me instantly. My daughter would now be sitting alone at daycare because I was gossiping about some guy.

As my pained expressions flashed across my face, Parker motioned for me to leave straightaway. Her sad smile revealed that she knew the day's short get-together would now be another thing of the past, along with my carefree attitude.

The next time she ran into me, I would make some excuse not to sit down and joke around. As much as we both wished I was the same person she grew up with—making the same jokes, teasing each other—we knew I had changed.

I was trying to be a mom and a dad, and I wouldn't let failure be an option.

I was strong enough to be both—even if that meant cutting everything and everyone who used to make me smile out of my life.

FIVE

COOPER

I FINALLY GOT to train as the starting running back during practice. I didn't have to stand around for some imaginary amount of time that Coach Hardy believed sent a message to jealous freshmen and other walk-ons. When I shook off Andy—the 240-pound star linebacker who everyone calls D—coming at full speed as if he was a restless puppy, Coach Hardy's eye started to twitch.

I hung around Coach a bit as the boys headed to the showers. Not to say anything; I got the feeling my mere presence and the smiles the assistant coaches were sending my way was enough to piss him off. I was tempted to be a dick and ask him for some extra pointers, annoy him by enquiring about how I might improve my already *innate* abilities. There were just two things stopping me. The first was I needed Coach to put me on the field during a game for longer than fifteen minutes as soon as possible, and I figured stirring up trouble wouldn't help my case. The second was if I went to see Coach, I was going to be late to class—late to see her.

I didn't just want to stare into her deep blue eyes. I planned on giving

Flash her stupid charm back today. I wasn't going to wear the thing everywhere I went anymore. The small gold house was almost feeling like a part of me, and I couldn't allow that to happen. If it wasn't going to be a reminder to stay the fuck away, I needed to return it like I'd planned. As much as I was tempted to see my hand sliding through all that red hair, I had a job I needed to do.

I walked in the side door of the lecture hall and moved up the stairs. I didn't look around the large room because I felt everyone's eyes follow me. Their judgmental gaze wasn't surprising.

It was never lost on me that I didn't exactly fit in there, whether it was in the quad, the cafeteria, or class. It wasn't just my leather jacket and old ripped jeans that set me apart; it was the fucking stench of entitlement that seemed to pulsate from everyone else on campus, a smell I clearly lacked. My stench was more of the old meat wafting into my cheap-ass apartment sort of smell.

Thankfully Flash didn't exactly blend either. Her bright hair acted like a beacon among our drab and dull classmates.

"Move," I said firmly when I reached the row she was sitting in and was faced with lanky guys blocking me from getting to her chair. If Lizzie were there, she'd tell me to be polite, following it up with a fast kick to my calf. But I couldn't help but think *Screw them*. They acted scared of me, so I might as well use that to my advantage. I made my way toward the chair to her left in a record time.

As I sat beside her, I didn't bother looking straight at her. I even went so far as to pretend like I didn't even notice her. It was a bullshit game, one I hadn't played since getting locked up, but it also allowed me to check her out without having her run away. I'd noticed most of the girls on campus looked my way, but the moment I got close they headed for the hills. Way too scared.

Thank fuck that campus wasn't too far from the bars I was used to. After two years on the inside, I didn't care if it was cheap pussy, pussy that liked the scent of incarceration or the look of my bike. I just wanted to get laid.

Now I knew I didn't get to touch Flash; girls like her were untouchable for guys like me. They would only fuck with the future I was working toward. A mess I didn't have any business wading into, but damn it, I was going to take my time looking at her.

Each time I saw her, I remembered how Jake was looking at me when I was looking at her. And how, once upon a time, my life wasn't nearly as screwed up as I thought it was. I'd decided before I got to class that I'd allow myself this lesson, quietly stare at her and get my fill. Then after she left the hall, I'd pull off the charm and chase after her, tell her I found it on the fucking floor or some place. Then she would go back to ceasing to exist, and I'd go back to the bars and chicks I belonged with.

I leaned back in my chair and tilted my chin, allowing her to slide into my vision.

What the fuck?

She was in a short skirt, and peeking out the edges were sexy-as-hell stockings attached to sexy-as-fuck lace garters. Was she filming a porno after class? Outfits like that only led to a shitload of trouble for girls like her.

I wanted to turn in my seat and demand to know what the hell she was trying to play at. Look her in the eyes and tell her to go get changed. Instead, I tried that stupid breathing crap they made me do in the joint when I felt like hitting another inmate. When I felt like getting involved in drama that often nearly saw me serving an additional five years on top of my sentence.

In. Out. What did I care if she was stupid enough to dress like a hooker? She was nothing to me. *In. Out.* What if she wanted to attract every dickhead on campus? It wasn't my problem, even if there were dickheads who were a lot worse than me.

In. Out.

Dickheads who wouldn't worry about destroying their last good memory with a friend.

In. Out. In. Out.

The breathing didn't do shit.

I couldn't control myself. She'd get hurt parading around in that shit.

Before I took my next breath, I found myself turning, staring into her big ocean eyes, and demanding, "What the fuck are you wearing?"

MILLIE

I WOULDN'T LIE, when the fallen angel walked into class, I let out a sigh of female appreciation. Then like everyone else, when he started walking up the lecture stairs, I enjoyed the show, tracking his muscular body with my eyes and enjoying the way his jeans sculpted to his thick thighs. I was even a little excited when I noticed him stop at my row. I watched him in amusement as he scared the freshmen boys out of the way before he headed right to me.

When he sat beside me and didn't bother even acknowledging my presence, I was a tad annoyed. Okay, I knew we weren't exactly friends—he'd spoken to me for a whole of two minutes at the last lesson—but would it have killed the guy to say hi? The least he could do was try and mend fences a little, so I felt completely justified objectifying him in my mind.

Before I had a chance to really convince myself that I could damn well ignore him if he could ignore me, I noticed his eyes make a slow perusal of my outfit just before hearing the stupidest of questions hissed at me.

"What the fuck are you wearing?"

"Excuse me?" I managed to whisper, noticing the fury swirling in his eyes.

"You trying to improve your grades or some shit? Get into the professor's pants?"

"Because I'm in a skirt? What?" I asked in shock, feeling the embarrassment bloom in my cheeks.

"It's a *fuck me* outfit," he muttered in disgust, causing me to lose my shit completely.

"Ah yes, a girl couldn't *possibly* want to wear pantyhose because it makes *her* feel good. It has to be in the pursuit of a penis," I replied.

Okay, so maybe I had a love-hate relationship with thigh-high pantyhose, and I only wore these because I had to leave school early today to work a double shift, but he didn't know that. I had also thought that my skirt covered the over-the-top lace garters. When I sat down and realized I had miscalculated the amount of skirt material working for me, I was a little annoyed. But I was also a big believer in wearing whatever the fuck you wanted to wear, so I wasn't above taking offense to the stuff he was saying. Screw any guy who thought he had the right to tell me or any girl what they could or couldn't wear. Plus, the skirt was basically covering the garters, and my loose cobalt blouse didn't even reveal the corset. As far as I was concerned, he was whining about a little lace trimming, which was ridiculous.

The blush of embarrassment coating my cheeks transformed until my whole face was red in anger. "For your information, I'm not looking for anyone to *fuck* me. I just like to look good."

"Problems going to come your way dressed like that."

"Is that right? Well, thanks for the advice, *Simon*, but I can take care of myself." I didn't think I'd ever been so furious at a total stranger before. First class, he called me rude, and now he was basically implying that I was a slut. I didn't even know his name and I hated him. Good looks didn't save anyone from a shit personality. I was picturing ways to dump his body. Sure he was big, but I was feisty and creative. If only I was in a lecture theater learning from Annalise Keating. Professor Bradbury discussing color theory was in no way helping me work out how to deal with the pretty but clearly bossy idiot who sat beside me.

"Where are you going after class?" he grunted.

"Why would I tell you that?" I replied.

"Because if I'm going to make sure you don't get attacked, I'd like to know how long I'll be following your crazy ass around."

"Don't worry, *Simon*, I'm leaving campus straight after class today. No need to get your panties in a twist."

"Name's not Simon," he muttered.

"Really, and yet you feel like you can say what I can and can't do? Well color me surprised."

"Flash, don't be a bitch. It's not attractive. And the name's Cooper."

He had to be kidding. No guy was so good-looking that he could insult my clothes, call me unattractive, and then tell me his name in one conversation. I wasn't even willing to stick around.

Screw class today. If I leave now, I'll be able to see Jessie at daycare before Tahnee picks her up and I have to work.

I grabbed my handbag and threw it over my shoulder. He sat still, like a sleeping volcano; I could tell he wanted to erupt, spit more rubbish my way.

Damn him if he thought I'd be giving him a chance.

———

COOPER

I DIDN'T CHASE after her.

Not straightaway.

I gave her a good head start.

Then I followed her as she made her way across the quad toward the parking lot. It was nice to see that while she was bitchy, she wasn't a liar.

I kept my distance as I watched her climb into a pickup truck: a polished, probably fucking expensive black Chevrolet Silverado. It had to be her boyfriend's, a guy who clearly gave more shits about his car than the safety of his girl if he let her run around looking like someone could buy her. Not caring in the slightest that when she climbed into that pickup in a short skirt, you could see her fucking panties. He probably had a daddy who replaced the whole fucking truck when the douche scratched the bumper.

I wanted to hit him. I pictured smashing my fist into the face of a fancy college boy. It wouldn't be the first time I'd hit a rich kid who deserved a lesson. I imagined the joy of tarnishing Flash's boyfriend's overpriced threads with blood might even be more satisfying than when I beat the college kid who tried to turn Jake into a dealer when he was nine.

"Who's the chick?"

Fuck. I didn't even need to turn around to know who that voice belonged to anymore—Kyle 'Trick' Sullivan. Since chatting on the field, the lost puppy followed me around: when we watched film, when we strapped on our pads, when we took them off. The only person who didn't seem afraid of me also couldn't take the hint that I didn't want to be his friend.

"Just some girl in my art class."

"She's hot. I suggest you do some figure studies."

"Dude. No."

"Hey, just trying to help my moody teammate get some action. I've got class in five. You done?"

"Left class early. Going to get food," I told him.

"You know what? I'm starved. I'll join you," he cheerfully replied.

"You just said you've got class."

"Yeah, I'll just text Veronica later."

"Veronica?"

"Just some girl who offered to take notes for me if I ever don't turn up."

"Girls offer to take notes for you in the off chance you decide to skip?" I asked, incredulous.

"Hey, don't be fooled by my cheerful demeanor. Girls love them some Trick,"

"Dude, did you just refer to yourself in the third person? Don't do that shit around me."

"Noted, bro. And yeah, I've got a girl in nearly every class who'll take notes if I don't turn up. Some don't even know I play. Apparently I look like some dude from that movie *Magic Mike*. Really appreciate that movie, man."

"You like *Magic Mike*? You leading all these girls on, Trick?"

"Oh nah. Don't get me wrong, I don't appreciate it like *that*. I'm definitely all about the ladies. I just like how it's helping me out here."

"Great. Now that I know all about your minions, are we going to stand around chatting all day or we getting food?" I finally asked him, accepting the fact that like a tiny splinter, I would have to put up with Kyle's presence embedding itself into my life until I did something that would dislodge its presence for good.

I HADN'T EATEN on campus before that point. I had been doing odd jobs late at night for the butcher next to my house, which meant I got mediocre pay and a lot of leftovers. If I was desperate, I would come in and grab a slice of pizza to go; I didn't ever sit down and chat.

When Trick and I walked into the cafeteria, I took a look around the room, inspecting the crowds of people, beige walls, and long wooden tables. I couldn't help but think what a stupid decision it was to go in here. I could sit in a classroom pretending I belonged, but I didn't think I could socialize or talk about my damn life. I was about to turn around, give Trick an excuse, and walk out the doors.

"Oh hey, D and Gray are here," Trick exclaimed as he spotted the guys from the team sitting at a table in the back.

"No," I stated clearly and without room for discussion.

Trick, like usual, took less than a minute before ignoring my assertion and insinuation. He kept moving toward their table. "Daniels, I know you aren't Mr. Friendly, but Gray is our star QB and captain. You want Coach to stop giving you such a hard time, Gray is the one who can fix that shit for you faster than you can blink," he told me as he gestured for me to follow him across the room.

"I can fix that shit on my own. Don't expect me to kiss Grayson's ass," I muttered.

"Geesh, dude. Sit next to D, then," Trick chuckled as he picked up his pace and maneuvered quickly through the masses. I watched him get to the table faster than I could blink; the puppy was fast on and off the field.

I followed halfheartedly, taking the time to accept that in the long run, it really would look better if people had seen Grayson Waters and me getting along. That didn't mean I wasn't bracing myself for a sit-down lunch with the star quarterback of the Herons, the prodigal son of the whole fucking town.

I decided if he looked at his own reflection when using his fucking cutlery, I was leaving. I didn't give a shit if everyone thought he looked like a movie star or that three men's health magazines had approached him to shoot a cover—no guy should stare at himself in a fork.

"Leyton call you yet?" I heard D, the hotshot linebacker and Thor look-alike, ask Gray as I finally reached the table. "Coach said he left for New York a month ago."

"Nah, he's probably too busy settling in and training with the Giants," Gray responded, then looked up at me after he took a bite of his bologna sandwich.

"Yeah, probably. Damn though, can't wait for that to be us, man. One more year and we'll be killing it in the NFL. This weekend is the beginning of the end, man," Andy replied before noticing my presence. "Daniels, dude, welcome to our cafeteria table."

"D, we don't own the table," Gray muttered before nodding in my direction.

"Semantics."

I took a seat and waited for the inquisition to start, figuring these guys would want to bust my balls, ask me shitty questions about prison or how I ended up on the team after hearing the shit Coach had yelled at me. I hadn't exactly been forthcoming about my past life. I was also waiting for Andy to start slinging shit my way about blocking him during practice.

So I was surprised to find that aside from the animated rambling between Trick and Andy about which of them would be the superstar that season and Grayson texting some chick, I was left to eat my lunch in silence.

It had been a while since I had socialized with guys my own age.

I couldn't help but imagine what the guys I ate lunch with in prison would think if they saw me now. I knew some would be laughing pretty hard at my place at a table with the elite inner circle of Penmore's football stars. Until they worked out exactly why I was sitting there, and then they would want in on my plan.

SIX

MILLIE

I KEPT TRYING to picture Jessie's smiling face and shaking hips as I pulled off my blouse and slipped into my floor-length sparkling dress.

I loved watching Jessie dance at daycare. I knew what twenty-month-old little girls did with their bodies to music might not necessarily be considered *dancing*, but that's what Jessie thought she was doing and she loved it. Every time she laughed while swinging her body back and forth to music showed me that while she may not look like me, she truly had inherited my personality. The carefree one I hoped she never had to lose.

She wasn't even a year old when I worked out that if I did a Fouette turn in front of her, she would stop crying. A week after that, I learned that she'd burst into giggles if I did a barrel roll. When she laughed, her green eyes sparkled and she looked so much like Nathan that Tahnee usually started crying. Big fat tears that slid down her cheeks and caused Jessie to stop giggling and try to catch them like snowflakes.

It was hard for me to encourage Jessie to dance at home anymore for fear of upsetting the one woman who had done so much for us. I now only encouraged Jessie's hilarious wiggling at daycare and in the car until

I had to leave and go to work.

As I prepared for my shift, I imagined our own lounge room. A room big enough for her to do any form of dancing she would like across the carpet. Once a vision of her was firmly in my mind, I started the arduous task of pinning on my wig.

Some shifts, I let my hair fall naturally, blasted Kings of Leon's "Closer," and waved my feathers around like they might burn anyone who dared get too close to me. Surprisingly, my tips were always better with the red and an added touch of superiority in my dance moves. But sometimes when I was on stage, I needed to pretend to be someone else.

That night, I was going to be Dita Von Teese. I could always enjoy the dressing up—wearing short black curls and applying a fake beauty mark made me smile—yet as soon as my costume was perfected, I found my smiling stopped. The red flashing lights slipping through the black curtain, the chatter of the other girls in the change room, and the beat of Cindy's number often made me go into a trance. A sultry exterior hid the numbness I desperately needed to handle my surroundings.

I didn't think, I didn't feel, and I didn't care—not until my shift was over and I was soaking in the tub at home. Sometimes I worried that with each performance it was becoming harder and harder to snap out of the trance, to melt the hard shell that coated each muscle and hair on my body. Then I would remember Jessie's daycare dancing, and suddenly I didn't care if I ever smiled again as long as I was working toward that little girl remaining carefree.

"Millie, you're up," grunted Lucille, one of the club owners, known as Lucky to her friends and Getting Lucky to her enemies. I plastered a smile on my face, waved extra big at Lucille—even though I sort of hated that bitch—and approached the curtain. I quickly checked that my gloves were pulled up past my elbows and my sparkling silver dress was ready, Velcro tabs and all, then waited for the music to hit my cue.

Nina Simone's "I Put a Spell on You" started and my character began. It was one of my slower, more seductive dance numbers. With my eyes closed, the music blaring, and satin beneath my fingers, I could almost pretend that this was a fancy burlesque nightclub with elite clientele. Picture someone sitting there appreciating the art form.

It wasn't until I heard the repulsive howling from the audience as I slipped off my first white satin glove while rolling my hips invitingly that I was reminded of where I was: a hole-in-the-wall strip club called Poison. A dump that after it got shut down a couple of years ago had repackaged itself, removing the silver poles, inserting chandeliers as well as red velvet as far as the eye could see, and replacing the word 'Gentlemen's' with 'Burlesque' on the front door. A place that could renovate the entire neighborhood, jack up their prices, and still struggle to attract anything other than truck drivers, addicts, and bored businessmen.

I turned my back to the audience and slowly undid my dress, letting it slip to the floor. While I stroked the sides of my body with my hands, I blocked out the lewd calls and prepared for the removal of my corset. Before I started counting out the steps that led to revealing the pasties attached to my nipples, I reminded myself why I did this job.

Big house.

Rooms where Jessie can dance.

Big future.

Independence.

One . . . two . . . three . . .

AFTER HOURS OF dancing, slinging drinks, and avoiding grabby hands, I packed up my belongings, wiped off my makeup, tied up my hair, and threw on my sweatpants. I was almost ready to swing by the twenty-four-hour supermarket on Broad Street and then drag myself home.

I took a quick look around to make sure I hadn't forgotten anything; even though I'd be back there the following night, I never wanted to leave something behind. It was a bitter pill to swallow, needing to be there to make my life happen. I wasn't ready to ingest the thick smell of cigars and appraising looks when I didn't have to.

As I made my final check for a possible forgotten tube of lipstick on the dressing table, I caught my reflection in the mirror. There were still hints of stage makeup near my nose and mouth, and I had pulled my hair into a tight bun. It was an old forgotten habit.

I couldn't help but think that I looked like a normal tired dancer. No different than if I had just performed for the American Ballet Theatre.

I immediately pulled my hair out of the bun, letting the red curls tumble across my shoulders.

My becoming a prima ballerina had been my parents' dream, born from the careless mistake of my dance teacher. She thought my parents needed to know at six years old that I was *gifted*. She couldn't have anticipated how that information would change them—change *us*. She had no clue that their dream furniture company had burned down a month earlier and that they lived with the constant feeling of defeat by working menial jobs to pay the mortgage. Our house kept slowly falling apart around them without any possibility to fix it up. She couldn't have understood that hearing their daughter was gifted was like a life raft to the future they had dreamed about and lost. Unlike my love of Jessie's dancing, which had to do with the way it made her smile, their love of my dancing had everything to do with status. Money. Security.

Unlike their forgotten furniture company, they latched on to the potential of my future with everything they had; the notion that they might watch me, Camille Monroe, grace the stage in *New York City* invigorated them. To see me not only be good at something but to excel beyond everyone else inspired them to work harder than they ever had before. The possibility that I could have more money than I or they would ever need altered how they treated me. I believed that, once upon a time, they truly loved me; they just came to care more about the choices I made than the person I was becoming.

They ignored me when I tried to tell them at fourteen that I no longer wanted to keep dancing. When I discussed at sixteen my fear of living in New York by myself, they laughed. With every fiber of their being, they refused to believe that I just wanted to be normal. By eighteen, I had stopped talking to them, deciding I could live my dreams without needing to share those dreams with anyone.

I didn't mention that my best friend's excitement for college and living on campus had inspired my own curiosity to look up every community college and university in the area. I didn't disclose how I had become so sick of bandaging and wrapping my injuries that I tended to spend more class time instructing others rather than dancing myself. I definitely didn't tell them how helping others and choreographing routines had gradually become my passion, or when I realized that teaching kids the arts would be my future. My deep-seated knowledge that small classes and the occasional school recital—not long rehearsal schedules and tireless workouts—would lead to my happiness was never spoken of.

In my final year of high school, I hid in my best friend Parker's bedroom for as long as she would let me, gossiping about boys and eating chocolate. If I *had* to go home, I would drag Parker with me. My parents never voiced their disapproval about missed dance rehearsals around company; in front of Parker, they acted like we were the perfect family.

I didn't reveal my complete rebellion to them or Parker until I graduated and sold my small car. My parents had bought me the car as a birthday present, which allowed them to boast to other parents about my ability to go to early morning dance classes. I used it to buy college courses.

My parents were furious, claiming I didn't learn a single thing from their struggles, yet they remained steadfast in the belief that I would see the light. They thought I would get through the first semester of college, find it completely unchallenging, and change my mind. They even told me they had a small bank account ready and waiting for the day I decided to move to New York.

The looks on their faces when I finally sat them down at nineteen and said the words "I'm pregnant" instead of "I'm ready to become a prima ballerina" were worse than I could've imagined. They were gutted. With two words, I destroyed their delusions.

I watched the color bleed from their faces. I watched them cry.

It was more than just the usual parental disappointment.

I'd killed something in them.

Still, I hadn't anticipated coming home from my second ultrasound to find my bags packed for me, the two people who always said they had my best interest at heart handing me a new ultimatum: home or baby. Unlucky for them, they timed it poorly. They should've challenged me when I was crying on the couch after hearing from Parker that Nate was gone. I was scared out of my mind then, but after hearing my baby's heartbeat, I had new strength. New determination.

I didn't even say goodbye as I grabbed my bags and walked out the door. They were trying to kill something in me, and unbeknownst to them, they were successful. I no longer gave any thought to their pain. My love for them was gone. I used the number Tahnee had programmed in my cell phone during Nate's funeral, straight after our first awkward introduction, and never looked back.

I knew Tahnee occasionally sent them photos of me and baby Jessie. I think as a parent who lost a child, she couldn't imagine voluntarily missing out on the future of your child and grandchild. I didn't bother trying to explain to her that my parents were a lost cause. Photos wouldn't change their insensitive beliefs.

I couldn't help but imagine what they would've said if they could see me now. Tahnee knew what I did to make my money. She disapproved, but instead of voicing her concern, she just kept reminding me that she would support Jessie and me no matter what. I chuckled when I thought about sending my parents a photo of me on stage with my tassels spinning in the wind. It shouldn't surprise them, because as far as I was concerned, my parents got their dream. I was now on stage every night, under the spotlight with adoring fans cheering my name.

I grabbed my bag and headed toward the exit, knowing I would still rather be dancing on this stage every night than in New York City.

SEVEN

COOPER

LUNCH WITH THE boys was okay, but after leaving campus, I decided I shouldn't do that shit too often. If I sat with them every day, I'd fuck something up. I wouldn't be able to stop myself from saying something I shouldn't.

I was way out of practice for that sort of thing.

Where I came from, there weren't too many guys my age wanting to come hang out at a group home. When I was a junior, there were some guys I threw a ball around with and they seemed friendly enough, but it was short-lived. I got involved in some petty fight over a girl, and the next day my foster parents were calling me "troubled" and I was moved.

I never did graduate to drinks by a bonfire with the boys. I certainly didn't shoot the shit with anyone the first time a girl let me touch her. Al bought me condoms when he found a bra in the workshop, and Lizzie made jokes if she saw me look at a girl a second too long.

Before today, they were the only ones I'd ever sat down with long enough to eat a sandwich.

Which was why I found myself walking into the supermarket past midnight following my late-night shift at the butcher. If I bought my own food, I wouldn't need to step into the college cafeteria for the rest of the week. I also liked the fact that none of the streetlamps worked in a five-mile radius around the store, and the only thing that shone in the darkness was the crappy neon sign that hung above the door. It meant less people went here late at night. Grocery shopping over the past few months, dealing with aisles of food going to waste and bickering customers complaining about a thirty-cent price increase, almost made me miss prison food.

I was just able to make out two other trucks in the parking lot when I stopped my bike. I could handle two people. It was unlikely that either of those guys will bother me.

I turned down the first aisle, making my way toward the bread, when I saw her.

I was stuck staring at the way her sweatpants hung low on her hips, exposing her lower back. and how her long red hair almost touched her ass as she reached for a bag of chips on the top shelf.

I couldn't help but take a look around to try and spot the boyfriend. She was alone. And I was pissed. She had a fucking death wish. Again.

"You think this shit through?" I asked her loud enough to be heard from the end of the aisle.

"Excuse me?"

Turning around, her eyes widened in surprise as I strolled toward her. I could tell when she recognized me though, as I was soon glaring into suspicious slits. I found myself unable to ignore her complete disregard to safety, even with the fire in her eyes. Fuck if I hadn't heard inmates joke about hunting grounds and empty parking lots. Her walking off into that dark lot without a clue was something she'd soon realize was a shit idea, even if I had to be the one to point it out.

"Your choice to do some midnight shopping in this place makes me think you're looking for trouble. You're not even trying to blend in. You should wear a coat and a hat, hide your hair and body. Do something to disguise that you're a woman all by herself, for fuck's sake."

"Look, Simon Says, I love that you feel like we have this relationship where you can walk up and start spouting shit about my outfits. But let me remind you, *we don't*. I don't know you. All I do know is that you were much more attractive when you were talking to yourself. Please, let's go back to that," she snapped before turning back around and scanning the lower shelves.

"Flash, if you think turning your back on me is going to get me to leave you alone here, you're wrong."

"I cannot believe this," she muttered before she turned toward me, her red hair flying. "Give me your jacket."

"Huh?" I'm too distracted to realize what she said. The heat in her face made her look amazing. Her rosy cheeks, sparkling blue eyes, and wild hair flying around her face resembled a mermaid coming up for air. I could almost lose myself in imagining her in a tiny shell bikini.

Then she tugged on the corner of my jacket and I remembered. It was late. She was not a fictional character. She was a serious danger to herself. She might even be deranged.

"You're telling me—a grown adult, mind you—that you won't leave me alone until I'm safe. Apparently you also think that if I hide my hair and my body, people will think I'm a man and leave me alone, so hand me your jacket. I'll return it in class and you can leave me the hell alone. Now."

"No. I'm walking you to your truck."

"I'm sorry, what?"

"You might not be putting on a show, babe, but that doesn't mean people haven't been watching. I'm not taking any chances. You can keep calling me Simon instead of Coop and lecturing me if it makes you feel better, but tonight I'm walking you to your truck."

"You do realize that *you* are the scariest thing in this supermarket, right? And the idea of you walking me into a parking lot with no light isn't exactly a comfort."

"You got mace?"

"What?"

"Mace? Pepper spray? A pocketknife? Some form of girly protection?"

"No, I don't carry an arsenal in my purse."

"Then we go by the cutlery aisle before we leave. You buy a fork. You feel afraid of me, go ahead and stab me with the fork," I told her, smiling.

"I think I'm feeling scared right now," she replied, arching her eyebrow.

"Funny. But Flash, just so you know, no matter how many times you stab me with the fork, I am walking you safely to your car. Tomorrow you buy an arsenal and a coat, and you can walk yourself."

"I can walk myself tomorrow? Gee, thanks." She sighed. "Look, I don't even care anymore. I'm tired. I ducked in here to grab milk and cereal on my way home. You want to follow me around, fine. Just stop talking."

"Done."

IT WAS THE longest grocery shopping experience of my life. And I didn't even buy anything. I just watched and followed her stubborn ass in silence.

After her taillights faded off into the distance, I decided to go for a ride. Groceries could wait. Sleep could wait. Consumed by my frustration over things I couldn't change, I needed to forget. Just forget who I was, where I was going, and focus on the air, my bike, and the road.

I cruised past trash cans that had been picked at by the desperate, ignoring the homes that only housed the hopeless, and the harsh looks from the few who lurked in nearby alleys eager for a fight.

My motorcycle was good for times like this, when I needed an escape, when I just wanted to ride and not have to listen to anything or anyone. A limitation of my parole and future plans was that I couldn't pop a pill, couldn't turn to the one thing that helped me silence the screaming in my head while in prison, which meant my bike was more than just a means of transport in my life. She was my lifeline.

The moment I saw her in the junkyard, I knew she had to be mine. I wasn't allowed to travel too far, but that didn't meant shit. On the back of my bike, I was happy to ride around aimlessly.

On Jake's birthday, I did twelve laps around the same block.

After following Flash around all evening, pretending like smelling her faint perfume wasn't one of the best things I'd ever experienced, I figured I'd probably need to do ten laps at least, until I forgot the challenge I saw in her eyes. Overlooked the desire I had to show her how much she liked having me standing close. Made myself numb to the fact that I couldn't touch a dream I had before everything went to shit.

I had to remember that cold air and speed were all I needed.

MILLIE

I TOLD MYSELF that I didn't find the fallen angel attractive anymore. His clearly psychotic "me Tarzan, you Jane" tendencies far outweighed how well his jeans clung to his ass. His outspoken critiques of my outfits definitely tarnished the seductive tone of his voice. Not to mention his completely overbearing presence was without a doubt the most painful and unwanted aspect of my evening.

So I felt a little safer walking to my car. That wasn't that big a deal. I also might have realized that maybe his personality wasn't as shitty as it came across in our last class. He just had a hero complex. Unfortunately for him, I didn't need a hero.

And as soon as I told him to stop talking, he followed me through each aisle in silence. He didn't even laugh as I spent the longest time deciding between Cocoa Puffs and Lucky Charms. But even with the gorgeous way his lips twitched in amusement, I've decided he was no longer going to be someone I sought out with my eyes. He wasn't starring in any more of my daydreams, and I would not be thinking about how it might feel to run my fingertips along each of his tattoos. Nope, I wasn't even going to let the fact that I now knew he rode a motorbike influence me. I was completely prepared to forget that when he straddled his motorcycle, he looked just like Jax Teller, ready to make all my fantasies come true.

I was actually already a little proud of myself.

I didn't even look that long at him when he threw his legs over the glistening black machine—ten seconds was a vast improvement from five minutes.

And I was sure I wouldn't even remember the way his eyes burned into the back of my truck when I climbed inside, as if he could strip each part away with a flick of his wrist if he needed to get to me.

I definitely didn't look more than once in my rearview mirror to see him patiently waiting for me to turn onto the well-lit street.

I was clearly ready to have nothing to do with him.

He completely repulsed me now.

Nothing was attractive about a motorcycle-riding, overprotective fallen angel with deep green eyes and a chiseled jaw.

Crap, I'm screwed.

EIGHT

MILLIE

AFTER I GOT out of my car, I slumped down on our rickety porch swing, carefully leaning back and gazing out at the empty street, the gravel pavement glistening in the night. The neighbor's tabby cat glared at me from the wire fence that separated our two yards.

It was peaceful in the early hours of the morning. This seat and Jessie's perfectly painted bedroom were the only spots in this ramshackle house that didn't cause me to sigh in exasperation. I felt the stress of the day drift away as I slowly rocked back and forth on the swing.

I needed more than a moment to collect my thoughts and calm my feelings before I went inside the house. When I walked through the doors, I needed to be in mom mode. I needed to put away the groceries I'd picked up from the store. I needed to do a load of laundry. I needed to check on Jessie before also checking on all the mess she'd made today. I knew I shouldn't spend long out on the porch.

I still didn't move.

Every activity would take twice as long if I was still thinking of green eyes and a motorbike. Sleep also scared me. Like many early mornings, I contemplated staying awake, planning and plotting my future. I figured with enough time I could devise ways to avoid Simon Says.

I had just worked out my first idea when I heard him.

You shouldn't have skipped your afternoon classes. It's too much.

"I need the money," I choked out, still staring at the empty street.

I tried not to cry. At times like these, when I imagined Nate talking and sitting beside me, I always cried. If I kept staring at the neighbor's cat or the empty street, I was usually able to keep the tears at bay. It was when I looked at him, with his brown hair falling over his forehead and his playboy smile wide as if nothing ever happened to him, that something inside of me broke. Letting my exhaustion and loneliness toy with my sensibility eventually caused more pain than pleasure.

It was worse than the dreams.

The first time it happened was right after Jessie was born. I figured it was a teenage girl's reaction to feeling completely alone. Abandoned by her parents. Living with basically a polite stranger. Not to mention the fear. Jessie was so tiny that I was afraid to pick her up. I was worried about bathing her, certain I might break the best thing in my life. What I felt was the only thing in my life. It also wasn't meant to be like that. We were meant to have a future together. A damn dog. Two kids. I wasn't meant to be doing it all on my own.

I pictured what it would've been like if I had gotten the future I was meant to have. It was supposed to be a careless daydream.

"If you were here, I'd make you do this shit," I said out loud to the Nate of my past, imaging him squatting beside me in that small bathroom.

I nearly had a heart attack when I felt his hand rest against my shoulder and heard, *Pamela, no way would I be helping you right now. Nope. No way. I'm leaving you in here while I try and haunt my mom enough to change the channel on the TV. It's like she doesn't know it's game night.*

I wish I could say it was a fleeting moment of weakness, but when Jessie would learn something magical, like wave goodbye, wink at Andy, or yell at the top of her voice if Gray left the room, I imagined Nate beside me. I talked to him so often in those first few months that after a while, all I had to do was walk into the house and I'd see him sitting on the couch, as if he were just waiting for me to come home. And now I didn't know how to stop it from happening.

I had opened the door, he strutted in, and I couldn't push him out.

I no longer needed to fear taking care of Jessie. Tahnee had grown into the quietly caring mother I never had. I didn't need his company. I didn't *want* his company. But just like my dreams, I couldn't escape my fucked-up ghosts.

You don't need to work there anymore. With everything else going on, school and Jessie, you need a break.

I thought about not replying, wondered if that would stop it all. But I made a mistake and turned to look at him. Nate's challenging glare was so clear that I couldn't help but reply, "We've talked about this. I promised just this year. Then I'll have enough saved—"

I don't want you girls to move out. You study, Mom can watch Jessie, and you can always pay to have the cracks fixed.

"I love that you want us to never move away, but you know as well as I do that it's a waste of money fixing this place up. In this neighborhood, this place is never going to be a gold mine. Not to mention if I start fixing things, I'll just find more things that need to be repaired."

I don't want you to leave.

"We won't go far. We'll still need your mom," I explained.

But you don't need to work there.

"I'd live here forever if I thought it was best for Jessie," I whispered, thinking of that future we were meant to share.

I know, Pamela. But I just don't want you working yourself into a breakdown trying to get a house you don't need.

"If it was too much—" I started to explain.

You'd still do it. For her. I just need to remind you that you don't have to.

COOPER

IT HAD BEEN three weeks since I spoke to Flash in the supermarket. I planned on handing over the charm in my pocket and making it to week four. I was done playing bodyguard.

Shit would get too complicated if I spent any more time with her. It was best I stick to my original plan; then I could go back to the life I wanted—long periods of nothingness.

I walked into the only class we shared, ignoring the girls who were following way too close behind me. When I felt their tits brush against my back and their breath chase across my neck, I planted my feet to the side of the doorway, forcing them to walk around me or appear like bitches in heat. I looked past the inviting grins they threw over their shoulders while they worked their way toward the back of the hall as I scanned the crowd.

The giggling I heard fading into the distance reminded me that pretending they didn't exist was the best response. In my last class, I'd tried to glare at the college chicks trying to seductively smile at me, had sneered at their designer clothes and expensive accessories, but it was like I'd flashed them my cock. Their eyes burned with hunger as they giggled even louder.

Apparently after a month of seeing me around campus, girls weren't running scared anymore. Some had seen me with the football team, noticed the seconds I'd graced the field in our away games. They'd heard rumors about the new walk-on that could be the Herons' very first Burlsworth Trophy recipient if given the chance to play a whole game.

The more daring girls were now looking at me like a challenge. I had become a meal ticket.

And yet Flash, the only one who had looked at me with heat in her eyes before anyone started whispering about the infamous walk-on, was clearly coming up with ways to avoid me. It had been amusing watching her tactics.

The first week after we ran into each other in the supermarket, she didn't show up to class. The week after that, she arrived seconds before the class started, sat right next to the door, and was gone before the professor had finished his final sentence. Last week, she sat in the front row, surrounded by hippies. She thought she had shielded herself because of their proclivity for waving their arms and the occasional chant. That was my favorite. From my careful distance, I could see how their tendency not to bathe regularly had not factored into Flash's plans, much to her horror.

I chuckled each time they raised their arms, cheering the professor for mentioning any artist involved in the psychedelic movement.

I was excited to see what she planned for today.

I started scanning the crowd for her red hair and smiled when I spotted her in the middle of the hall with the seat to her right empty.

When an arm slipped across the back of her chair, I processed her new ploy. The anger began to boil.

I used to have more control over myself. I could rein myself in. Those with control always had the upper hand in a good fight. The ability to surprise an opponent should never be discounted.

Attacking the dick sitting in the left chair beside Flash, drooling into her cleavage, wouldn't end how I wanted it to. There would be no surprise. No grace.

I still couldn't stop myself.

I glared at the fuckwit sitting like a king on a damn throne as I moved toward them. I didn't take my eyes off my prey in his fancy threads and black-rimmed glasses, throwing carefree smiles to everyone who walked past. Clearly unaware that with each chuckle and casual stroke of his fingers against her bare shoulder, he was eliciting my primal urge to hear the sound of his bones breaking.

"That chair's taken," I told him forcefully when I stood directly in front of him, with no room for argument. My anger was chained only by the very last tether of my remaining restraint.

"Sorry, bro, didn't know it was yours. Maybe you can sit there," he replied casually, pointing at the empty spot on Flash's right.

I didn't look at the empty chair but deep into Flash's eyes. I could see her fury, the way her cheeks flushed. Her eyes narrowed, leaving no doubt in my mind that this scene was something she was going to give me shit over. I could see the words she wanted to scream at me in her eyes. *You do this, make a scene, there will be hell to pay.*

Babe, you started this.

I did? You egotistical ass! He just sat there!

Babe, you let him sit there and didn't say shit about his arm. You hated it and then decided to use it to avoid me.

I did no such thing.

"Maybe I should move?" the idiot asked as he looked back and forth between the conversation Flash and I were having with our eyes.

"Sounds good to me," I said firmly, my anger ebbing the longer I watched him twitch and give up.

When he was long gone, I planted myself in the seat he'd vacated, leaned back against the chair, and made myself comfortable. I rather enjoyed not only the sight of watching him run with his tail between his legs, but the heat radiating from Flash as she looked me up and down.

"I cannot *believe* you did that," she gritted out between clenched teeth.

"Flash, you should be thanking me," I replied, turning my head to check out her rigid posture. "He looked sleazy as fuck. You didn't like his hands on you. I didn't like how *he* couldn't see that you didn't like his hands on you. Even from across the room, I could tell his arm against you wasn't something you wanted. You think I didn't see each time you cringed? You were leaning so fucking far forward to get away that your boobs were practically falling out, and all he could do was stare at them. You talked to him. Smiled once. He doesn't get to fucking touch you because of it."

She didn't deny it, and I watched the heat in her eyes die down. She exhaled her anger and then, with an eyebrow raised and a smart mouth, asked, "Do I need to start paying you?"

"Paying me?" I asked, distracted by the sudden shift of light in her eyes. The beauty that seemed to slam into me from every direction.

"For this fucked-up protection service you think you're running. Or are you like an undercover cop?"

I burst out laughing.

"Why is that funny?"

"Flash, I just got out of prison," I told her without hesitation.

"Who are you, Allen Iverson? The administration isn't worried in the slightest about letting you study here?"

"What can I say? The dean loves me. I've also been on my best behavior." I smirked at the shock plastered on her face.

"Damn, if this is your best—"

Before she could finish her sentence, the noise in the lecture hall amplified. We realized everyone was chatting excitedly with the person sitting beside them.

I looked at the girl sitting above Flash, "Yo, what's everyone talking about?"

"Didn't you hear? The professor just announced that our major assignment could be done with a partner. He's also sick of marking incomplete assignments, so he's giving us the rest of the lecture time to research together. I guess everyone's excited about having free time. That or they're finding a partner before they get stuck with the spare hippie," she said before turning to the person sitting beside her and smiling.

I took a quick look at the five hippies in the front row, saw the fifth smile widely at the room. Yeah, that wouldn't be happening. Although it would be funny watching Flash try to work with her.

I slowly twisted my head to make the suggestion only to find Flash's narrowed eyes on me. Before I got the chance to suggest she join the hippie in the front row with a shit-eating grin, she gave me a sharp look, flicked her hair behind her shoulder and, like a queen dismissing a peasant, simply said, "No."

Now, I was pretty sure after suggesting she work with the hippie, I would've gotten up and walked out. I hated working with others. I also kept meaning to stay away from her. Couldn't do that shit if I was expected to study with her. Fuck, I wasn't even going to talk to her that day. I was just going to give her that damn charm and walk away. But she had to get on her high horse.

Lizzie used to tell me that whenever she wanted me to do something, all she had to do was tell me I couldn't. Apparently she always thought I had issues with authority and staying out of trouble.

I always thought that was bullshit, but fuck if I wasn't about to show Flash that I didn't take kindly to being dismissed.

And now that she'd made such a big deal about it, I fully intended to introduce her to her new partner.

NINE

MILLIE

I MADE IT into the quad. Then heavy footsteps fell beside me.

"No," I repeated without looking at him. I refused to even use my peripheral vision while I made my way toward the campus library.

I didn't need to see his face to know he was the one beside me. Didn't need to run my eyes over his imposing body or rebellious gaze. As soon as I left the hall, I knew he would follow me. I wasn't stupid—though flatly refusing a convicted felon probably wasn't my smartest move. After I worked out how to get him to leave me alone, I'd be having a very serious conversation with myself.

Especially seeing as I was already angry at myself for getting turned on as I watched him intimidate the guy who had sat beside me earlier. Sure, I was pissed when Simon Says yet again started treating me like I couldn't take care of myself, but my body hummed. He took two steps toward that stupid guy, his strong arms clearly tensing beneath his jacket, and sweet baby Jesus, I was fidgeting in my chair because every part of me had started tingling. I was a hot mess.

Thankfully I was angry enough about his continued rescue efforts to mask any signs that revealed the real cause of my flushed cheeks and unsteady breathing. Because it didn't matter how hot he looked trying to protect me, I'd finally started taking care of myself this year. I was no longer in need of anyone's help. His gestures weren't wanted or necessary.

Furthermore, I didn't want to help others, and the longer he did things for me, the more I'd feel like I was duty bound to help him.

But I wasn't going to be his partner. Or anyone's, for that matter. I didn't have the time in my day to put up with anyone's issues. I had more than enough of my own.

I figured if I kept walking away, pretended he didn't exist, he'd disappear. I hadn't exactly met a lot of guys with a hero complex, but I was laying my money on it being an attention thing—just like when Jessie helped me put away her toys, always anxiously waiting for the pat on the back. The moment she was lavished with attention, her enthusiasm always diminished.

Simon wasn't getting jack. No smile. No undying gratitude. I was sure he'd go look for another helpless damsel in distress when he realized the most he was getting from me was the cold shoulder.

I walked in silence all the way to the big timber doors of the library entrance. As I reached for the handle, he stepped forward and held the door open. I walked through, my head held higher than I'd ever held it before, yet I still caught the hint of a smile coupled with bemused eyes.

"You know, Flash, I don't think I've ever had a girl tell me no before I've even asked her a question. Maybe I don't want to be your partner. Maybe you're not smart enough to work with me." He laughed before pausing in the entryway. It was the first time I'd heard him laugh. Deep. Infectious. Potent. I really wanted to turn toward that noise, take his ridiculous bait and argue with him just to see how his face changed with each chuckle. Did his forehead crease? Did that sinful mouth stretch or stay the same? Did he have dimples?

But I couldn't. I had to stay strong.

I reminded myself he was arrogant.

He was bossy.

He was a damn felon!

No girl in her right mind should be turned on by his dangerous, domineering crap. And while I couldn't always be considered in my right mind, today was different—today I was sane.

I was also done with men. Stupid men with their stupid pretty faces and nice-sounding laughs that turned me into a fool. No sir, I was not responding to his lunacy. I was just going to keep trekking toward the art section at the back of the library.

As soon as that girl in class stated we were given time to study, I struggled not to cry tears of relief. I rarely had a chance to hide in the library and complete my homework in silence. I usually worked on my assignments in a bathroom; sitting on a toilet by myself, with someone shouting for me to do, fix, or flirt in the distance, was the only study time in my life. I was very ready to embrace the smell of moth-covered books and the glare of cheap orange lights, so I kept walking. I passed the section with all the science and mathematics textbooks—the subjects the school had deemed important enough for the front aisles. When I reached the dark area designated to art history, I knew he'd continued to follow me. The heat radiating off Simon Says's body seemed to press against my back the farther I walked down the aisles. I wondered what it was he was thinking. Was he looking at the books or at me? Checking out my ass or the stacks? Planning on begging for me to do the entire assignment myself?

As I stopped in front of the rows that held the books of all important art movements, I just stared aimlessly. I had no idea where to start. All we had to do for our assignment was research any movement, present a small talk to the class on the artists involved, and discuss their impact on art today. I just had to pick a book—any book. If only I was a tad bit better at making small choices. Big life-altering decisions came easy to me—I always went with my gut feeling—but I had no gut feeling when it came to choosing between painters who liked squares and painters who liked circles.

I heard a deep chuckle behind me and I couldn't help it. I gave in. I turned around and looked at the fallen angel. *Sweet baby Jesus, he has dimples.*

Stay. Strong.

"Something funny?"

"This is going to take as long as the Cocoa Puffs and Lucky Charms decision, isn't it?" he mocked as he leaned against the shelves. It was like he had studied every bad boy in every teen movie. His lean was equal parts relaxed, cocky, and sexy as fuck.

I had no response. Mostly because the answer was *yes, it most likely will*. Defensively, I rambled. "I'll have you know I'm smart. I'd wager that I'm smarter than you. Not that you'll ever find out because I'm not working with you. If you think following me will convince me otherwise, you've got the wrong girl. How about you try and grab one of those *friendly* girls you walked into class with and go annoy them. I'm sure one of them will *eagerly* help you."

"Flash, I wouldn't expect you to do all the work. And I'm a Harley Quinn sort of guy, not Poison Ivy. Those girls are welcome to some other hopeless fool who can't see past their tits," he said, smirking.

"You do realize I have red hair, yes? I've been confused with Poison Ivy many times."

"Ah, but Flash, those people aren't looking at you as closely as I am. I've seen your temper. You're more likely to set people on fire than ever toss around a love potion," he chuckled. "You're red, but you've definitely got a dark side."

I couldn't deny that. There had been more than one occasion when that was the only side I wanted to embrace.

"And if you let me work with you, I'll make the choice of what we'll discuss," he continued, gesturing toward the stacks, clearly amused at my indecisiveness.

He didn't realize that he'd just hit my Achilles' heel—avoiding small choices.

"And if I say no, you're just going to keep standing there watching me, aren't you?"

He flashed me that smirk once again.

I sighed, contemplated the benefit of not wasting the next fifteen minutes staring at the books and how thoroughly I was probably going to screw myself over in the next five minutes. *I'm a fool. A total idiot.* "Fine, stay. We'll work together, and then you can go off to save other damsels in distress. I just have one condition: no more calling me Flash. I don't want any cutesy nicknames. I've had enough of that for my entire life."

"Done. Although that means you need to tell me your name." His words glided across my skin as his eyes shifted from amused to serious.

I hadn't realized that I hadn't told him my name. I remembered when he told me his—Cooper—but I never thought about my response. Now I almost wanted to retract my statement about working together. And about no cutesy nicknames. Telling him my name seemed too personal, as if calling him Simon Says and him not knowing my name kept us further apart.

Without that distance—

No. Nothing's going to happen.

Not this year.

Not in this life.

I'm a single mom, and he's an ex-con.

He probably doesn't even think of me that way.

I breathed in and felt the air shudder out.

I was an idiot for thinking otherwise.

"Millie. My name's Millie," I said quietly.

He held his hand out and I felt like whimpering. It scared me—the calloused, rough, and beautiful hand of a man who I should keep very far away from. He was potentially dangerous. He was overtly bossy. He was sinfully attractive. All things that didn't need a warning label to predict doom for a girl with a foolish heart. A girl who had spent the last year locking down her impulses to live in the moment.

I watched as it enclosed around mine. It was too comfortable, my hand in his.

The warmth seemed to protect and hug my skin, trailing along and down my body until it reached my core. I was transfixed on where our bodies touched. I forgot that I hated him, forgot the ghosts that haunted me. I was focused on the fact that I was a woman who hadn't been touched in years, and I wasn't exactly sure how I'd survived.

My heartbeat increased and I shifted my gaze from our joined hands until I was staring into his dark green eyes. I lost myself in their mountain valleys and rolling hills.

"Hi, Millie," he murmured, and I couldn't explain it, but I wanted to cry.

"Hi, Cooper," I whispered, feeling the heat bleed into my cheeks. I prepared myself to pull my hand out of his and turn our attention back to the rows of books that related to art, get my body under control and my head back into studying.

Then I heard his soft "Fuck it."

Suddenly that same hand was squeezing and pulling me forward. My chest was hitting his chest and my mouth was slamming against his mouth.

He was wrong.

It wasn't me who was setting him on fire.

It was him who was destroying me.

With every stroke of his tongue, it was as if he was pouring gasoline on a spark inside my body, encouraging it to build and flare. Become wild and uncontrollable. I couldn't help but react. I had kissed people before, soft and sweet while tentatively trying to work out if we were compatible.

This wasn't that.

This was rough, aggressive, and had nothing to do with compatibility.

Hell, we'd talked three times before that day. I already knew we weren't compatible.

This was more like battling each other. Only we were doing it with our mouths, tasting and testing each other's pent-up desire, determining who was stronger and both realizing we were weak to whatever we had started. It was like parts of me that I thought were broken were suddenly switched on and given life again.

When we grabbed each other harder, our hands roaming over each other's bodies, I felt myself go crazy with need. Gone was all sensibility as I yanked him closer by his jacket and he pulled me in tightly by my hair. Damn, it hurt, but there was something about the pain. It caused heat to pulsate through my body. It revealed our desperate need for one another.

Immediately after pulling me closer and feasting on my mouth, he was tugging my hair toward the ground, exposing my neck to his teeth, scratching and licking along my skin. I loved it. We were brutal with our hands, our mouths. There was so much craving inside both of us, only revealed by his inability to control himself and the way my heart wouldn't stop ripping from my chest.

This wasn't love. This was lust. Or it was some sort of war my body had enlisted me in without my permission.

My daughter was proof that I hadn't exactly been saving myself for marriage. I wasn't naïve about sex, but I had never experienced anything like this. My previous sexual encounters occurred pre-pregnancy in the first few months as a freshman at my community college. Most of those kisses were from barely-out-of-high-school boys who didn't know what they were doing. Nearly all of their kisses demonstrated that I had a habit of picking boys who had yet to learn that their tongue was *not* meant to be anything like a turtle's head poking in and out of a shell. Nate was the only one who knew what he was doing, but even those encounters had been tentative, subtle explorations of how far I would be willing to open. A growing friendship that shifted into a slow exploration of each other's bodies.

Cooper, however, clearly knew what he was doing and didn't give a shit about being subtle or waiting to see if I was going to open for him. He was demanding it. As he continued to explore my mouth, he started unzipping and pulling down my jeans. I knew if I was going to object, I needed to do it now. If I was going to walk away from doing something crazy like having sex with a stranger in a public place, this was my only chance.

As he traced his fingers over my drenched panties, I knew I wasn't going anywhere. If I was going to lose control, it was going to here and now, with someone I knew wouldn't make this more than it was.

I was also just as hungry as his eyes revealed he was for whatever I'd been missing for years. I was ready to beg, plead for him to slip his fingers beneath the white cotton fabric he'd exposed and help return my sanity. Except no words escaped my mouth. I became lost in the sight of him trailing open-mouthed kisses along my exposed thigh beside the edge of my panties. It was as if I was intoxicated, drunk on the sound and feel of his lips against my skin. I barely registered when he stopped, shifting his position so he was standing before me, looking directly into my eyes before he lifted me from my pants. I was adrift in the wanting.

When he lifted me into his arms like I weighed nothing and pushed me against the stack of books, the feel of his hands on my ass and my knees wrapped around his waist entranced me. Until his left hand started running along my hip and calf as he helped stabilize our position by placing my foot against the opposite rack of shelves. His fingers traced their way back across my calves toward my ass and spurred me on. I looked into his eyes, burning the image into my mind, and reached for his zipper. He ripped my cotton underwear and before we moved, both exposed and ready, we started kissing. He gripped the side of my face, pulling me closer, pulling me under. Furious and desperate kisses coupled with the faint air between us teased me and built the ache inside of me until it was drumming in my ears. I barely heard the rustle of the wrapper ripping, and as his hands dropped from my face to help align our bodies, I was ready to scream from the need to be filled.

As he entered me, his mouth muffled my surprised cry. I'd forgotten how much sex *hurts*. It had been nearly two years since someone had been inside me, and in that moment, it was like it was my first time all over again. When he pulled out and thrust back in, I decided that the momentary pain was worth it. The feeling of him sliding back in, hitting the deepest parts of me, was like a prize at the end of the battle. The glory all fighters desperately wanted.

When the pleasure built, I couldn't help but start rocking toward him, creating an effortless rhythm between our bodies. Fuck, it was amazing. He continued to slam inside of me again and again; the books behind my back shifted and fell to the ground on the other side. I would be mortified about that later, would worry if someone heard us or saw our actions through the fallen books. Wondered if they had stopped and kept watching us. If they'd seen my face as I climaxed while holding onto Cooper's shoulders for dear life. However, even then I wouldn't be able to deny that this was incredible.

Foolish and reckless, but incredible.

COOPER

WE WERE GOING to kill each other. I always knew my number would be up before I reached old age. And if this was how I was going to go—with her in my arms, struggling not to scream out loud, her body rocking hard beneath mine—I was okay with that.

Watching her come was fucking spectacular, finding a new grip that allowed me to use my fingers and encourage her to fall again phenomenal.

I promised myself that I wasn't going to get involved, which I fucked up the moment I touched her.

She was a glimpse into the past that I couldn't have back, no matter how much I wished I could change it.

She pressed her mouth into my arm, struggled to muffle her moan, and I decided that I didn't regret my actions for a second.

I can't change my past, won't change my future, but I can enjoy the fuck out of my present.

When the whirlwind stopped, the sound of my breath was like a fucking steam train. I barely had a chance to rake my hand through my hair and calm myself before I realized she'd grabbed her stuff and run.

Gone in a flash.

Well, fuck.

TEN

COOPER

I ARRIVED AT the prison thirty minutes before visiting hours. The wind was howling, the clouds hid the sun, and the cement structure looked more austere than when I'd first laid eyes on it from the back of a police car. The barbed wire curled around the impenetrable walls. The gate groaned with each gust of wind. This place didn't just hold criminals until their time was up—it caged people until they turned into animals. The lucky ones came in that way; the unlucky took a week before they accepted the transition.

Nonetheless, the parking lot was crowded with families and friends, cheerful everyday men and women chatting and laughing, removing things from their pockets, preparing for their pat downs. Completely comfortable with the inspections and the loss of their dignity to see someone they loved—or, more often than not, someone they worked for.

I shouldn't be here.

Until my parole ended, I wasn't allowed to step foot behind those gates. Getting caught with a fake ID was a risk I shouldn't take. The long-sleeved flannel T-shirt, John Deere cap, and sunglasses I was wearing helped me look like the damn farmer I was pretending to be. I knew, however, how quickly shit could go wrong inside those walls. My beard was half the size it was when I'd walked out, and from the look of every other dickhead lining up to get in, if I kept my eyes down, it would help me blend in with the crowd. That didn't mean another inmate or a guard wouldn't recognize me, of course. I knew this was idiotic, but it was a risk I was willing to take before I did something worse than get locked up again.

Like fall in love with a fiery redhead.

Like forget everything I had planned for a girl I'd had once.

Three days had passed since the library and I could still taste Millie on my lips, feel her hair under my fingers. See that look in her eyes when we finally let go of each other, both spent and reeling from our fall back into reality.

I could've said something, in those seconds before we let go of each other and she ran away. I could've told her that I'd fucked up, lost control. But even if taking her there in the library where anyone could've seen us made me an asshole, I didn't regret what we did in the slightest. Feeling her was the best thing to happen to me in two years.

I just knew it would only make things worse. To continue playing whatever game I started when I picked up that golden charm would be a huge fucking mistake.

She was meant for a different life.

Hence why I stood silently as she hurried out of the library. I didn't chase her down to try and convince her to stay with me.

When I got back to my apartment, stroking the small charm beneath my T-shirt, I made the call. I needed to remember what the fuck I was meant to be doing out here and *why* I was doing it.

Tony had it all sorted. All I had to do was follow the plan. From the numerous aliases on his visitor list, the guards he knew could be bribed with a measly twenty bucks, and the notes I'd found in the apartment. It was like he knew I'd need to come back. I'd need to hear his pain, his anguish, and remember why I volunteered.

Why I'd told an old man I'd avenge his dead son.

And how I planned to spend my time on the outside, however long or short that may be, destroying the only other son he had.

—

ANTHONY WATERS LOOKED like shit. His hair was nearly completely white, his complexion gray, and his orange jumpsuit looked two sizes too big.

He was a fucking mess.

"You eating?" I asked him.

"Yeah."

"Bullshit. You're wasting away again. You were meant to get your shit together when I left."

"Coop, it's hard. Not knowing. Thinking about what happened to Nate. It eats me up. I shouldn't . . . I don't deserve to live," he muttered before starting to cry.

It wasn't the first time I'd heard Tony cry. First night he was moved into my cell, all he did was fucking cry. It was the background music to my life for a year and a half. When I learned the reason behind his tears, I couldn't help but wonder if my father had ever shed a tear over the crap that had happened to me. I doubted it.

"Tony, shut up before you draw attention to us. You know I get it. That's why we're doing this. That motherfucker will pay. I'm already so close. I'm on the goddamn team, for Christ's sake. Coach Hardy will have to start me next game. All we need is one brawl and Gray ends up at the bottom or in the path of a punch. He'll be benched, and not just for a couple of games. I'm damn good at making people want to take a swing at me. As soon as I get my shot—"

"You shouldn't," he mumbled like a timid mouse. "There's no way it'll look like an accident. With your record, no matter how friendly you guys look, you'll end up back in here. Or worse, he'll retaliate. You might end up like Na—"

"Tony, we discussed this. If I'm going to end up back in here, at least I'll have done something worthwhile in my time out. And maybe you'll finally get some fucking sleep at night."

It shocked me how any judge would throw this guy in prison. A guy who clearly couldn't take care of himself. For as long as I'd known him, he didn't do anything but cry and pace like a nervous meth addict. He reeked of desperation and depression. I could see him committing a white-collar crime sure, but assisting the mafia? Picturing teary Tony in front of the mob was like picturing a fish working with a cat—they would've eaten him alive.

"You have to be careful, Coop. His connections are serious. I think I was wrong to turn to you that night, to accept your help. Even now, you're risking so much to visit me—"

"This is important. He sent his old man to jail for shit he orchestrated while walking around like a god on campus. I can fix that. I just want you to be alive to see it."

"Coop—"

"No. I told you I would fix this."

"You won't kill him though, right? I don't want another dead son. I know h-he's—"

"Tony, we already talked about this. We'll just damage that fucking professional career he thinks he has all lined up. If I can make it look like an accident, no one has to know."

"I can make some calls," he whispered.

"You don't need to do anything," I said firmly.

"You shouldn't have to deal with your ghosts anymore either. I know it must be hard to be clean. You're on the team now, so you could probably get away with some—"

"We'll worry about my shit when justice is done. I got through the withdrawals better than even I thought I would. I think looking at the way everyone treats that scumbag keeps me straight. Let's not risk the plan."

"O-okay, if you're sure," he muttered, a single tear falling down his face.

"I am," I asserted before I stood and headed toward the exit, not bothering to say goodbye.

I'd gotten what I came for—the reason I had to avoid Millie.

I was reminded of a wrong that needed to be right.

I needed to remember that Millie was in my past and destroying

Grayson Waters was my future.

ANTHONY

I NEVER TIRED of it: the game, the pretense. Watching the boy walk out with purpose and a grim expression because every tear was delivered so superbly.

I wanted so desperately to laugh. He wanted to stick to *the plan.*

It really was becoming too easy.

I almost wished the guards would grab the fool now. The boy was bound to get handcuffed eventually. He'd be pushed to the floor and treated like the trash he was, and I really did deserve to witness the moment I'd spent so many hours preparing for. The exact moment when Cooper realized how stupid and pathetic he'd been was bound to be glorious.

It would only take a whisper—the right name in the wrong ear.

But I knew I had to wait. I had to be patient.

The kid was only one con. One game. The more I pushed the right buttons, the better the finale. Hell, I hadn't spent my time in prison pretending to love a bastard child for an arrest inside these walls with no cameras.

There would be a bigger show. With the right amount of pressure on the right people, I'd get everything I wanted.

The best game was a long game.

ELEVEN

MILLIE

I HAD BRUISES everywhere.

On my knees.

Near my hips.

On my arms.

Anywhere I was grabbed and manhandled in that library three days before, I now saw a purple and green reminder. I didn't own large-enough clothes to cover the clues of my past actions, so I had to apply extra layers of makeup to hide what we had done. I'd gone through almost an entire bottle of concealer to cover the damage each night for work.

At least the visual reminders were something I could manage. I couldn't seem to switch off the memories. Each moment from the time he'd followed me through the library until the time I stormed out kept replaying in my mind. When I sat across from Tahnee all week talking about her new promotion, I couldn't control the unexpected flashbacks. Mouths. Tongues. Hands.

I was no longer forced to relive my final moments with Nate when I went to sleep now. Feel that pain of losing him. Instead these nights I found myself eager to go to bed, my mind filled with Cooper. It almost scared me how I had begun to dream again, how desperate my body was to return to those damn stacks and see if this need inside of me could be sated again.

Even now I was sitting on the couch, my ear pressed against my cell phone, trying to listen carefully to everything Parker was telling me. But my thoughts kept drifting to the memory of looking into Cooper's eyes as he thrust inside of me. Witnessing his hunger transform into acceptance, as if he knew exactly how it would feel when we finally came together. As if he knew the consequences us being together would bring and no longer cared.

He had turned a switch on inside of me, and I was shocked at how much I worried about it turning off.

"Millie?" Parker asked, pulling me back to reality.

Shit. Please be a yes or no question.

"Yes."

"You're sure? You really don't need me to organize the party? You're completely okay with having Jessie's party while Tahnee's away for business and you have to organize all the food?"

"Umm, sure. Definitely. Yes, of course. It's only party food," I replied, completely hiding the panic.

"Okay great, because I was worried that Jessie wouldn't get a cake—"

"Parker, I'm fine. I agreed to let you and Grayson take Jessie tonight while I have work, and I trust that you have everything under control. When the party comes, trust that I'll have everything under control. I can cook a damn birthday ca—"

Before I had a chance to finish my sentence, I heard a noise through the baby monitor. "Mine."

"I actually better go check on the soon-to-be birthday girl. She's awake and I hear her using her new favorite word," I laughed. "I'll see you later."

SHE'S BEAUTIFUL. THAT'S mostly me, but I'll give you credit for her personality. I was never that possessive.

"Thanks," I choked out. Half laugh, half Sob.

I was sitting in Jessie's bedroom watching her pick up each of her toys, look at me with suspicion, say, "Mine," and then drop them in a pile near her bed.

All while I was chatting with her dead father beside me.

Let's go back to my main argument. You need to hire a party planner or at least ask Marissa.

"I know what you're thinking, but you're wrong. I can handle a little girl's birthday party by myself. Parker is just being ridiculous."

Please just buy a cake, babe. Remember, we want her to have lots of birthdays.

"I only gave Tahnee food poisoning once," I replied defensively.

You know, it's a few weeks away. Maybe just don't buy any ingredients. Think about other options. Hey, in another week, you might not have to do it alone. That guy definitely doesn't seem like the type to leave you in the lurch.

"Tell me you're not trying to imply that I ask a convicted felon to help with our daughter's birthday."

Why not? I think he's a good guy. Sure, he's not as handsome as me, but we both know you won't find that. At some point you're going to have to lower your standards. Plus, I'm committed to any plan that helps save my baby from your cooking.

"You're dead, which means you aren't handsome anymore. You're blue. That being said, if you were alive, after your comments on my cooking, it wouldn't be for long. Also, you couldn't possibly know that he's a good guy. He's a criminal. He said so himself."

Real criminals don't tell you they're criminals, Pamela.

"Or maybe they do in order to distract you."

You know that's bullshit. Plus, he's going to frighten away every boy who tries to take Jessie on a date, so he has my vote.

"She's not even two yet, so that's not exactly a pressing issue. What if he was in jail for kidnapping?"

Ask him.

"I shouldn't. I need to focus on work and school. I need to get Jessie out of this house, remember? Plus, I probably won't even see him again. I ran out of the library like a crazy person."

Didn't you decide to be partners? Now what sort of partner abandons the other? I bet he's in the library. I bet he'd be willing to help fix this house up. I bet you could ask him what he was put away for.

"You're only saying this because my stupid horny subconscious wants to go back to that damn library and is looking for excuses."

Or maybe your subconscious is ready to share some of its thoughts with someone who can actually reply.

"Then why are you still here?" I asked before I looked up to see Jessie had stopped her hoarding and dropped her most tattered plush at my feet.

"Yours," she told me with a sweet smile.

COOPER

I LEFT THE prison repeating to myself that I was staying far away from Millie. With my fake ID still in my pocket, I thought about going to the nearest seedy club and toasting to the demise of Grayson Waters. I knew I needed to get back to the life I'd planned, one that existed in dirty establishments and didn't have me wondering about the safety of a redhead.

I need to get drunk, forget Millie, and take one of the girls dancing on stage home. A girl who knows the rules. One who's pretty enough to fuck, doesn't make me want to take another look, and is too busy dealing with her own shit to affect me and mine.

I'm not meant for libraries and college chicks.

As if possessed, I found myself driving to campus anyway, ignoring everything I'd told myself to pick at some invisible splinter embedded under my skin. I parked my motorcycle in the lot closest to the library, exhaled my self-control, and then followed the path across the quad toward the last place I should've been heading.

As I reached the library doors, I replayed our conversation in the stacks in my head. I recalled telling Millie that I thought of her as a Harley Quinn—a villain. After leaving a prison filled with the scum of this town, it was the last thing I really thought. I knew what real villains looked like, and although I saw her temper, I also noticed the vulnerability. I should've called her a princess, told her she was precious, even if she got pissed at me because she hated asking for help. The invisible splinter embedded in my skin that couldn't let go of Flash urged me to make amends, and fuck if I wasn't going to follow through with it.

I'd research a group of dead artists, write the whole damn assignment, and give the girl a break. I had already blown off my morning classes to go to the prison, so I figured I might as well blow the rest of them off for the real-life princess who was probably used to people waiting on her. Even if that did piss her off. The best part of my plan was it also meant I didn't need to spend any additional time with her.

I promised myself that I was really minimizing the distractions. I wasn't following my initial thoughts to fuck others and forget about her, but getting this shit out of the way would allow me to focus on football. With a bad block or tackle, a few words to the opposition about their shit skills, I'd help Tony get his revenge and my time at Penmore would be done. I'd already accepted that I would probably end up behind bars, but with Lizzie and Beth protected, no connections, that wouldn't be a problem. And after I helped Millie with this damn project, she wouldn't have any ties to me either. It was the perfect solution.

When I found my way to the back of the shelves, I swore the place still smelled like her. The faint mixture of exotic spices and common flowers that seemed to linger wherever she went invaded my senses. I felt like one of the arsonists I'd met in lockup.

Addicted.

Crazed.

Sniffing the air and wishing I could get closer to the flame without getting burned.

Determined to leave before someone caught me staring at the stacks, I started pulling art history books quickly. Made a damn mess and didn't give a damn.

"Were you in prison for kidnapping children?" she murmured behind me.

Fuck me. I turned around and Millie was standing at the end of the row, her arms crossed and her eyes narrowed. I almost couldn't decide how I liked them better, widened in pleasure or spitting warnings at me. *Damn, she's gorgeous.*

"Nope."

"Did you rape and kill women?" Her solemn attitude almost made me want to laugh. I was tempted to tease her, make up some ludicrous story to match her crazy questions, until I noticed she was biting her lip. She was worried about who I was, afraid that she'd let a monster touch her. I'd never cared to explain myself, but something about her false bravado got to me.

"I beat the shit out of a cop," I replied honestly.

"Oh."

"Yeah."

"Did he deserve it?"

"The judge didn't think so," I muttered.

"But the dean did?" she deduced, the realization clearly calming her fears as she stopped biting her lip. When she ran the tip of her tongue along the part of her lip where her teeth had been earlier, the point of the conversation was lost on me. I wanted to replace her tongue with mine, forget about the assignment or understanding each other and focus on feeling our way to a shared familiarity.

"Mostly he wanted a new running back. But he might have used the rumors about the cop's willingness to look the other way when it came to child abuse in foster and group homes in the area to get the other bigwigs on campus to let me in," I said quickly, shrugging off the harsh realities I had to deal with.

I started leaning into her body. I should've been keeping things platonic, but I just needed to smell her. I caught the widening of her eyes before she looked off into the distance to process what I'd said. While she was distracted, I took a step forward. Like an addict, I was incapable of following my own decisions to keep away from her.

"Damn, the law can really be screwed up." She let out a soft sigh and turned her gaze back to me. She took in the limited distance that now existed between our bodies and I saw the heat ignite. "Okay, um, so I'm happy to still work together," she murmured, her voice thick with desire. "We just need to have boundaries. This is probably a crazy suggestion, and if you just lied to me, potentially dangerous, but I think we should study at my house."

"Something wrong with the library?" I asked, smirking at her. I watched the blush creep across her face until I saw her steel spine snap back into place.

"We go to mine and you'll have a chaperone. You won't be so inclined to say, 'Fuck it,' and we might actually get work done," she replied haughtily.

"Who do you think will prevent you from running your hands over me?" I moved until I felt her chest pressed against my own. I was seconds away from sliding my hands around her small waist, completely prepared to say to hell with my decision to stay platonic. With firm hands, I would remind her exactly how good we felt together and how much she wanted me. "Or will be able to keep my hands off you?"

"My daughter."

TWELVE

COOPER

"YOU HAVE A kid?" I asked, my hands frozen at my side.

"A little girl, yes," she said, smiling wide. "She's nearly two."

"You have a boyfriend or husband as well?" I growled.

"If I did, I wouldn't have let you fuck me in the library shelves," she hissed. "If you want to say stupid stuff, you can stay here." She turned dramatically and headed toward the exit.

Unlike her last library escape, that time I followed her silently, too shocked to speak.

Princesses weren't single mothers. Princesses lived lives full of frivolity. They needed people to take care of them.

Single mothers were tough. They were warriors and saviors, women who took care of their children without support and with the determination of a pit bull.

Lizzie and I decided at a young age that single moms were like the pot of gold at the end of the rainbow: elusive, mysterious and utter fiction. Neither of us had mothers willing to go it alone without our father's help. Sure, we'd heard of people talking about single mothers, but we had also heard people talk of leprechauns.

I took another look at Millie as she strode across the campus. She was wearing skintight black jeans that hugged her hips and fit tightly into her gray ankle boots, a long-sleeve white shirt, and a gray leather jacket, her hair falling in curls over her shoulders. She didn't look like she'd struggled. She looked amazing. She looked like a mythical fucking creature come to life.

Fuck me.

"This is my car. We can take it my house, and then when I head to work, I can drop you back at your bike," she told me. "I'm a mom, so I can't just hop on the back of your motorcycle."

I finally snapped out of my daze, staring at her pickup truck.

"All good," I murmured before asking for the keys with my palm out.

"It's my car."

"Babe, I'm still driving."

"*Babe*, you don't even know where we're going. And I'll repeat, it's my car."

"And I'll repeat, I'm driving," I informed her. "I'd also like to point out that it's a pickup truck."

"Yes. *My* pickup. Which is why I'm driving."

"Flash, a man does not sit as the passenger in a pickup while a woman drives him around."

"That's ludicrous, not to mention sexist."

"Could be Beyoncé's pickup and I'd still make her give me the damn keys. You want to call it sexist, go right ahead, but I'm going to call it being a gentleman and ask for the keys again."

"Gentleman, my ass. And by the way, no one would demand Queen B sit in the passenger seat."

"Babe, I doubt Beyoncé sits anywhere but the passenger seat. But we can continue arguing this fact, wasting study time, or you could just give me the damn keys."

I held back the smirk as I watched her contemplate how long it would take her to win this ridiculous argument. Then my smile widened as she huffed and stomped her way toward me.

"This is ridiculous. Just because you're male does not mean you need to be the one to drive a truck. There's a car seat in the back, which makes this a *mom's* car. Moms drive the mom car!" she rambled as she climbed into the passenger seat and buckled up.

"Millie, I'm trying real hard to ignore the fact that you went batshit crazy and tried to turn a pickup into a mom car. But I'll also shock you by saying that if this shit was a Volvo, a mom's car Volvo, I'd still be driving. Now do me a favor and help by telling me which way I'm going."

"I wouldn't have to tell you if I was the one—"

"Millie," I interrupted her firmly. "Address."

I turned my head to watch her chew on her lip again.

"I changed my mind. Maybe we should go back to the library."

"If you're backing out and don't tell me where you live, I'm just going to drive to mine," I told her, my voice dipping low. "Where there are no chaperones."

"Two lefts. Then keep driving until you pass the traffic circle."

"You live a block away from the old trailer park?"

"Yeah."

"It's not a good neighborhood."

"Umm, okay, so I know it's not ideal, but maybe you should wait until you see it before you judge my neighborhood."

"I grew up in your neighborhood. I know how bad it can get."

"Oh."

THE TERMITE DAMAGE exposed a lot of the wood that enclosed the porch. The faded blue paint was peeling from every corner. The front window was boarded up with old pieces of wood. The whole house was an eyesore. I was surprised it was still standing. The city should've torn it down already.

"How is this place not condemned?" I muttered as we made our way up her hazardous driveway.

"I have no idea," she laughed, carefully maneuvering her way across the dangerous cracks with ease. "It's not so bad on the inside."

"And you live here alone with your daughter?" I asked, keeping the concern out of my voice. The last thing I wanted was for her to become pissed at me again and lock me out of the house.

"It's actually my daughter's grandmother's house. The day I told her I had nowhere to live, she called a real estate agent and sold her townhouse. This was the only house in her price range that she could buy that same day and gave us all our own rooms."

I read between the lines. Her daughter's grandmother—not her mother. Nowhere to live—I wasn't surprised. In this neighborhood, I was sure being related to a deadbeat dad and having shit parents were prerequisites.

"Sounds like an impressive woman. She going to be here?"

"She's the most impressive woman I've ever met, but you're not getting that honor today. She's at work, but my best friend will be here. She came by to take Jessie for a sleepover and let me duck out to the library to get more notes. I'm not a deadbeat parent, if that's what you're thinking. I don't leave my two-year-old in the house by herself," She raised her eyebrows as if waiting to be challenged. When I shrugged, letting her know of my indifference, she continued. "You do realize you only recently told me you were an ex-con? While I trust that you didn't lie about why you were put away, I'm not going to pretend that I don't feel safer knowing we aren't alone."

"I get it. Hell, the more the merrier. I could invite the whole team over if it makes you more comfortable."

"Team?"

"The Herons."

"Simon, the team wouldn't just show up for some fan to help him score with a chick. You can't tell everyone what to do and expect them to follow your orders," she laughed while unlocking the door.

"Probably not, but I'm on the team."

"You're not on the team," she said firmly as she abruptly blocked the doorway.

"Babe, I am." I chuckled as I realized there was annoyance brewing in her vivid blue eyes.

"No, you're not. You can't be," she repeated.

"I'm the new walk-on. I trained over spring. I haven't been doing much at the past few games but warming the bench, but I'm on the team, even if the coach hates me."

"Great. This is just fantastic," she muttered.

"You know, you're the only person I've met who's been pissed that I'm a part of the team," I responded, smirking.

"It just means we're going to see each other more than I ever thought we would."

"Is that so? Babe, you a team groupie?" I teased. "Am I gonna get to see you checking me out from the stands? Shit, do I need to worry about tackling your baby daddy?"

"Funny," she retorted. "As if I would let a Heron touch me."

"Sorry to break it to you, Flash, but you already did. With me."

"Yeah well, I didn't know you were on the team then, so it doesn't count. And now that I know, it won't happen again. I don't sleep with people who play with my daughter's uncle, who also happens to be my best friend's boyfriend. Way too incestuous."

I didn't hear the shit about her daughter's uncle. I didn't think to ask any questions, too stuck on her comment that "it won't happen again." Like knives to my gut. After those words, everything else became white noise.

She was right.

I couldn't help but yell at myself. *What the hell am I doing here? Insisting on driving and coming to her damn house—where her daughter lives!*

I need to let her go.

I started making excuses, reminded myself that I kept my promises. Told myself that in that moment I had to fulfill my role as her partner.

I wouldn't risk her getting too close to the shit I'd agreed to do or the crap choices I planned to make after they were all done.

I was just going to help her.

MILLIE

LITTLE GIRL GIGGLES.

That was the noise we heard when we finally walked into the house.

All I wanted to do was follow the high-pitched squeals. I wanted to walk down the hallway to Jessie's bedroom and soak in her eyes and smiles. I wanted to join my best friend in basking in my kid's entire essence while I wasn't tired, when she wasn't hungry or grumpy.

I desperately wanted to forget all about the project. Avoid the fact that I'd agreed to be a college football player's partner for a class assignment—a clichéd recipe for disaster.

But I knew if I didn't finish the work now, there would be no time to work later, when she was demanding my attention or when I was struggling to keep my eyes open. So I ignored the sounds that pulled at the core of my being and led him to our small kitchen table.

I'd probably made a terrible mistake bringing him home. I was thinking all about sexual self-preservation in the library, about the encouragement my imaginary Nate had given me. I wasn't thinking about the realities of having a stranger in my house, about the invasive questions this invited. I had forgotten about the photographs I kept around the house that exposed my life.

Deciding we would prepare our speeches at the kitchen table, I hid my panic in a strong stomp straight to the kitchen, avoiding the furniture that allowed for horizontal activity or ornaments that might've led to quizzical looks. I would kick him out before he could blink, and then I would be able to get to work early.

"So, you live here long?" he queried as he looked at the small kitchen and high chair.

Great. Small talk. I needed to move faster.

"We moved in just after Jessie was born." As I leaned over the table and started laying out the notes, I felt his eyes scanning the house, so I pretended that I was completely engrossed in deciding upon an art movement.

"We have all night to do this assignment, Flash?"

"No, I've actually got work in a couple of hours."

"Then maybe you should stop that."

"Stop what?"

"Trying to make a decision. It's painful to watch. You should stop and let a pro handle this."

"Already predicting a professional career, huh? A tad conceited, but hey, you want to prove to me that you're not a dumb jock, go right ahead," I replied. "But I'm going to keep looking at the different movements until you decide to stop examining my house and put your money where your mouth is."

THIRTEEN

COOPER

SHE WAS BAITING me.

She was trying to tease me with her words, but it was her body that tormented me. Leaning over the kitchen table spreading out her notes caused her jeans to stretch across her ass, and my dick started twitching. It wanted me to grab either side of her hips and claim what was on display. It took every bit of my self-control not to press myself against the tight seam between her cheeks. It didn't matter that it had only been minutes, I was already struggling to stick to the plan.

I tried to keep myself in check by looking around the kitchen to find reminders that she was a mom, that we weren't alone. However, there was nothing personal in the kitchen—only a rectangular wooden table, daisy-yellow cabinets, and an old white fridge. The space was clean and friendly, but clearly no one in this house spent very much time in this room.

I needed her little girl to start giggling again.

When we first walked in, I'd heard her down the hall and it was like an ice bath. A cute but strong reminder to get out of this house as fast as possible. I knew we needed to select an art movement, outline speaking roles, and divvy up responsibilities before I could leave. I planned on getting all that done in less time than it would take me to buckle my seat belt and drive away.

Unfortunately, the house had gone silent. I could see the notes and pages of information we needed to shift through, but each time I looked at that damn table, my eyes were drawn to her luscious body. Every time she reached for another piece of paper, all I could see was red.

When she groaned in frustration because a stack of her notes fell to the floor due to too much shifting, I felt it in my dick and gave in to temptation. I stepped directly behind her, pressed tightly against her ass, and reached for the paper directly in front of her thighs. I let my thumb casually brush against the edge of her jeans.

"This one," I told her huskily.

The sound of her swallowing was her only reply. She was frozen.

I pressed tighter into her ass and heard the soft exhale.

"Read the name, Flash," I whispered into her ear, stroking her earlobe with my tongue as my thumb lazily drew closer to the heat between her legs. I watched her bend her head, taking in not only the piece of paper but also my hand moving against her inner thigh.

"De-De St-Stijl," she stammered.

"They look good?" I pressed my fingers firmly between her jeans and ran the length of her seam.

"Ye-yes."

"How good?" I asked as my thumb found her clit and began rubbing hard circles over the warm fabric.

"S-so good," she moaned, pressing her backside into me.

"How about now?" I couldn't help rocking my hips into her ass as my fingers started working her harder and faster with each new rotation.

"Oh God, yes—"

"Hey, Mill, Jessie and I are ready to take off—" Suddenly a hot brunette walked into the kitchen with a baby on her hip. And as fast as she entered, she was walking out, yelling behind her, "Shit, so sorry. I didn't mean to interrupt. Um, Jessie and I will be on our way—"

While the brunette was rambling in the doorway, Millie and I straightened up. Her eyes were wide with shock and horror at being caught bent over the kitchen table. I couldn't help but smile at her beautiful blue eyes, which suddenly filled with wrath. Directed straight at me.

Thankfully whatever verbal lashing she wanted to send my way was saved by the sound of the front door opening, because she immediately turned toward where her friend had just left and called out, "Parker, get back in here. It's nothing. We're just studying."

I was hoping her friend wasn't an idiot. I hoped she left and took the toddler with her, so I wouldn't be meeting them both with a raging hard-on.

When I heard footsteps getting closer to us, I remembered that I was not that lucky.

"Well, studying art sure looks different than how I did it in high School," her friend stated, struggling to swallow her chuckle. "You're lucky your daughter is obsessed with playing with my earrings or she might grow up very confused when she has to study *art*." She then turned her amber eyes to me and said, "You must be Simon."

"Cooper," I corrected, glancing quizzically at Millie.

"Oh, sorry, Cooper. I'm Parker. It's really nice to meet you. I'd shake your hand but mine are kind of full here with this munchkin. Not to mention Jessie and I are all packed for our sleepover. And we really should be going."

"Damn. Sorry. You shouldn't have to rush off because of—"

"No, it wasn't you. I promised my boyfriend I'd only be gone an hour. He doesn't like it when I get more time with Jessie than he does. He's a whiner when that happens, and I love him, but even I can't stand listening to his jealous whining."

"You're also rushing out of here so you can save all your good jokes for when I'm alone," Millie scoffed as she walked forward to kiss her daughter's cheek.

"I don't know what you're talking about."

"If you say one word about us being in the kitchen, I won't let you take her."

"You wouldn't dare. Plus I know how little action this kitchen has seen, so I'd hate to joke about it. Gosh, did you even know you had this room?"

"You're hilarious," Millie deadpanned.

"I try. Anyway, Cooper, it was nice to meet you. Mill, pickup tomorrow round four?"

"Sounds good," Millie agreed.

I stood there in silence as I watched Millie kiss the head of a little girl with brown curls. Thankfully I couldn't see her face because she was too engrossed with playing with the brunette's dangling earrings. I thought it was the only reason why I wasn't freaking out.

How could I forget that she's a single mom? I shouldn't be touching her.

No matter how much my fingers burned to continue what they started, I needed to remember that no single mom deserved the life that came with me.

When the front door closed, she turned her mermaid eyes toward me and I shrugged off my self-loathing. "You couldn't help yourself, could you?" she asked mockingly.

"Babe, you were bent over the table," I tried to explain.

"It wasn't an invitation," she returned.

"The fuck it wasn't. You were seconds away from begging me to lick the damn envelope."

"That's ridiculous."

"What's ridiculous is snapping at me because you're embarrassed and trying to act like you weren't moaning beneath my fingers five minutes ago. You're as guilty as I am prosecutor. Now if you're done pretending that wasn't mutually awkward as fuck, I've only got one question. How many names have you got for me? And if they exceed two, why the hell am I not allowed to call you Flash?"

I watched the blush bloom across her cheeks. Then just as quickly, I noticed her inner steel straighten her spine. "You know what? Call me whatever you want," she told me as she began to collect all the paper into a big pile. "I'm really too busy to argue with you."

"Yes, princess. Although I thought you were never too busy to argue. Now if you're finished putting me in my place, why are you packing up? We not studying anymore?"

"Clearly nothing stops you from touching me, so I think it's best you leave."

"You know, most girls would take that as a compliment."

"I'm not most girls," Millie stated as she turned to me and trapped me in her eyes. "I also don't have time for whatever your presence might lead to. Now, I need to get ready for work. I'm happy to pay for the cab back to campus for you to grab your bike."

"You want me to leave so you can get ready for work? Right now?"

"Yes."

"You're full of shit. You're afraid of whatever this is and worried that we can't seem to stop ourselves from giving in to each other. We couldn't in a crowded library or in a room right beside your daughter. We can't seem to get our act together, but I'll concede. I'll leave so you can get ready for work, but we're still doing the damn assignment together."

"Okay."

"Okay?" I repeated.

"If I said no, would you listen?"

"No."

"Then you can start the assignment. Next class, give me whatever you have done and I'll finish it."

"Sounds good to me," I told her. "Before you push me out the door, you got a bathroom here?"

"Sure," she replied, rolling her eyes. "Second door on the right. I'll just pack all this up for you to take with you."

I nodded and left the kitchen, running my fingers through my hair in exasperation as I made my way down the hall.

I'm full of shit too.

I have no control over whatever's developing between us.

If I had, I wouldn't have been looking for family mementos as I made my way through her house, desperately hunting for more reminders that would cement the feeling I had when I saw her kiss her little girl.

I was so close to dragging her into my world, making her one of those women who only got to see her partner in visitor rooms, across tables with guards watching close by.

I needed something—anything—that might've been able to keep her protected from the need I was struggling to control when I was around her.

I was hoping to discover the ropes that bound her to a future of school dances and dentist appointments.

I found what I was searching for on a small table just past the bathroom: a collection of eight-by-seven-inch photographs documenting a teen's journey into motherhood. I smiled at the photo of Millie sitting by a Christmas tree wearing a sweater with Rudolf the Reindeer's red nose protruding due to the width of her growing pregnant belly. Examined the photo of Millie in a hospital bed, her red hair sticking to her forehead and a 'just try and fuck with her and see what I can do' expression on her face as she held a newborn wrapped in pink.

However, I decided to memorize the image capturing her dozing beside a sleeping baby on a picnic blanket. Both of them were in identical sleeping positions, their left arms beneath their heads with their mouths pouting.

Two beautiful girls I would destroy like everything else in my life if I decided to bring her into my world.

I was about to turn back toward the bathroom when I saw them glaring at me from the end of the table.

I sucked in a breath when I picked up the small silver-framed photograph. The guy could be a fucking model with his perfect hair and bright green eyes leaning against a bar. The next star of that stupid show where dozens of girls lined up to win the chance of wearing his engagement ring. It didn't take a genius to figure out that this guy must be the dad—the baby had the same dark curls. I struggled not to snarl. *He should be here. He should be protecting her from me and everything else that this fucking life throws at good women.*

I put the frame down and with tentative fingers picked up the last photograph on the bench. The black-and-white photograph that sent the breath I was holding wheezing out. Even in tones of gray it was clearly documenting the baby's first birthday—filled with cake, a candle, and a big number one balloon. At the center of the photo was a high chair, a little girl's face covered in bits of cake with only her pigtails free from icing, and her small family surrounding her. My eyes glossed over Millie, the grandmother, and the hot brunette I'd met earlier.

Instead they focused on the only guy in the picture. The one with his arms around the brunette,. a 'World's Greatest Uncle' T-shirt and the same smile the media captured when he won the Heisman Trophy his sophomore year.

A smile that made it into fucking prison because everyone was so enamored by the local town hero.

Grayson Waters.

A smile I'd promised to destroy.

Things just got really fucking complicated.

FOURTEEN

COOPER

I DECIDED TO walk back to campus. I didn't say a word to Millie, just grabbed the handful of documents she held out to me and walked out the door.

I needed to process the shit I'd just seen. The family and the smiles. The photo of a guy I'd been told was a scumbag—a fame whore who didn't give a shit about his family. Flash's photo of him smiling like the only thing that mattered was a little girl's first birthday didn't make any sense.

My facts weren't adding up. If Parker was wrapped around him, then he was the boyfriend. He wanted to watch a two-year-old, and he whined about not getting the same amount of time with Millie's daughter. He was *not* the guy Tony described.

How the hell was he the same guy who threw his dad into prison? The same man who let his brother get gunned down by mobsters because he didn't keep his gambling accounts paid in full?

I had always been a skeptic, distrusting the words that fell out of people's mouths from a young age when I realized sooner or later they revealed something very different. But Tony had been crying about Nate since he'd stepped foot in the prison. Never once did he waver in his pathetic appearance and distraught attitude. He kept me up most nights with his pacing, talking about his guilt about not stepping in soon enough. After a year and a half, I believed him.

For *once* in my life, I finally thought a father might give a damn about his son.

I wanted to stand for that. I wanted to help *that* man, the man who knew how it felt to have no control over losing someone so fucking important.

I couldn't have been wrong. I couldn't have let a mobster convince me that he was the victim, his eldest son a victim and the youngest a criminal.

I was not the idiot who got manipulated.

I was, however, that fucking unlucky.

Promising to help tear apart the few people in Millie's life. The one girl who almost made me forget the demons I lived with every day.

I needed time. I needed to work out what was real before I did anything.

———

I GOT BACK to campus and was lost in my thoughts. I was only a few feet away when I saw him leaning against my fucking bike.

I was tempted to turn around, leave it all behind.

I hesitated a second too long.

"What? No warm hug?" Eli called out as he straightened his cop's uniform and smiled at me.

"What do you want?" I asked, approaching with clenched hands tightly constrained in my pockets.

"Now is that any way to greet your brother? I miss your grand exit, and the first chance I get, I come to visit and you aren't pleased to see me. That hurts, little bro." He chuckled.

"What do you need?" I muttered.

"It's not about what *I* need. It's about what *you* need. I got a call today. One of my boys on the inside mentioned that you were in the visitor section today. Except apparently you aren't Cooper Daniels but Billy Nolan.

I thought, 'well that's mighty strange. Maybe I need to go find my little brother and see what he's up to.'"

"Nothing that has anything to do with you. And if you want to turn me in because you're afraid of what I might be up to, well I'm happy to follow you back to the station, Officer. Sign away my life to you and yours. Again," I drawled.

"Always so dramatic. Coop, you know that wasn't me. I was in the hospital. You did that. Attacking a police officer in front of witnesses? You think they would just look the other way? That because of the blood we share you'd get a free pass?" He laughed lightly, then straightened and took a step toward me. "You always had delusions of grandeur, bro."

"You turned up to his damn funeral in your fucking navy blues," I gritted out, braced to receive or throw a punch. "You let me pay you off that same fucking morning and still you contacted the Walters. If you hadn't—"

"The orders came from above. I just followed them. Whatever you believe about me calling all the shots is wrong. I've always just followed orders. I did, however, go to the funeral for you, and for Lizzie," he told me, flashing his white teeth.

"Neither she nor I needed you. I've told you from the very beginning to stay away from her. You weren't prepared to be there for her when we all shared the same roof or when sick social workers started cornering her in the group home. Social workers you were in charge of monitoring. Why you thought she needed you to watch Jake be put in the ground—"

"Shit, Coop. Not even prison has changed you. Always so dramatic," he chuckled. "You know we could've avoided all this if you hadn't been such a dumbass that day."

"Is that so?"

"You know as well as I do that I've been protected. The moment I put on the uniform and the sleaziest of the government workers of this town knew I would follow their rules, I became important to them. You put me in the hospital for three weeks. Two broken ribs, a concussion. There was going to be retaliation. Two years in jail was lucky compared to what they could've done."

"I'd do it again."

"You keep wanting to blame me, but my phone call wasn't what ruined that day. It was one delinquent kid doing what delinquent kids usually do when they fuck up: fuck up some more. You're just pissed that when I left the group home, I joined the system we grew up in instead of trying to fight it."

"That's not all I can be pissed about. That phone call—"

"Fine, whatever bullshit you've twisted in your head, I get it. Make me the baddest of the bad guys. With the savior complex you like to rock, I know you need someone to blame. I understand that you're still trying to avenge him in some fucked-up way and I'm the one you've decided upon, even though you fail to remember that no one ever fucking avenged shit for me. While you were bouncing around in your first foster homes like a cute wounded puppy, I was moved straight into the group home with guards a lot worse than you all experienced. No one protected me, so why you think I was duty bound to protect all of you escapes me. I lived in the same home. I saw the same troubles. I just decided I was done eating shit. I figure maybe my seven years on earth before you made me smarter, because, little brother, *I* survived that place. I wasn't the one trying to bite the hand that fed me. You work with the enemy and you no longer have any reason to fear the enemy."

"Your logic was fucked back then, and it's still fucked up."

"I have a system that protects me. And what do you have, Coop? How's your savior complex working for you? Notice you haven't been exactly starting in any games lately. This fancy college's charity program doesn't extend all the way to the field, does it? Hate me because I turn a blind eye like everyone before me did and everyone after me will. I don't live with the threat of being thrown in a cage though, which is more than I can say for you."

"Doesn't mean you're not their pet."

"Jesus Christ, no wonder Dad hit you the most," Eli muttered. "Stop making stupid mistakes, little brother. Don't go back to the prison. This is as generous as I get."

I watched him walk to his car, the pain and anger and fury building. I let it feed me.

I'd failed Jake, failed Lizzie and Beth. I'd failed myself.

And now after a fucking day with a redhead, I was afraid I was going to fail her as well.

Before I could drive off, the cocksucker pulled up beside my bike and threw a small orange bottle of pills at me. I caught them on reflex.

"I figure your supply is running low these days. Can't be easy to get a hold of oxy out of the joint and with your parole officer coming around all the time. Don't say your big brother doesn't look out for you," he told me before driving off.

I stared at the small bottle.

With all the control I had, I pushed it deep into my pocket. The lifeline I found in prison. It annoyed me that he knew, that he had something else to taunt over me.

Thank fuck I knew the parts of this town where nobody knew jack about anyone else and liked it that way.

MILLIE

I LEFT MY house straight after Cooper stormed out without saying good-bye. I could've stood in the kitchen and imagined what might've happened between us had Parker not walked in, but I knew it would've led to something ridiculous like my chasing him down the street.

Arriving at work early was the smarter choice.

I waved at Clint, the bouncer, and entered through the back door. I knew if Getting Lucky spotted me before my shift, she'd make me manage the bar. Hopefully if I caught one of the girls who had a soft spot for single mothers, they'd swap shifts with me. I'd go on early, they'd go on later, and I would make it home in time to snuggle on the couch and watch *Outlander* with Tahnee.

As soon as I saw Anna at her small dressing table, I knew I was in luck.

"Hey, An—"

"Thank God! You want to change shifts?" the cheerful blonde asked as she spotted me sitting down opposite her.

"Yeah, if you don't mind."

"Not a problem at all! Mike just dropped me off and was sulking that we can't spend more time together. Boyfriends are so hard to make time for, right?"

"Umm yeah, boyfriends—"

"Anyway, I go on in ten. Do you think you can manage that?"

"I can definitely manage that."

"Awesome. I'll be back in an hour for your shift, right?"

"Yep."

"Okay, toodles." She raced out the door, a complete whirlwind of bubbly enthusiasm.

I waved goodbye and not for the first time thought how much I would probably hate her and her perky California girl attitude if she didn't give me her shifts whenever she couldn't be bothered to turn up, or swapped at a moment's notice, saving my ass.

With only ten minutes to get ready, I started pulling out my supplies.

Every Thursday night I played Jessica Rabbit. I swept my hair so it all fell over my right shoulder in loose curls, painted my lips a blood red, and wore long purple satin gloves. The floor-length strapless red satin dress I used to complete my costume was my favorite burlesque gown.

It was also the most expensive outfit I'd bought for this job. With its sweetheart neckline, exposed boning on the bodice, and a cutout at the front of the skirt that ended at my thighs and revealed nearly all of my legs, the gown was the perfect outfit of a classy seductress. One of the other dancers had a cheap sequined red dress she offered to share when I first started that would've also passed as a perfectly good Jessica Rabbit costume, but when I saw this one in a window after coffee with Parker, I knew it was meant for me.

After slipping it on, I was almost able to overlook the fact that I would be revealing my matching thong to the audience after only a couple of minutes. The soft fabric sliding down my skin made me feel like I was waiting for a real party to begin. A party that started with a prince and a horse-drawn carriage.

Unfortunately, it wasn't a prince who ended up calling my name but an angry, middle-aged woman.

"Millie, you swap with Anna again?"

"Yep."

"All right then. Be warned though, we got a bachelor party out there tonight. You get too close, you're on your own."

"I'm sorry, what?"

"All my other bouncers called in sick. Can't risk Clint now or I'll be closed for the rest of the night. You think about doing something stupid, just know that I've given strict instructions that no one's going to rescue you."

"I cannot believe you're telling me this right now."

"You have a problem, I'll get one of the other girls."

"No, no problem. I'll just keep my moves short."

"Perfect."

With those parting words, I walked toward the stage curtain and posed.

Even with short moves, in this dress with a bachelor party going wild in front of the stage, I was ready to make enough money to buy my own damn carriage.

FIFTEEN

MILLIE

THE FIRST LYRICS of "Hotter than Hell" started and I began my transformation. The song was faster and more modern than my usual numbers. The seductive tone and lyrics, coupled with my satin red dress, made me feel every bit the she-devil. I couldn't help but roll my hips slowly and move my arms across my body freely. I knew the crowd loved it when I heard their cheers.

After dramatically throwing my gloves into the audience, I bent over and slowly slid my hands from my calves to my exposed thighs. I started picturing the path Cooper's fingers took earlier in the day. It was as if my body was back in that kitchen, recalling the feel of Cooper pressed against my back. I closed my eyes, fantasized that my hands were his as they moved across my cleavage and the boning of my bodice that cupped my breasts.

I got so turned on by the idea of Cooper's fingers running across my skin and tight dress that I missed the sound of a glass smashing and guys having words at the front of the stage. Lost in the music and my desire, I kept rolling my body to the beat, posing dramatically each time the song reached a crescendo.

Before I realized it, I'd moved too close to the edge of the stage. I remembered the wild bachelor party too late. When a calloused hand grabbed my ankle from amongst the crowd and stopped me from my next dance move, I fought the panic I felt. Instead I focused on looking for someone behind the bar to help. When I finally caught sight of Clint's look of defeat and Getting Lucky's shaking head, I realized I was on my own.

The hand moved from my ankle to my hips. Before I could blink, I was thrown over the shoulder of a muscled man and carried outside the club.

With as much gusto as I could muster, I prepared to scream my lungs out. When the cool air bit my exposed skin as we exited the building, my fear sky rocketed. With a renewed sense of self-preservation, I took a deep breath to fill my lungs, but when I opened my mouth to start wailing, I was abruptly dumped to the ground.

My seven-inch heels wobbled on the gravel, and the air I had sucked in wheezed out like a dropped balloon. I tried to stabilize myself and quickly came up with a new plan. The silence in the parking lot reminded me that in this neighborhood, I could scream all evening and no one would come to my rescue, so I put on my saddest face and looked into the eyes of my kidnapper, ready to beg.

I was, like always, ready to save myself.

"You're not going back in there," Cooper announced when my eyes locked on his angry stare.

I let out a sigh of relief. I didn't need to beg. I wasn't being kidnapped. I wasn't about to be assaulted.

I was about to be lectured. Again.

"You're not doing this anymore," he demanded.

Fuck, where was a kidnapper when you needed one?

"I'm so sorry, *Simon*, but just like in the supermarket, you can't boss me around."

"You're a mother, for fuck's sake."

With those words, something inside of me snapped.

"You did not just say that to me," I growled.

"Mill—"

"You think I want to do this? That I don't wish I could spend every night with my daughter? You think I want to dance around with things attached to my nipples and pretend I love every oily fingered man in there?" Before he had a chance to respond, I continued. "Unfortunately, I don't live in a fairy tale. No one is picking up one of those gloves I dropped in there, checking that it fits, and buying me a castle. Every week there is food, clothes, diapers, and toothpaste I need to buy. Me. Only me. And if I want anything left over to actually improve my life, I need a fuckload more money than they pay at the local diner. So yeah, I'm a mother, *for fuck's sake*, and I'm a *damn* good mother *because* of this fucking job."

"Babe, you don't belong here."

"You think I don't know that? No one belongs here. But all this is just my prologue."

"Your what?"

"The part of my story that explains how I got Jessie and me into a nice three-bedroom house that doesn't look like you'll break your ankle walking up the stairs. Or how I'll afford an SUV that has working airbags should a dipshit think of hitting my girl and me rather than drive around in a used pickup. So yeah, my job isn't pretty, and it isn't perfect, but I can handle it. It's a far cry from being an escort and a step up from a stripper. Hell, burlesque can be an art form."

"Babe, you're forgetting that I grew up around here. Places like this lie with their fucking use of the term *art* and their ability to offer anything other than grief. They're calling it burlesque to jack up the prices, but Poison is still the same strip joint I grew up around. And babe, you're kidding yourself if you think the women who work here end up in pretty houses. They end up in hospitals, rehab facilities recovering from the shit they've had to ingest to sleep at night without visions of the creeps who have come in and out of doors just like those. It'll harden you beyond your years. It'll destroy you."

I couldn't help but laugh. It rumbled deep from my gut until I was bending over wiping away tears.

"I forgot," I managed once I had myself under control and stared into his eyes, smiling.

"You forgot what?" he asked, looking at me like I was a lunatic.

"That we're strangers. Sure, you've sat beside me, followed me around a supermarket, bickered at me some. And yeah, you've been *in* me. But you're kidding yourself if you think that means you *know* me."

"What the fuck are you trying to imply?" His eyes hardened.

"It means I'm already hard, you asshole. I've been hard for *two years*. I'm not some naive young girl anymore."

"You don't think you're naive?"

"It's difficult to remain unscathed after you spend a night with a beautiful man, get pregnant, and then have to go to his funeral *the day before* you go to your first ultrasound," I replied, my eyes glassy with unshed tears.

"Babe," he murmured softly, reaching for me. "You aren't as damaged as you think."

I shook off his outstretched hands. "I hide it better than most, but don't confuse me with some carefree college chick. I lost that innocence a long time ago. And it wasn't from taking my clothes off. In case you haven't experienced it, having no hope for the future does that. This place, this money, it's giving me my hope back. It's giving me *me* back."

"I get it. Probably more than you realize. But if you won't change your mind, then once I get off work, I'll be by the stage each night. "

My eyebrows rose. *He has to be joking.* "You've got to be joking."

"I just grabbed you off the fucking stage and no one did shit."

"They're short on bouncers. I was warned. I just got distract—"

"That's not good enough. You tell me your shifts and I'll be here." He crossed his arms over his barrel chest to emphasize his point.

"Cooper, you trying to save the world one damsel at a time isn't getting you laid tonight."

"That's not me. This isn't about me getting laid."

"It looks like it from where I'm standing."

"What did you call us? Strangers? Guess you were right about that."

"I'm right about a lot of things. Like how you shouldn't be here."

"It's a waste of your time trying to change my mind. It's not happening. Instead, let's fix this shit."

"What?"

"This stranger crap. Hell, you want to go back in there after they did jack shit to help you?"

"No. But my purse is inside. With my car keys."

"All right, we'll go get to know each other. Partners should know each other. Then I'll bring you back to get your purse and keys afterward. Hell, you can tell them I kept you against your will and still demand to get paid."

"That still doesn't change the fact that my keys are inside. If you think I'll get on your bike in this dress, think again."

"Then the first thing you get to learn about me is that I can boost a pickup."

"You told me you went to prison for beating up a cop."

"I didn't tell you I had a squeaky-clean record babe."

"Great. In case I forget to mention it later, this show-and-tell time is likely going to traumatize me." I begrudgingly led the way to my car.

"You have no idea."

SIXTEEN

COOPER

"SOMEONE NEEDS TO go get more beer. We're all out," a guy yelled from the back of the frat house.

I was momentarily repulsed by the circus of activity. Smoke polluted the air. People were standing around in small groups everywhere, laughing and dancing. Music blared from high-tech speakers. Drunken sorority girls kept singing off-key each time a song hit the chorus. It was a madhouse. The chaos was worse than the prison yard during a riot.

The pulsating pop music was already giving me a headache. I wanted to walk out as quickly as I walked inside. Unfortunately, my gut told me that this would be the best place to get answers from Flash. A place where we could be talking amongst a crowd of people and nearly all of them would only be hearing the latest hit on repeat and focusing on the drink in their hand.

"This is where you bring me? A frat party?" Millie asked, crossing her arms in front of her fucking gorgeous tits. Her nose twitched, probably due to the smell of cheap perfume and spilt spirits.

"It's better than my place, trust me." I reached for her hand and dragged her toward the back door, hoping it led to a patio deck and some privacy.

"I'm a little overdressed for a house party." She looked around, staring at the girls in cutoff denim skirts and tank tops.

When I noticed her tugging at the side of her floor-length red dress, I squeezed her hand. "You look fucking amazing, and if someone wants to say otherwise, they can go through me," I informed her firmly. I noticed a few girls look our way with jealousy in their eyes and venom on their tongues. Seeing my eyes narrowed and shoulders braced, they quickly turned back to their conversations and drinking games.

When I opened the back door and saw a small patio with two empty chairs, I turned to Flash and smirked. "Looks like it was all set up for us."

"Seeing as they're turned away from the party and look almost as excited as I am to be here, you're probably right."

"Now don't be such a killjoy. We sit out here, we can hear some of the music, chat a little, see the stars and maybe we won't be so keen to kill or jump each other in the future. How nice does that sound?"

"Peachy. Although I'm skeptical that sitting down and sharing our life stories will make you less of a control freak. And just in case you were curious, generally that's what makes me want to hurt you."

"Or maybe it's just your pent-up desire to have me, Flash." I grinned, secretly hoping that with each joke, casual smile, and personal story I told, she'd loosen up enough to tell me all about Grayson.

She shivered slightly in the cool air and I shrugged off my leather jacket, placing it over her shoulders and taking a seat. I noticed her weariness but let out a breath of relief when she pulled the jacket tighter and took a seat.

"Yeah, that's exactly what's happening here. Now what do you want me to tell you?" She sat in the chair, staring up at the stars and putting her high-heeled feet on the patio's rail.

I was momentarily distracted by the way the skirt of her dress fell on either side of her legs. "Umm, maybe let's start with simple stuff and work our way toward the big stories, like why you're working at Poison and are harder than you look."

"Simple stuff?" she whispered.

"Like your age, favorite color or ice cream flavor."

"Well, I had my twenty-first birthday last month, green's my favorite color, and vanilla is my favorite flavor," she told me while still staring up at the sky. It was as if telling me things about herself was something she could only do if she was pretending she was a world away.

"Vanilla? Seriously?" I chuckled, causing her to turn to me with narrowed eyes.

"Hey, it's delicious. Not everything has to be filled with bells and whistles for it to be amazing. Some of the best things in life are the things everyone usually overlooks."

"I won't argue with that," I murmured, admiring the way the moonlight hit her legs.

"How about you?"

"Well I'm nineteen, am a chocolate man, and I think after tonight red is definitely my favorite color."

"You're lying."

"Flash, if you could see you in that dress, your favorite color would be red too."

"Not about that, because yeah, this dress is awesome. You're lying about your age. No way in hell are you nineteen."

"Prison will do that to you. Not much else to do but work out."

"Shit, does that make me a cougar?"

"Well you did leave scratch marks." I smirked.

"I did not." She blushed.

"Babe, you want to see the scars, I can strip off and show you, but that would defeat the purpose of why we're here. You'll see me with my shirt off, and then we won't be talking."

"I'm sure I could restrain myself, but I think you need to explain why we're here anyway. Surely we could've just gone to a coffee shop?"

"I was invited. It's a good luck celebration for the game against the Wolverines on Saturday. First party they invited me to. I guess the whole team's meant to be here. I was going to blow it off, but aren't frat parties where college guys and girls are meant to get to know each other?"

"The whole team is meant to be here?" Her eyes widened.

"Most yeah."

"Except Gray won't be because he's watching Jessie," she said softly, her eyes turning glassy.

I didn't bother stopping myself—I reached out and laced my fingers with hers. Without any other questions, she started talking. I listened to her story. She told me about Grayson Waters, the small-town hero, her best friend's crush turned boyfriend. Then she told me about Nate, Gray's estranged brother who worked with Parker at Lucky's and could've passed as Gray's identical twin were it not for his eyes.

My jaw clenched when she explained how Nate was a one-night stand, but before he knew he was going to be a father, his life was cut short due to his own negligence and devious father. A man Gray and Parker tricked into admitting his role in Nate's death, but who still was able to cut a deal and remain in the local prison.

A man I now knew without a doubt conned me.

Fuck my life.

As she told me about her parents kicking her out and Gray fulfilling Nate's role in her daughter's life, I struggled to hold in my rage.

When she mentioned that this was just one of many nights that Gray gave up his old college ways to help her, I was suddenly really fucking grateful that I'd learned all that shit that night. Gray wasn't Eli. She revealed the guilt she carried when she didn't take Jessie to the games and how she could barely manage to sit through a whole game herself to support him.

"He know you're dancing?" I asked, reaching for one last reason to be pissed at the guy.

"Oh no, Gray would be furious. Ever since I moved here, he's acted like I'm his little sister. Hell, Parker would probably be concerned as well. Sure the club says burlesque, but everyone knows Getting Lucky doesn't run a classy, artistic place. They both believe I work night shifts as a telephone operator."

"They never questioned it?"

"Well Tahnee never mentions it, and I have a deal with one of Gray's best friends, Marissa. She's part owner of the club with her mother, and she mentions that she occasionally works with me at the operator place for extra cash so they don't worry."

"She a good friend of yours?"

"Marissa?" She laughed. "No, not really. I . . . well let's just say the day I went to audition at the club, I saw something she doesn't want Gray to know about. So, we do each other a solid and keep each other's secrets."

"You should take your girl to his games. It's an easy fix to your guilt. Then you should tell him about where you work," I said sternly.

"You're right about Jessie going to the games. But this is Gray's senior year at Penmore. Everyone knows he's going to be drafted in the NFL, and soon he'll have to move away. I know he could've graduated already and been drafted earlier, but instead, the year Jessie was born he became a redshirt player. He told the coach it was to help him focus on his studies and writing, improve his results without distractions, but he was constantly helping me. Filling in where Nate would've wanted to be, building cots and painting bedrooms. If Gray knew I needed more than a phone operator's allowance to survive, he'd quit for good. I know it. He'd put off his entire career for Jessie and start working. I love that, but I won't allow it. I can do this on my own."

"You got a thing about doing shit by yourself, don't you?"

"Don't you? Doesn't everyone want to be independent after they leave home?"

"I guess I've never had anyone try and help me, so I wouldn't know. I've always had to take care of myself."

I felt her fingers tighten on mine. When her eyes shifted to mine and her lips parted, I knew she was waiting for me to explain. It was my turn.

When I came up with this idea to share, it was a means to an end. Getting her to tell me all about Grayson. I wasn't going to reveal the skeletons in my closet.

But staring out into the dark, her hand gripped tightly in mine, I started to tell her about my parents. The sporadic highs and lows that came with living with heroin addicts. My first memory of my dad shooting up, then deciding to sit me on a kitchen stool and teach me all he'd learned. I explained that the punishments that came when I couldn't recite his teachings at five years old were worse than any other age, because at five my bones had grown enough for him to get a good grasp on me, but they also broke easily. I told her about Al finding me in his car and calling social services.

When I felt her lift our joined hands and press them against her wet cheek, I realized she'd been crying.

"Life hasn't been pretty for me, Flash," I murmured. "I'd keep sharing, but it doesn't get better. Even after I got put in the system, most of the stories I have aren't pleasant."

"You don't have any favorite memories?" she asked timidly.

"A few. Not a lot."

"Tell me one of them," she whispered.

I thought about the stories I could tell about Lizzie, Jake, or Beth. Only I didn't have many memories where they didn't start with one or more of us getting hurt or acting out. I also wasn't sure I could talk about any of them without getting angry, so I thought about a time when I wasn't burdened by life.

I quickly realized what story I needed to tell her.

A moment in my life I used to wish I could forget.

Until I stood in line at student services holding a little gold charm.

"I went to the café a couple of years ago. Day after Halloween," I started softly. "It's a fair bit away from campus, not in the greatest area, but it's still nice. It has these big cups with pictures in them. I'm not big into art, but a friend was, so I always went there with him. They also serve damn good bagels."

"I think I know it."

"Yeah, that doesn't surprise me," I muttered. "Anyway, this one morning I'm sitting with . . . with my friend, and I see the prettiest girl in the world. She has all this wild red hair, and even from a couple tables over, her blue eyes slay me. Watching her laugh with her girlfriend was like a punch to the gut. I'd had a seriously crap morning, but staring at her laughing, I was reminded of fairy tales and shit—even though she was sipping coffee from a to-go cup."

I heard her inhale sharply.

"I didn't go up to her or interrupt the conversation she was having with this nerdy brunette. Almost as fast as I had forgotten, I remembered all of the shit in my life I had to deal with, so I walked away. It was a nice moment though, even if it was over in a *flash*."

"Th-that's a favorite memory?" she choked out.

"It was the last good thing to happen to me before I was sent to prison."

When I stopped talking, we sat in silence, our fingers laced as the music from the party seeped through the cracks in the door.

We didn't move a muscle, but we kept holding on.

MILLIE

I WASN'T OKAY. Listening to his story ripped something open inside of me. I didn't know what to say, so I decided to do what I did best when I was scared: I became a character. I pretended I was aloof and superior. I was the frigid ice queen.

I knew he could tell the difference.

I was suddenly afraid that he saw more of me than anyone ever had before. That he understood my life like no one else.

But I couldn't let it affect me, couldn't let it melt the shell I'd spent years building.

After we sat in silence for what felt like eternity, I stood up, gave him his jacket, and started walking toward the exit.

If I could handle my own life, I thought I might've had the words to express what I felt for his. If my heart hadn't led me astray too many times to count, I might've leaned over and kissed him, soft and sweet. I would've told him what it meant to me, to be sitting on that patio sharing my life story, hearing him pouring out his heart and not hiding behind his beard, ink, and badass persona.

In the silence, I wished I were brave enough to fight past the last few shields he kept between us, to demand he tell me everything I knew he wasn't saying. Ask about his prison sentence, the cop, and how he felt about Penmore. What he felt now when he saw me. I just knew that if I did that, I'd be stepping over some invisible line.

I would end up needing to protect *him*.

I just hadn't worked out how to be this new me yet. I constantly had Tahnee, Parker, or Gray preventing me from drowning. I kept talking to a ghost to distract myself from the loneliness I felt.

If I can barely help myself, how could I ever be enough to help someone else?

WE PARKED AT the back of Poison. I slipped my heels off and carefully climbed out of the truck, not bothering saying goodbye as I headed toward the entrance on my tiptoes, heels in hand, to collect my handbag.

"You still think we're strangers?" he called out to me, leaning against the driver door.

I paused, exhaled my nerves, dropped to my feet. Before turning around, I fixed my mask.

"We shared a few shitty stories each. I don't think it means we know each other. Maybe we aren't strangers, but you telling me about how you saw me sitting at a café before my life went to shit also doesn't distract me from the fact that you didn't tell me about why I should let you keep up this protection gig."

"Flash—"

"No. We work together, finish this class. You want to come to this club every night and sit by the stage, I won't stop you, but if it's for that girl in the café, you know now that she's a ghost."

"I get it," he murmured, walking toward me. I didn't move, frozen as his large hand reached out to stroke my cheek. "You're too busy trying to do shit on your own."

"Good," I whispered, not sure if his words were patronizing or understanding. Then I reminded myself.

I wasn't meant to care.

SEVENTEEN

MILLIE

MY LATEST CHARACTER was the unfeeling ice queen. I had perfected the art of the cold shoulder. There wasn't laughter or smiling, just cool indifference.

I went to all my classes, didn't try to avoid him. I made myself be seen around the quad, and I even sat in close proximity to Cooper during class. I simply ensured my head was always turned toward the teacher, or my nails, or my handwriting, or my cell phone. With every movement of my body, I demonstrated that I was sincere when I'd told him that we would remain strangers.

However, I was constantly replaying the conversation we had at the frat house in my mind. Hearing his story softly whispered over the cold wind. There was no outward sign, but my heart had yet to stop bleeding for a little lost boy and an oblivious girl who had their futures shattered without warning. My eyes were empty of the emotions that wanted desperately to escape and run down my cheeks. In my dreams, I was no longer in the library; instead, I was on that back deck.

The first time I saw him sitting at the edge of the stage as I danced since we'd shared our secrets, I made sure to greet him afterward at the bar. I was *Basic Instinct* indifferent—tight white dress, sweeping heels, acting all superior—while managing to keep my legs close together as I sat beside him. I slid the completed assignment across the counter, watched his arched eyebrow and smirk, and returned to the dressing rooms as if I had no care in the world. I didn't take in his gorgeous green eyes laughing at me or feel the urge to wrap my arms around his waist, bury my face in his broad chest, and cry.

Every night after that I kept my distance. He came to each show, but neither of us made a move to show that there was any familiarity between us. I never acknowledged the fact that I saw him follow me home on his bike and wait until I was inside before driving off again.

I had everything worked out.

I was under control.

My life was all about avoiding disaster.

Well, except during those rare moments when my best friend got involved.

In a moment of weakness, I told Parker about my conversation with Cooper, minus the dramatic stage exit. I talked about the frat party and his description of us in that café—happy and unmarred by the darker aspects of life. I told her about his suggestion to take Jessie to one of Gray's games and my decision to keep his offer of friendship at a distance. I ignored her pleas to reconsider and her arguments for me to stop building walls around myself.

I just didn't have any energy left when she told me how excited Gray was about the idea of Jessie coming to his next game. When I finally agreed to go, I decided it would all be fine. I was good in the lecture hall. I was good at the club. I could damn well be good at a damn football field.

"HERE THEY COME," Parker said from beside me, and I felt the bottom of my stomach drop.

I tried not to look at the field and instead focused on Jessie sitting on my lap. She was adorable, her big white jacket with Gray's number 27 stitched into the back, little blue skirt, and long yellow socks making her look like a mini cheerleader. Her curly brown hair was up in pigtails with blue and yellow ribbons attached to her hair ties. If she weren't driving me mad trying to pull off her noise-canceling headphones, I probably would've insisted she sit on my lap for every game in the future. The cuteness factor alone was enough for me to ignore the gnawing tension I felt bubbling inside of me.

The excitement in the stands as the team entered the field distracted Jessie enough to stop her fidgeting, so I turned and watched the crowd with avid interest. Every spectator seemed overwhelmed with anticipation. The atmosphere in the stadium that had been building during the day had finally reached boiling point as all the people from our school started cheering.

Between the new action on the field and the spectacle in the stands, Jessie gazed around as if in a brightly colored candy shop. She reached for Parker, as if already aware of who would put her closest to the action. Parker immediately opened her arms wide and settled Jessie on her hip. She started swaying in time with the crowd's cheers, causing Jessie to giggle and clap her hands.

I should've taken a photo, recorded this sight for Tahnee—Jessie's first football game. I tried to dress us similar for the photo opportunities: matching blue shirts, big white jackets, knee-high yellow socks, and pigtails. I had it all planned—if I was too busy taking photos, I wouldn't focus on Cooper. I wouldn't spend the entire game watching his every move on the field.

But I didn't take a photo. I was too nervous. Without any control over my actions, my gaze kept moving from player to player. Searching for that thick brown hair and don't-mess-with-me attitude.

"He usually stands around the back," Parker told me, grinning. "Next to Trick."

"Gray's at the front. Don't worry, I saw him," I let her know, lying to myself, pretending I didn't know exactly who she was talking about.

"I'm not pointing out Gray. I'm pointing out number 32, the guy you're looking for. The guy I've seen pacing along the sidelines at the last couple games you didn't bother coming to. Although, I think my favorite memory of him is in your kitchen bending you—"

"Shhh. I'm not looking for him." I was sure my cheeks had bloomed bright red. I managed to hold out for five seconds before I followed her visual instructions and located number 32.

I soaked in his appearance, examining the tattoos that couldn't be hidden beneath his jersey, the way the pads attached to his muscles made him appear like a giant among men.

"Bullshit," Parker chuckled.

"Hey! Little ears," I chastised as my eyes drifted to Jessie. When I saw she still had her headphones on, I smiled.

"Like you haven't said 'bullshit' around her," she whispered.

"Yeah, but she's nearly two and she's starting to collect her words. Plus, I'm her mother. I swear she's already learned to ignore everything that comes out of my mouth."

Parker laughed and turned back to the field. Sitting on the edge of our seats, we watched the players assemble for the coin toss. Wolverines won the toss and decided to go on the defensive. Cheerleaders for both teams went crazy, twirling and throwing their batons in their sparkling outfits. The Penmore cheerleaders executed a quick dance routine, which distracted me from the action. I wondered if, in a different life, I would've been one of those girls. Could I have been a girl known for her cheer? I could rock the pigtails, but could I have been that happy?

"Looks like Jordan is sitting on the bench tonight with an injury," Parker told me, pulling my head back into the game. Her eyebrows rose as she turned and asked me, "Did you know your boy was going to start?"

"Not my boy," I informed her. Pretending that I didn't care what she was telling me, I put on my bitchiest tone and ignored the fact that she could see right through me. When she didn't hold back her snort, I continued, "You know, sometimes I miss my friend who knew nothing about football except for the scientific statistics."

"Yeah, yeah," she replied, winking at me, "Blame the boyfriend and his game tapes." She turned back to the game and then started commentating for me, explaining the plays and occasional player gossip. I chose to focus on Jessie's reactions to the crowded atmosphere.

I adjusted Jessie's socks and contemplated getting her a snack when

Parker's comments seemed to only be about Cooper. "Wow, that must've hurt. I wonder if he practices that move at home. Oh my God, did you see that? Millie, your guy is blocking everything that comes at him like he's swatting away flies. Did he just jump over that guy? I can honestly say that after this game, you're probably going to be the only girl *not* offering him your undivided attention."

With those last words, I gave in, looking up just in time to see Cooper score a touchdown. As the crowd and boys on the field went crazy, I murmured, "So he's good. I figured he had to be pretty good to get on the team."

"You're not wrong, but there are athletes and then there are *star athletes*. Not to mention running backs are usually just fast. Unless they're running for a touchdown, they aren't doing anything too impressive, but your boy is fast *and* strong. He's also reacting so damn quickly. He's already made two knockdown blocks."

I tried to ignore Parker's words. With the Herons' defensive line taking center stage, I was able to watch the game and tell myself that she was just misinformed. I witnessed each defensive player perform like an iron fist, smashing down every play with little effort. The crowd was screaming just as loudly as they had been before. Cooper wasn't being treated any different. He was just another player.

Nothing was different.

When the offensive line came back on, I finally didn't turn away.

I scrutinized Cooper in the scrimmage, then watched with bated breath as they began another play. Cooper led the way for a touchdown; every Wolverine player foolish enough to go for the ball went down fast and hard. Half the time he didn't bother avoiding their attempts at blocking him. It was like watching them run straight into a brick wall and fall down. If you blinked, you might've missed his

The crowd went wild, crazier than their cheers before.

He was a monster wrapped in pads and a jersey.

And they loved it.

"Everyone at school is going to start worshipping him now, aren't they?" I said softly.

"With how much this school loves football and winning? Probably."

Her words didn't fill me with joy.

Instead I worried.

I worried how a lost boy who wasn't used to anyone caring about his actions, would handle thousands of people caring *too* much.

Without really caring at all.

———

COOPER

THEY WERE CHEERING: the fans, my teammates, complete strangers.

It was all over. We defeated the Wolverines 42–13, but the crowd was cheering like we had just won the state championship.

Between the chanting of Gray's name and D's name, I could hear my own. People I'd never met now knew my name. All because of a game.

My head was fucking throbbing.

I walked on the field with a history of keeping my word and a reputation for living dangerously. And I had friends on the inside hoping to see me do more than just tackle men on a patch of grass when I finally made it onto ESPN. There was meant to be much more blood and the shrill sounds of an ambulance siren.

But I didn't fulfill my promise to Tony. No one got near Gray.

I didn't start a riot. I didn't say a word. I just played the game.

Hell, I scored more touchdowns in that game than any game I'd played in high school.

It wasn't because I thought it was the right thing to do. I'd *never* given a shit if I was doing the *right* thing. Mostly because the people who were deciding what was right and wrong in my life were always into sketchy shit up to their eyeballs.

I just couldn't bring myself to fuck with a guy trying to help Flash survive.

Now everything that was meant to happen after I helped end the star quarterback's future NFL career would no longer transpire. If only an unknown future didn't screw with my fucking head.

The moment the last touchdown was made, heaviness settled around me. I suddenly understood that I didn't deal too well with the undetermined. Since I was thirteen years old, I'd ensured that my life was mapped out. I protected Jake, then Lizzie, then Beth. I worked toward getting us out of the system. I avoided Eli at all costs until he wouldn't let me ignore him. Then I was locked up and I was following orders. I met Tony and started plotting his revenge.

I loved it: the planning, the kept promises, the purpose.

The years with my parents and brother made me hate surprises. The smell of desperation and self-interest exuded from every pore of their bodies, and it wasn't a stench I ever wanted to worry about coming from mine.

I was meant to be something different—a fucking martyr if necessary.

However, in a crowded stadium, a glistening future now laid out before my feet that might only have to do with me. I couldn't help but get pissed and feel a little unhinged. I missed Jake, was desperate to see Lizzie and Beth. I was worried that Eli was right—I wasn't surviving.

It was as if in that moment, their absence was physically hurting me. If I were a fisherman, they had been my lighthouses, and now I felt like I was wrecked. Crashed on coral and rock without a guide, without a light that showed me what I needed to keep fighting toward. I was drowning in a sea of cheering fans.

I walked off the field while the team was still celebrating behind me. Coach tapped me on the shoulder before I was able to completely extract myself from the group, his expression a mix of awe and pity. With one look, he cut me to the bone. It was as if he knew that I had just done the hardest and easiest thing in the world. As if whatever hard-ass mask he'd been wearing every time he looked at me was slipping.

"They didn't have a lot of film to watch and prepare themselves for you," he muttered. "That won't be the case for the next game. You going to be ready?"

"Yes, sir," I replied.

"You're going to need to spend more time lifting," he told me sternly. "Hang out with the others. Trick is always working out around noon. He seems like the only one who doesn't piss you off. Join him."

"Will do."

"You did good, Daniels. Whatever shit you're trying to handle, just know, on that field tonight, you did damn good."

I nodded.

"I hear you're skipping any more classes though and you won't be starting again. I don't give a shit how good your grades are, but your academic advisor calling me isn't shit I want to handle. I've given you a chance. After how hard you worked tonight, I'll give you another. But you fuck it up, it's now on you. No one will roll out a red carpet into the NFL, but if you want it, I'd be damn proud to help you get there."

I just looked at him with dead eyes, already locking down my emotions. Barring the confusion that came with the idea of playing football for a living and the notion that I was the one who would be helped for a change.

"Okay, Coach," I replied dismissively, then headed toward the locker room. Ignoring all the other pats on the back and jostling, I started thinking about the pills my brother gave me. They were just sitting in my medicine cabinet in my apartment, itching to be touched.

When I first got them, it took all my strength not to tip them into my palm and start counting them. The idea of doing anything my brother expected kept my shakes and thoughts at bay.

I'd been sober for nearly nine months. I wasn't going to risk it for that asshole. But right then I felt lost.

There was no plan anymore. No purpose.

Nothing to focus on that eclipsed the memories and needs that wanted to pull me under.

And if I was going to drown, I wasn't sure I wanted to feel it.

EIGHTEEN

COOPER

I MOVED SWIFTLY, past parked cars and tired families. I heard the rumbling complaints from Wolverine fans and the sighs of disappointment. I was almost home free. Seeing my ride, I felt the pressure dissipate. I could almost taste oblivion.

"So, you're a superstar athlete," I heard Flash call out behind me, stopping me in my tracks. "Guess we didn't get to that portion of the show and tell."

"I guess not," I replied, not looking back. I forced myself to keep walking. Chose to keep making my way toward my bike. My salvation.

"Want to tell me why you're sneaking off? Not celebrating your victory?"

"Maybe I've just had enough shower time with other guys to last me a lifetime," I called out as I walked, trying to ignore her presence.

I had managed throughout the game to pretend she wasn't there, even after I heard Gray and D talking in the tunnel earlier about her finally coming to a game this season. Granted, it was easy to do when I thought Millie would go out of her way to avoid me. After she had made it pretty clear at

Poison that she was going to pretend that whatever was between us wasn't important, I'd received a lot of cold shoulders. The shitty move of doing our assignment without me and then acting like she had something stuck up her ass every time I walked by didn't exactly invite further interaction.

I sure as hell didn't expect to have her breathing down my neck when I felt lost and fucked-up inside.

"Makes sense. Except I saw you sneak out of the locker room while the guys were still walking in. You didn't even notice that I was standing there by myself. I could've been crushed under the excited mob without anyone looking out for me, and you didn't lecture me once. I figured something must be up."

"Babe, can we leave this play-by-play for class or the club? I'm tired, and I just want to go home. Leave it alone."

"I thought you didn't want to be strangers anymore. And now I have questions."

"Text them," I replied, still ignoring her.

"I don't have your number," she called out. "And can you hold up? It's really hard to chase after you, talk, and carry a toddler on my hip."

I turned around to see her standing in the parking lot balancing her little girl on one hip and a big-ass handbag on the other. I hadn't really looked at the kid when we had been in her house; she'd had her face turned away from me, burrowed into the best friend. Now a foot away from me, I couldn't help but notice that she was pretty cute, her brown curls all done up in pigtails. She was clean and smiling—not how I often saw kids growing up.

When she waved at me, even with my shitty attitude, I couldn't stop the grin that pulled at the edges of my lips. Damn, she was adorable.

Staring at the little girl still waving eagerly at me, I couldn't help but note her dimples and her obvious disregard to stranger danger. I suddenly saw the family resemblance. She might not have her mother's red hair, or blue eyes, but she was total trouble.

Flash walked toward me until she was in touching distance. The little girl started yawning, clearly fighting to keep her head up and her green eyes wide open.

"After that game, I realized when we told our stories, we left some important stuff out," Millie whispered.

"Is that right? I thought you were done with us talking to each other?"

"You want to give me a hard time about how I've been acting, go ahead. But I'm here now, ready for a do-over. And you never met Jessie. You said you didn't want to be strangers, right? Well that means you need to meet my kid."

"A do-over?" I asked.

"Yep."

"And you want this sharing to happen now, I take it?" I muttered in exasperation.

"Unless you hate kids," Millie replied.

"Don't hate kids, Flash. But you're changing your tune damn fast. Hell, last night at the club you were too busy to look my way."

"Yeah well, let's just say I've had you stuck in my head like a bad pop song, and I've decided that maybe if I listen to it on repeat, I'll start to hate it again."

"You want me to tell you stuff that will make you hate me?"

"To start," Millie said softly.

"You're not going to admit it, are you?"

"Admit what?"

"That you're trying to be that girl, looking to make my problems disappear."

"Look, let's not get too philosophical about all this. You can tell me why you aren't celebrating with the guys or you can tell me to move along. This time it's your choice."

"You want to know why I'm not celebrating?"

"Yeah."

"Your truck here?"

"Of course. Although this time I'm—"

"Keys," I ordered with my hand out stretched.

"Seriously?" Millie groaned.

"Do you want to be standing in the parking lot talking? You chill, I'll drive us somewhere, and you can keep at me, yeah? Otherwise I'm getting on my bike."

"Bike, Mama! Wanna see bike," Jessie said to Flash, still struggling to keep those pretty eyes open and speak without yawning but reminded of her latest infatuation. "Mama, see." The slight whine that escaped her pursed lips was almost as adorable as her drooping head.

"Okay. Here, take the keys quickly," Millie sighed. "She's just about to fall asleep and you said the B-word. If we're lucky, she'll forget about it. If not, I'll be living with my nearly two-year-old in an arm cast. Now move. *Move*." She pushed me toward her truck.

—

MILLIE

WE WERE IN my car, my hand resting close to his.

We hadn't spoken since I'd silently strapped a sleepy Jessie into her car seat and thanked him for holding the passenger door open for me. After I climbed in and we drove off, the tension built to mammoth proportions.

We didn't say a word as we passed the campus. The local coffee stores flashed by and I held my breath as we entered my less-than-ideal suburb. The radio kept playing classic hits from the seventies and eighties. Slightly embarrassed by my musical taste, I kept wishing it would turn into hip-hop or chart-topping music. Unfortunately, almost as soon as we drove away from the stadium, I became too nervous to change the station. Jimmy Cliff started singing "Many Rivers to Cross," and I couldn't do or say anything. The song and the tension in the car were freaking me out.

When we drove behind a row of run-down houses and reached a small park, I was shocked. Nestled amongst the trees was a picturesque little playground. From the parking lot, it was almost hidden from view, untouched by the grime that covered everything else within a five-mile radius.

If I weren't panicked about the secrets he was about to tell me, I might've stared at the park with wonder and excitement, imagining Jessie's future play-dates.

Instead, the consequences of my actions were plaguing me. I still couldn't believe that I had chased after him. Ordered him to share what was bothering him. I was meant to stay away, protect myself from the foolish ways I could end up hurt. I was meant to be strong. The cool, unfeeling bitch mask was to be duct-taped to my face. Instead, I'd noticed him on the field, detached from everyone, alone and hurting. And I became the bleeding-heart fool who always got me into trouble.

I watched him walk off the field as if he were immune from the joy around him. And I saw myself at Nate's funeral. The damaged girl, incapable of smiling or laughing. I recognized the loneliness that cloaked his body. The type that transformed how you walk and talk, that helped push everyone away. The type that convinced you that any hand reaching out might latch on, turn into an anchor, and drag you to the bottom.

So, I grabbed my bag, my girl, and ran—toward him and everything I told myself I would stay far away from. I didn't explain myself to Parker or anyone as I maneuvered through the crowd, pulled by some invisible string. I knew when I got to him that he might not let me get close because of how I'd been acting, but also because when you feel like you're about to self-combust, you just want to be alone.

But I decided to try. Even if nothing had changed since our last discussion. Even if I still felt ill-equipped for the job of helping someone else sort out their problems. I wasn't the cheerful girl in the café. I didn't have any answers to find happiness.

All I knew was he didn't have a family.

He didn't have friends.

He didn't have anyone forcing their way in to help.

I was pretty certain all he had was *me*.

NINETEEN

MILLIE

WE SAT IN silence for a little while, staring at the park.

When he finally reached for the door handle to climb out of the truck, I noticed Jessie had fallen asleep. "Do you mind if we don't go too far?" I whispered. "She's probably exhausted after the game, and I really don't want to wake her. She'll be grumpy. We can still talk though, get some fresh air. I'm sure she'll be fine in her capsule. But I can't go too far. Mom fear. Unless, of course, you didn't bring me here to talk. Then we can just stay in here. Not saying anything. Staring at nothing." *Dear God, I'm rambling. Stop it. Just stop talking.*

"Yeah it's all good. I was just going to walk to the park bench. That close enough?" he asked, pointing to the small bench opposite the jungle gym a few feet from the car.

"Perfect."

"And I think I need to talk." His voice was hoarse and thick with emotion. "I think after that game, I need to just say all the shit that's in my head, and it's probably best if she can't hear."

"Okay," I whispered before I opened my door carefully and climbed out.

When we both sat down on the bench, it was as if we were strangers. Our knees were held stiffly and pointed straight ahead. Cold air slithered like a snake between us.

"I left the field tonight because I don't know what's going to happen when we go back to school. And I don't deal well with surprises," Cooper told me softly.

"I get that—" I began to tell him when he choked out a laugh.

"Flash, you couldn't possibly get that. Unless you know what it's like to fear everything in your life. Be weak. Indispensable. The only time I haven't hated my life is when I used to focus on a plan. Taking care of the kids in the group home was the only thing that kept me sane."

"Kids?"

"Yeah, when my foster homes kept bouncing me around for boosting cars and just general rebellious teenage antics, I landed in this group home. Everyone usually kept to themselves, praying that they'd be the next to bust out. Pretending like the disgusting shit the social workers and cops were doing in the home wasn't happening.

"Most of the kids had been older than me when I arrived. I was the first young one to be sent there because my older brother had been there since my parents lost custody. We hadn't seen each other in years, and I'll just say that there wasn't a dramatic reunion when we were put under the same roof again. I still felt pretty much alone. That was until I was thirteen and Jake turned up. He was seven and a total punk. Kept at me because he heard my social worker explaining to a potential foster family how I ended up in the home. Jake wanted me to teach him how to boost cars. Told me he was gonna open a chop shop."

"Please don't tell me you helped—"

"Babe, his feet couldn't even reach the pedals. I took him to the community library, told him I learned all about the engines from a book, so if he wanted to boost, he had to learn to read. Lied through my teeth, but he fell for it and learned to read crazy fast. I decided to keep him safe, from the cops and the staff. I was big for my age, so no one messed with me. I had a guy who had failed at adopting me, but no matter what, he watched out for me when I was about Jake's age, so I decided to do the same. I used to bring him to this park for his birthday. He was too cool for it at first, but when he watched me go down the slide, he slowly got into it. Not too many people know it's here because of the trees."

Picturing the big teenager trying to teach a little boy to read and play in the park had my eyes stinging. I reached for his hand, pressed the side of my thigh against his, and rested my head on his shoulder.

"We never really talked about it being our tradition. Then the girls came, Lizzie and Beth. Lizzie was just a year younger than me, and Beth was the same age as Jake. They just seemed to tag along at first, came with us here and to the library. We were all struggling with our pasts, but together it felt—"

"Like you weren't alone?" I whispered softly.

"Yeah. We never really said that, but yeah. Anyway, after that first year, Jake gave up on wanting to chop cars. He wanted to be an artist. He was a damn good drawer. Plus, he found a book in the library on Paris and the Louvre. He used to make me go through all the pictures with him. Jake liked the landscapes the best. It wasn't enough for him though, to only get to see the pictures when we went to the library on the weekends, so he tried to steal the book when he was nine and got banned for the rest of the year. He cried and cried that night, stopped talking about learning to paint big landscapes, going to Paris. I think he just started giving up. Never wanted to go back again. Started hanging with some of the kids in the home who were into tagging the train tracks. I should've stepped in, but I hadn't been living a law-abiding life myself, so I didn't really know what to say. I should've gone back to that stupid library and stolen the book for him. Maybe then he would've trusted me. He would've had it as a reminder that he could rely on me.

"We were always getting put in new foster homes. They don't like to keep us in the group home for too long. For a while, we would all do whatever it took to end up back together, until Lizzie needed to stay away from the cops and social workers who were on the take, Beth was moved so far that we weren't sure she'd end up back with us if she acted out, and it looked like Jake actually landed a good home. Then we were all about just waiting until we hit eighteen and could officially adopt each other."

"So why aren't they here today?" I whispered, squeezing his hand.

"The Walters, Jake's last foster home, were going to send him back to the group home—when all of us weren't there—after finding out he'd been caught tagging trains. The cops called them—my older *brother* called them, even though I paid him not to. I should've known there was always a better deal in the works with Eli. Once they found out about the vandalism, about his visits to the police station, the Walters made their decision. They were waiting outside his foster house when I took him home, the same day I saw you for the first time.

"They had all of his shit already packed up. Laziest fuckers I've ever met, hid it behind their age. They never had any fucking time to sit down with him, but they packed his clothes for him," he told me, his knuckles going white as he clenched the fist he had resting on his knee.

"Coop, look, I know I asked, but you don't have to tell me," I murmured softly, my tears already collected in the bottom of my eyes.

"No, I do. I haven't . . . I've never spoken about it before. I think . . . fuck, I think it needs to be said out loud." He nodded at me before continuing. "I started fighting with them, the Walters. I was angry with them for calling social services without talking to me. To him. For not even giving him a chance to explain or offer a warning to fix his behavior. I'd already scared him, had already convinced him to get his act together. Reminded him of Eli's deal with the deadbeat pedophiles. Damn it, he panicked, too worried about going back without us. We'd all seen things in that place that we never wanted to feel. He panicked and thought he'd make a run for it. He fucking ran and tripped.

"Little shit was always forgetting to tie his shoelaces. I used to tease him. He could pick a lock to a five-hundred-dollar safe, never forgot to look out for security cameras. Real badass. But remember to tie two stupid thin white laces so they didn't come undone? That shit he struggled to remember. One second he's a deer in headlights, running away from us out the front of the Walters'. The next second he's smashed his head on the cement curb. Bam. Seconds. It took seconds and he was gone. Such a stupid way for him to die, tripping over his goddamn shoelaces. Paramedics said they'd never seen anything like it, a kid hitting his temple on the damn gutter.

"I just fucking stood there. When I told Lizzie, she collapsed at work, stopped talking. Basically went catatonic for a week. I knew how she felt. When it happened, Mrs. Walters started screaming loud enough for their neighbors to come rushing outside. They were the ones who called the ambulance.

"I just stood there staring at his fucking sneakers. I knew he was gone. The light and the fear I had helped put in his eyes weren't there anymore."

"Cooper," I choked out, my face a wreck with tears. My heart was breaking for him.

"I had to make the choices by myself. I offered to pay, so the government let me pick his casket. Pick the damn rock that I get to look at if I ever want to talk to him. Then my brother came to his funeral, the one who'd called the Walters. The one who took bribes and looked the other way when social workers at the group home climbed into kids' beds. My fucking brother. When I saw him at the funeral, I jumped him. Broke his ribs and smashed his face in. Would do it again. Even though it means I can't see Lizzie or Beth because they didn't get locked up. He was never really my family. That word was full of shit. Even after I got put away, Lizzie followed the plan. She turned eighteen and started the adoption process. But see, you can't associate with criminals and still get to take care of someone from the system, so the two people who've ever given a damn about me are people I can't associate with."

"They'd have been proud of you today," I assured him. "You were amazing."

"That's just it. I just played in the fucking stadium that we only saw on our beat-up television screen and none of them got to see it. You wanted to know why I wasn't myself. Because I finally made a dream happen and it's too late. None of it will help them anymore. It doesn't matter. It's just a game now."

He sounded so defeated. I had no idea what to say, didn't have enough words. All I wanted to do was hug him and remind him that he wasn't broken and he wasn't alone. Neither of us was, if we just stopped being so guarded.

"Fuck it," I whispered before letting go of his hand and standing up. "Move your hands to the bench," I ordered.

Without making eye contact, as soon as I noticed his hands had moved, I climbed onto his lap. *I'm a fool for doing this.* I carefully positioned my knees to comfortably straddle him and not expose my ass to the elements.

"What are you do—"

"Shhh," I whispered as I put my weight on his lap and felt his arms quickly wrap around my back for support. When I knew I wouldn't fall, I exhaled, placed my hands on his shoulders, and looked into his eyes.

Lost in his irises' hills and valleys, I almost forgot why I'd decided that we needed to be this close. Why my head on his shoulder wasn't enough. When his hands squeezed my skin, as if he were afraid I'd disappear like a dream, I remembered.

I needed him to *see* me.

"You have a future," I said quietly. "It might be the game, or it might not be. You might let me in, or you might not. I *do* know it won't be anything like what you pictured. What you planned. Because if I've learned anything, it's that none of us get the fantasy future we paint in our minds. If anything, the shit going on in our heads is always working against us."

I bared parts of my soul and he didn't reply, just kept staring into my eyes until I felt like he was looking directly at my ghosts.

This time just keep talking.

"Sometimes that hurts. We find ways to forget, create a life where it's as if the picture is faded and kept in our wallet. On goods days, it's almost as if that picture is nonexistent. Of course, you always remember. You might even pull it out, start staring, and put yourself in a whole new world of pain. The truth is if you try and hold on to it even for a moment, keep the picture alive, it'll feed off you. I think the only way to survive is to make other plans and dreams so the picture moves to the back of the pile. Then if you're lucky, you forget to look at it at all."

When I finished my attempt to vocalize how it was like for me every day, I leaned forward and rested my forehead to his.

I felt his left hand move from my back until he was tugging on my hair. I shifted back and before I had a chance to react, he softly brushed his lips against mine. Time stopped. The taste of him on my lips, the way he encouraged my mouth to open and allowed his tongue to gently sweep across mine—I was captivated. It was nothing like the library; it was sweet and cautious and filled with so much emotion that I could hear each beat of my heart. My breath caught, we looked into each other's eyes, and then he kissed me again.

"What are you doing?" I whispered when our mouths finally parted and the ability to think slowly returned.

"Forgetting. Focusing on another dream."

"We're in a public park. My daughter's in a car only a few feet away. This might not be the best time—"

"Jessie going to wake up and need you?"

"She never does. She sleeps like a hibernating bear."

"Okay then, I want—no, I *need* you now. Don't give a shit about a better time. There are never *better times* in my life." And with that, his lips brushed over mine again, that time with a little more force. When I felt his hand slip beneath my skirt, I raised my hips to give him space to pull the thin layer of fabric separating us down my thighs.

"Shuffle back a bit," he whispered against my mouth, and then with a little maneuvering, I felt him pulling a condom from his pocket and unzipping his jeans. He looked into my eyes, paused, and murmured softly, "But fuck, if you want this to stop, worried someone might see us, you tell me and we end this. If you need a better time, a better place—fuck, a better person—I get it."

I stared at him before I rested my forehead against his again. Then for the second time against my better judgement, I started running my hands underneath his shirt as I settled back into his lap. Our bare thighs were cold to touch, but the heat in his eyes and the warmth between my legs distracted me.

I felt his cock twitch to get inside me, but he didn't guide it in. Cooper's hands moved to either side of my face and he kissed me slowly. With each brush of his lips against mine, I felt myself get wetter. I started moving my hips, letting him slide against me. When I finally rose high enough, angling my hips slightly, there was no need to guide anything; he slid inside as if that was where he'd always been.

I increased my pace, slid him in and out while we looked into each other's eyes. We were moving in complete silence, our connection palpable. We started going faster and I swallowed the need to moan. I felt his hand move to my clit and start rubbing. Harder and Harder.

Before I could scream my release, Cooper's mouth covered mine and we both let go. I thought to myself in that last moment before I felt his hands squeeze my hips or his mouth cover mine that this was a hell of a lot more than forgetting.

TWENTY

ANTHONY

I WASN'T SURPRISED.

Thankfully, I was prepared for this. After all, the guards and other in-mates were all just pawns. They weren't bright. They weren't tough. Their only value in society was standing in front of others poised to be beaten and captured. Collecting information and using it against the people in this place wasn't like watching any real entertainment, not when it posed such a little challenge. I was quite certain that I could walk out of this place like fucking Pablo Escobar walked out of his jail cell. This might not be Colombia, but as far as I was concerned, the people around me were just as incompetent. I just let them believe otherwise.

When the whispers started, the discussions about Cooper on the football field, it took less than ten minutes to hear an entire replay of his athleticism. His victory. The place was crazy for him. One of their own becoming a college football star was like they were all out on the field scoring touchdowns. No discussion of a riot. No mention of an ex-inmate showing his true colors under insane amounts of pressure.

Of course, it took even less time for me to get word out that it was time to deliver the package. My friends on the outside were some of my fastest assets. It also didn't hurt that I always had a strong intuition and in every circumstance had a plan B.

I knew from the very beginning that Cooper was more like my sons than myself. He had no real ability to play the game, no finesse or skill. A sheep that wasn't even able drink without leading him to water.

In those first few weeks sharing a cell together, I had the seventeen-year-old completely worked out. He was a ticking time bomb built from lies, bad luck, and pent-up emotion. The drugs were the easiest part of the plan. All I had to do was get one of his friends to offer the boy a means to turn off his emotions on his eighteenth birthday. The boy was so easily convinced after that; he just needed the right direction and trigger.

Of course, I had anticipated his ineptness. I never put all my money on red when it was equally amusing to win with black. I also knew even the best bombs needed some fine tuning before their showstopping explosion.

I do believe I would've actually been disappointed if this part of the plan hadn't been fulfilled. Sure, it would've been simpler if the boy had developed more of a dependence on the pills. If Cooper had relapsed just once since his release, I would've been able to use it against him. I'm also sure it would've made him more committed to the cause. Alas, the boy was single-minded in his actions and rarely strayed off course for individual gratification. Idiot. Although, with his mind clear, he'd understand how I'd been running the show all along. The satisfaction was always sweeter when the other parties involved felt my hand around their throat. Not to mention I made it my business to outmaneuver the rats that scurried in every alley in this town. They always forgot that this was what I did.

Even my stupid son.

It was nice to be able to send a reminder.

I imagined it would take less than an hour before Cooper was regretting the decision he'd made that evening to try and be a star. Victory on a field with children wasn't anything compared to the war being fought in the streets between men. I wondered how long it would take before my cell was opened to greet my old friend. It would be the first time I didn't greet my old cellmate with tears.

I wondered who I would pretend to be.

How delightful it would be to pretend to be just like dear Cooper's father for a change.

It was going to be perfect.

COOPER

MY BODY ACHED and creaked when I woke up. I stretched and adjusted my legs, which were pressed against the passenger seat of Flash's pickup, when I realized Flash was asleep, her head resting in my lap.

Her red curls were spread out over my legs and under her face. Even if I had been bleeding internally, I wouldn't have moved or disrupted her.

It had never been part of my plans to bring Flash out to this park, tell her everything about Jake, lose myself in her, and then climb into the back seat to fall asleep. It wouldn't have even occurred to me that something like this could've happened.

Staring at her, I wasn't sure I wanted to make any other plans in my life that didn't involve us coming to this park, talking, fucking, and falling asleep. As I contemplated what it was I should do, wake her up or go back to sleep, I heard cheerful gibberish beside me.

When I looked to my left and was caught in a little girl's smile with big green eyes sparkling at me, I flinched. "Mine," the cheerful toddler muttered, her big brown curls in loose pigtails made messy from sleep. I had no clue what she was talking about, but I was certain that whatever it was she owned, she wasn't wrong.

My slight movement and the clear word reverberating around the pickup for the second time was enough to have Flash's eyes snap open.

"Fuck," she said softly before sitting up and stretching her neck. "I feel like someone ran over my body with a bulldozer." She took one look at me and another at her little girl, currently waving at us both. "Oh yeah, I'm definitely winning Mother of the Year at the next parenting convention."

"Yeah, maybe sleeping in the back seat wasn't our smartest idea," I replied, feeling like a deer caught in bright green headlights. I couldn't help it, I started waving back at the bubbling little girl. "She keeps saying 'mine.' Should I give her something?" I wondered out loud.

"Even if you gave her everything in the car, she'd still keep saying it. I'm slowly suspecting she believes she owns the world." Flash ran her fingers through her hair.

"Do they really have parenting conventions where they crown the best mother?" I asked.

"God, I hope not. Geesh, if I'd realized how much of the seat you would take up, I would've just driven us home," Flash complained as she tried to move her leg off my thigh unsuccessfully.

"You fell asleep on me on the bench."

"I still could've driven after you woke me up."

"You were a zombie. I think you fell over twice getting from the bench to the truck."

"You could've driven, then." Flash blushed.

"My legs were cramping. It's a blow to the ego to admit, babe, but gashing the Wolverines' defense for 482 yards and following that with us on that bench, my body was on strike," I replied, chuckling. Then I noticed the scowl on her face, which made me ask softly, "You regretting last night?"

"No. No, not at all. My body just hurts. And okay, I'm going to have to admit that I'm not the best morning person. And maybe I'm also a little prissy before I've eaten."

"If I get you coffee and food, you'll stop staring at me?"

"Coffee and food would be amazing," she almost moaned.

"Great." I watched her adjust her little girl's pigtails and kiss her on the forehead. "Does Jessie like pancakes? There's an IHOP a short drive from here, and the waitress always gives me a discount."

"Pancakes would be great. Although I'm sure you walk in there with me and a toddler, you're going to lose your discount," Flash laughed.

"Babe, after last night, losing my IHOP discount would be worth it. Although, the girl behind the counter has to be like fourteen, so she could just be sweet to everyone."

Flash rolled her eyes. "I'm sure she's been dreaming about the tough biker since you first pulled your motorcycle into the parking lot. Not that it matters, because I can cover Jessie and me."

"Flash, I'm paying. Don't even think about pulling out your wallet. I nearly made some really shit choices last night, but didn't because of you, us, and sleeping here. I know I come from nothing, but that doesn't mean I don't know how to work hard to ensure that I have enough in the bank to cover breakfast."

"Okay then, let's go disappoint your IHOP girl."

WE DIDN'T JUST disappoint the IHOP girl, we made her cry. Thankfully, Jessie smiled at her and muttered some gibberish, and the girl could no longer hold on to her dashed dreams. Flash informed me under her breath as we walked to our table that no female could be sad around her smiling little girl in pigtails.

After Flash inhaled her first pancake and cup of coffee, I felt safe enough to ask, "What are your plans for today?"

"Besides getting us both out of these ridiculous outfits?" She gestured to their football game skirts and socks. "Not much."

"You okay if I stick around with you guys for a bit?" I wasn't sure if I was avoiding the pills I had back in my apartment or if the previous night had truly changed something between us and I was eager to not burst the bubble. All I knew was I wasn't ready to leave her.

It took her a moment to reply, and I could feel the uncertainty pulsating from her body. I knew she was contemplating the risks she was taking standing on the edge of the cliff and jumping off completely.

I took a breath and prepared to tell her to forget about it, that I remembered her words from the last time we'd shared our secrets: *"We shared a few shitty stories each. I don't think it means we know each other."*

I almost didn't hear it when she whispered, "You can stay with us."

MILLIE

I DIDN'T KNOW what I was doing.

I was freaking out.

I wasn't only on a weird pseudo-date, I was on a weird pseudo-date with my daughter.

When I watched him pull faces at Jessie until she had milk coming out of her nose and then make a quiet apology to the teenager with her first crush when she delivered our menus, I was lost for words.

Like the fourteen-year-old girl, I was afraid I was gone for him. It was a lost cause. I could no longer fight whatever was happening between us.

It didn't help that he was a total contradiction. There was the rough biker with a scowl that caused grown men to move away from him. With so many issues swirling inside his head, he could almost compete with me and mine. Then he was this knight in shining armor, willing to cut himself down if it meant protecting the ones he loved. He was walking up to and talking to strangers to ensure their safety if he felt that they were endanger.

The night before, I'd told him how I tried to distract myself from the pain in my past. How I focused on other dreams so the picture I'd once painted in my head of the future didn't haunt or feed off me. I didn't tell him that until I met him, as hard as I'd tried, I'd sucked at it.

It had occurred to me briefly that night, but now staring at him, I knew for sure that I was no longer at risk of going home to ghosts. No, I now had a whole new future painted in my head.

A future that had started and might end with a damn park.

I wasn't sure what I should fear more: him doing something to make that picture I was painting disappear, or become brighter.

TWENTY-ONE

COOPER

"THANK THE LORD, she finally hired someone."

I heard the words, but with a nail between my lips and my hands filled with timber and a hammer, I wasn't able to turn around immediately. Once I had the next-to-last piece secured tightly to the porch, I finally looked up into the warm brown eyes of an older lady. Her brown hair framed her face like a helmet, and she had these little black glasses perched on her nose. She was pretty in a soccer mom sort of way, and I had no idea what to say to the likely owner of the house I was working on.

"Don't let me stop you. I know you have your work cut out for you. Do you think you'll have enough time to look at our gutters? If Millie hasn't asked you to do them and you have another job, I completely understand, but I'd be willing to pitch in and pay you more if you manage them."

"Um, Millie isn't paying me, ma'am," I managed while trying to wipe away some of the sweat coating my forehead and make myself more presentable.

"Why would you be fixing our rotten porch if she isn't—oh," she murmured softly as she took in my appearance. "I understand," she continued moments later, apparently seeing something in my sweaty jeans and dirt and sweat covered black sweatshirt.

"We met in Art 101," I explained. "We were hanging inside watching a Disney movie, but I couldn't keep staring at this eyesore without fixing it. I didn't like the idea of the little girl running out here and touching it."

"You and me both, young man," Tahnee agreed before taking a seat on the porch swing. "I'm just going to have a little sit down out here with you before I go inside if that's all right. Don't mind me. If I go in, I'll be tempted to ask her a billion questions, and Millie is a little sensitive where I'm concerned. She'll likely think I'm sad about my son and will reevaluate having you here. That girl is constantly trying to repay me for helping her out when her parents forgot how to be parents. And seeing as I'm glad you're here, fixing our porch and taking care of my girl well I'm just going to take a moment. Maybe ask you some of my questions if that's alright?"

"Ask away, ma'am," I grunted. "I've just got another piece to fix. You okay if I answer while I hammer?"

"Hammer away." When she saw a tray with an empty glass as well another that appeared to be untouched lemonade, she asked, "Do you mind if I have this one?" before bringing it to her lips.

"No, don't—"

Unfortunately, it was too late. She'd already sipped and consequently spat the disgusting lemony liquid onto the ground. "Sorry. I did try and warn you."

"Millie made these, I take it?"

"Yeah, she was trying to thank me for fixing the porch. I don't think she knows you need sugar or something to actually make it nice."

"Gosh, I adore that girl. It seems that whatever she sets her mind to, she can achieve—that is as long as it doesn't occur in the kitchen," Tahnee laughed. Taking another look at the tray and the empty glass, she asked, "Did you manage to secretly tip yours into the garden?"

"Nah, I drank it."

"A whole glass?"

"When she brought them out, she clearly had no clue what she was doing and she was nervous about having tried. I thought drinking it was the least I could do."

"Are you going to drink this one after I go inside?"

"It's just a glass of lemon and water. I've drunk worse," I told her uncomfortably.

"And I'm done with my questions. I'm going to leave you to finish your lemonade and protecting my girls while I go see what trouble they've got themselves into while I've been at work. Even if Millie says otherwise, I want you to know, you're welcome at this house whenever you want."

AS I FINALLY made my way up the stairs to my apartment, the putrid smells and sounds didn't even register.

I was exhausted.

I didn't know if it was because less than twenty-four hours before, I'd started in my first college football game, or because in one night I'd told Millie more crap than I'd even shared with Lizzie, or because spending the day with an energetic toddler was actually harder than dealing with my fellow inmates in prison. But when I kissed Flash goodbye, breathing in her scent of spices and flowers, it turned me into a guy who forgot he had problems.

If being worn out was the price I had to pay, I was ready for it.

I just needed to collapse now. Sleep away at least one whole day and then maybe I would be better prepared for the look I'd seen growing in Flash's eyes.

"Will you come to Jessie's birthday on Thursday?" she'd asked me softly when she'd dropped me off at my bike, pretending she wasn't struggling with her emotions. When I'd nodded in the affirmative, she'd started babbling. "Great. Awesome. It really makes the most sense. Until you get your family back, you'll protect mine. Having a porch that doesn't look like a death trap isn't the biggest imposition. I'm learning. You're learning. I will no longer whine or get defensive. We're dropping our tough acts. It's all going to be good." I just grinned and kissed her forehead.

I didn't say anything about her programming her number into my cell phone or that as far as I was concerned, I didn't consider my tough nature an act. I just looked into her glistening eyes filled with determination, smiled at her, and then jumped on my bike and drove my ass home. I figured I'd give her enough time to remember who she was inviting to her house: the domineering ex-con. Let her build up the shields and masks she loved to wear.

I wasn't going to get attached. I knew better than to play with fire.

As I reached the top step, I saw a black duffel bag at my front door. With its nondescript labeling, I didn't rush to touch it. If it were left at an airport, I had no doubt dogs would be sniffing and barking. I wondered if it was another delivery from Eli. After spending time with Flash, I remembered I had a new focus.

A new distraction from the pills and pain.

I decided I might as well get it over with. Stepping closer, I carefully unzipped the top and was faced with hundreds of photographs of Lizzie and Beth. I froze.

I knew what this was. It wasn't a delivery from my brother.

It was a warning from my cellmate.

A reminder.

I picked up the bag and stalked inside my apartment, then slammed the door with the frustration and anger that was building inside me. *Fucking hell!*

I dropped the bag on my bed and stalked to the fridge for a beer, taking a swig before I looked back at the damn bag. I wondered how long it took them to deliver it after they'd heard that I didn't follow the fucking plan. If it had been sitting on my doorstep the whole time I had been acting like my life wasn't filled with shit.

The amount of fucking photos meant they had this in the works all along. Since the damn beginning.

I was an *idiot* for not realizing who the fuck I was dealing with.

I thought I was so careful. Didn't say shit to the cons who tried to get to know me about Lizzie and Beth on the inside. When I put Eli in the hospital, I knew there might be further retribution, a blood repayment of sorts. I was never certain who was and wasn't friends with dirty cops, and whether they would or wouldn't deliver a message to those who wanted to see me suffer.

It never occurred to me that my decision to help my fucking pathetic-as-shit cellmate would blow back on them. I never thought about the shit I told Anthony in the fucking weakest moment during my time in lockup. How in the early hours of my eighteenth birthday, the year I could've finally adopted Jake, I told my roommate all about the life I could've been living if it weren't for that fucking judge and a corrupt cop. The nice neighborhood Lizzie and I always talked about living in. How we planned to escape from the shithole we grew up in. I remembered his condolences, his compassion, and his fucking friendly prison drug dealer.

I took another swig of my beer, then let out a ream of fucking curses that matched the fear and anger swirling inside my body. I thought to myself about what an idiot I'd been. He'd been screwing with me from the very beginning.

I needed to work out what the fuck I was going to do. I walked to the medicine cabinet in the bathroom, opened it and stared at the little bottle of pills on the top shelf.

I should chuck them. They came from him, I knew it. I grabbed the little bottle and walked toward the trash. I had been coming home to these earlier. If Flash hadn't stopped me, I would've used them to block the pain.

Destroyed my potential NFL career.

I emptied the pills into the trash.

"Fuck!" I yelled out loud before slamming the trash can shut. I was not a coward.

I wouldn't be playing this motherfucker's game anymore. I knew someone would go after them. If after the next game I didn't make good on my promise, they would show me what happened to fucking cowards. The fact that Lizzie and Beth weren't my family didn't mean shit; these assholes knew that if they wanted to hurt me, all they had to do was hurt them. I wasn't sure how, but I wouldn't be letting that happen.

I prowled toward the bag and grabbed a handful of the photos. I couldn't help myself as I started looking at the life we'd always dreamed about. Photos of Lizzie doing people's hair at the salon. Beth walking in and out of school. Both of them playing at a park.

The more of their life I saw, the wilder I felt.

I couldn't let this shit slide. Someone invaded their privacy, took photos through windows and bushes. Dragged them back into the dirt they'd worked damn hard to climb out of. Someone would pay for this shit. I might've decided not to break Grayson Waters's legs but I hadn't decided to walk the fucking clean life. I would break the legs of the asshole who took those photos.

My fingers traced over their smiles and laughing faces. I started looking at every photo methodically, tried to calculate how long ago they'd been taken. Tried to put them in order to find a photo of Lizzie with her current hair color. If I turned up the next day, would I be able to catch the Peeping Tom?

I was almost at the bottom of the bag when I saw the photo. My heart stopped.

There in crisp color was Flash dropping her girl off at daycare.

I flipped the photo over and read the words written in black marker: *"Make a choice."*

—

I LOOKED AT myself in the bathroom mirror, studied the worn jeans, plaid T-shirt, and leather jacket, grimaced at the telltale signs of living without sleep. I knew I was not little girl birthday party suitable. I also didn't have anything else to wear and knew I couldn't avoid this shit any longer.

It was Thursday. Four days since I'd shared my baggage with Flash, lived a day free of worry, listened to her announce that it was okay now to protect her family, and then found Tony's fucking threat. The fact that I looked like a rough biker dealing with a hangover was the least of my problems. A duffel bag of photos. Oxy in the fucking trash. Some dickhead telling me I needed to choose between helping Flash's family or ensuring no one decided to destroy Lizzie's and Beth's lives. My life was a mess. I just happened to look that way too.

I needed to work out what the fuck I was going to do.

I had started riding toward Lizzie's home twice before turning around. I didn't know what the fuck I was going to do. Before I turned up on her doorstep throwing her and Beth's life in turmoil, I needed to know everyone here was safe.

As I stared at the holes in my jeans, I went through my options for the billionth time. I thought about calling Lizzie instead, telling her that someone was stalking her and Beth and instructing her to get out of Dodge. Immediately. I also thought about calling Al and getting him to share his motorcycle club connections. I knew his club would help Lizzie find some place to hole up in with Beth. They would even send someone out from Nevada to help me deal with the fuckers threatening to destroy Flash's family. Unfortunately, I knew they'd ask a lot of questions, or at the very least demand that I hole up in their fucking compound while they exterminated the pests I'd let burrow into my life.

I knew it was my best option, but I knew Al wouldn't let me punish the idiot who thought he could send someone to follow the women in my life. He still thought of me as a kid. Nineteen and a college football star in the making. He hadn't seen the man I had become since doing my time. I also knew the club wouldn't let a witness stand around as they chased these assholes down unless he was patched in. Therefore, it wasn't an option.

Tony needed to pay.

My phone went off again with another text from Flash, reminding me of the time and place of the party. If I didn't leave now, I knew I would be late.

I climbed on my bike and adjusted the rough backpack I usually took with me when I had a need to carry crap. It felt heavier than it ever had before. I chose not to think about how that didn't make a lick of sense seeing as the only thing in the bag was a fluffy pink bear with a giant yellow bow.

I adjusted the bag and pulled out onto the road, getting every green light as I rode to Flash's house. With every tree I passed, I thought about how my bike should've been headed in another direction. It shouldn't have been around a two-year-old. No good would come of this.

I was at Flash's door in record time and I rode past the damn thing, lost in thought. When I saw that I'd driven a block past her house, I slammed on the brakes.

Shit.

I pulled over, got off my bike, and took a fucking breath, staring at the dirt. I couldn't leave her yet. Not until I knew that she'd be okay. I had faced down a gang of skinheads wanting me to join their ranks behind the walls of a fucking prison. I could handle a gang of little girls and an asshole behind bars.

The photo told me to make a choice.

Thank fuck I'd stopped fearing the orders of sociopaths a long time ago.

TWENTY-TWO

MILLIE

I WAS GOING insane.

It was the only logical conclusion.

I needed to be committed. Immediately. I needed to be taken straight to a padded white room. A room that was absolutely silent, no little girls screaming and crying for attention. I didn't even care if my arms had to be strapped to my body. The idea of my hands being unavailable to get snacks or drinks for dictators in tiaras was heaven right now.

What the hell was I *thinking*?

Telling Grayson, Parker, and Tahnee that I had everything under control was possibly the first sign of lunacy. But they knew. Oh, those bastards, with their convenient excuses as to why they couldn't arrive until the party was almost over. I'd decided it was all an act. Tahnee with those unshed tears in the bottom of her eyes. Parker and Grayson with their dozens of apology text messages. I'd believed they were so sad and disappointed.

They had me fooled. They knew I would be dealing with bedlam, and they averted the chaos like trained Marines leaving a hostile country before it imploded. I was sitting there, all sweet smiles and naivety, planning my two-year-old little girl's party as if it would be just like a one-year-old little girl's party. None of them warned me. None of them told me that my sweet angel child would refuse to follow my every instruction. Tahnee and I had been unknowingly creating a devil by talking about it being "her day" for a week. How I rued the day I introduced the idea that it was "her day." It was worse than her obsession with "mine."

This year my girl knew it was a day about her and demanded as much attention as she could get. Thinking that there would be a sleep in, with Jessie not realizing that it was her birthday, was the first warning sign that my day would not go as planned. When I was unable to throw on a Disney movie and set up the decorations I had planned to have stylishly around the house, my day started unraveling.

Five hours later and there were too many of them. I was outnumbered. I didn't think three kids under three would be that hard to handle. Excited children were like Gremlins: completely unmanageable, eager for only dirty and dangerous activities. And I was the only one around to supervise.

When the doorbell rang I almost cried.

God, please tell me I didn't invite another one. I didn't care how cute they looked in their ribbons and party dresses. I couldn't handle another one.

When I tentatively pulled the door open to find Cooper standing all brooding on the doorstep, I couldn't help but mutter "Excellent" before grabbing him by the arm and pulling him inside.

"Whoa, hey, stop pulling," he grunted as I dragged him toward the lounge room.

"Nope, nope, I need you to go in and keep them occupied. Five seconds. God give me five seconds. Burn the house down. Set a doll's hair on fire. I couldn't care less. But you will give me five seconds of peace so I can go to the bathroom and get what I'm pretty sure is glitter nail polish out of my hair."

"Flash, I'm a guest. Goddamn it, stop digging your nails into me"

"Cooper, you are the only adult in this damn house. All others ran. They dropped their devil spawn disguised as princesses at my door and bailed. Unless you come with me, I will draw blood. I promise you."

"Flash, seriously, I'm following you, but I don't think you shou—"

I didn't let him finish, shoving him into that room alone before I made a run for it.

—

I LIED. I spent five blissful minutes in the bathroom. However, I completely forgot to wash out the nail polish. Instead I looked in the mirror, stared at the messy red bun, the freckles that danced across my nose free of the cloak of makeup. In all the drama of trying to wrangle three two-year-olds, I had forgotten about Cooper coming to the party. Sure, I had sent a couple of messages reminding him to come that morning, but I then came up with the brilliant idea of a pretend spa activity, and with little devils dictating my every move, I forgot my foolish plan to invite him into my world.

He's here.

I felt the tears threaten to spill over. "I know," I whispered to Nate.

I knew he would come.

"I just pushed him into a room of two-year-old little girls with a ton of makeup. He might be here now, but the moment I rejoin that room, he won't stay. He'll have some excuse."

Who you trying to kid with that crap? You don't really believe that. He's a fucking superhero. All that shit about his growing up in foster care, taking care of those kids he lived with, and then you asking for his help. You know the dude's a damn white knight in training. He'll stay.

"I didn't think about you both being here on this day. I forgot that you'd be in my head on her birthday," I choked out. "I . . . this . . . what am I going to do?"

Go enjoy our girl's party. Let them paint your face again. Laugh. Tell me about it later. Or maybe with him here helping you celebrate, you won't need to tell me at all.

With those last words, he disappeared. I wiped away the tears and opened the bathroom door.

—

HE WAS COVERED in bright red lipstick, his forehead, his cheeks, and his lips painted with a very thick hand. I was certain I saw glitter, nail polish, and princess stickers in his beard. I kept my chuckles silent.

"You knew."

"Oh I knew."

"They're so little, but together they're like a sixteen-year-old girl on steroids."

"Mama, wook! Pwetty man!" Jessie yelled out to me as she tugged on Cooper's beard.

"She's been saying that since you pushed me into the room," Cooper muttered as I surveyed the lounge room.

I snorted. I knew. "Pwetty" was her word of the day as she became a dictator that morning, ordering me to do her makeup after I did mine. Learning new words just to boss me around.

"I figured you'd be able to handle yourself." I grinned.

"Do I get a bathroom break now?" he asked with one eyebrow raised. I took in his appearance, all sparkling beard and 80s Madonna wannabe eye shadow, and without hesitation informed him, "No time. We need to exhaust these little devils so when other people get here, they'll think I've been in control the whole time."

"Babe—"

"Come on, you can do it. Thirty minutes tops. We let them do our nails next and then help them build a fort. Surely by then they'll want to watch a Disney movie and our job will be done."

"They already did my nails."

The look on his face, part horror and part shame, had me bursting into laughter.

"Okay, they can do my nails as you start building the fort," I chuckled.

"Fawt?" Jessie squealed, distracting the blushing biker enough for me to turn to the other little she-devils and start pretending that I was excited about the length of my fingers about to be painted.

IT WAS TWO hours and two bottles of nail polish remover later. Two moms had arrived to cart their sleeping babies away. Both of them apologized for having other commitments and missing out on all the fun. They were very good liars, but they weren't very good at hiding their shock. Only one of them managed to keep her tongue in her mouth at the sight of the overgrown biker asleep under three different princesses. I should've woken him up, or at the very least lifted Jessie off his chest. However, the sight was almost too much for me to handle.

I decided to stick to the kitchen. Parker was arriving any minute with Gray, and Tahnee would be there after that to help with clean up. They would wake Cooper up. They would take in the sight of my daughter asleep on his chest, covered in makeup and glitter, and not want to cry. They wouldn't know his background. They wouldn't struggle to keep their shit together. Their eyes wouldn't threaten to fill with tears that I wasn't sure would stop once started.

When a knock sounded at the door, I raced to open it, that time not out of excitement or desperation but to ensure they didn't wake my exhausted patrons.

"Hey," Parker greeted before taking a step back to let Gray inside, who was carrying a handful of pink balloons and a very large wrapped box. "Sorry we're late. I know you said it was okay, but Marissa needed help at the bar."

"It's all good," I whispered as I led them toward the kitchen, away from the sleeping girls.

"Why are we whispering?" Gray asked as he placed their gifts on the dining table.

"Well, while you guys were helping Marissa and every other child's parent had some engagement to attend today, I had three wild little girls on my hand. After pretend beauty salon, where I let them paint each other's faces with all my makeup, then help themselves to my nail polishes, and then destroy my lounge room in the effort to build their own pillow castle, the she-devils finally fell asleep," I responded.

"Shit, babe, not one parent stayed?" Parker's eyes widened.

"I told them I would be fine. That I had it under control." I rolled my eyes. "Three didn't sound like a lot."

"I don't suppose I can wake the birthday girl to give her these balloons?" Gray inquired.

"Do so at your own peril," I warned. I already knew him well enough not to waste my breath. He wouldn't be able to help himself.

I watched as he crept toward the door and poked his head in. When I heard him shout, "Daniels, what the fuck?" I realized I had left out a key factor in my retelling of the day's events.

"Dude, you shout again and wake this little girl up, I'm telling Coach," I heard Cooper angry-whisper to Gray, then watched as Parker's eyes grew as big as saucers.

"Is that—"

"It's a long story. I invited him after the game. He's been an amazing help today," I told her before Grayson joined us with fury in his eyes.

"What the fuck is Cooper Daniels doing in your living room? And why the hell is Jessie asleep on his fucking chest?" he demanded.

"I invited him."

"Do you not know that he's a convicted felon out on goddamn parole?"

"I never thought you were so goddamn judgmental," I whisper-yelled back at Gray, suddenly grateful I was an only child for most of my life.

"Who made Jessie's cake?" Parker asked me, obviously trying to change the subject.

I was tempted to ignore her like a stubborn child, wanting to tell Gray to get the hell out of my house if he had issues with Cooper being there. Unfortunately, as I watched her eyes get wider and wider, taking in the three-tiered chocolate mud cake masterpiece with decorative swirls and cascading icing, I interrupted Gray's drama and said, "Oh stop staring. I didn't make it, so it won't poison anyone. Cindy Shu brought it for me."

"Cindy Shu from the Chinese takeout place on Johnston street?"

"That's right."

"Millie, did you get your Chinese takeout lady to cook your daughter's birthday cake?"

"Yep."

"And you see nothing weird with that?"

"Babe, I don't think the cake is the weird shit we should be questioning Millie on right now," Gray muttered, clearly wanting to get to the sleeping giant in my lounge room.

Seeing as I had no idea how to handle Gray's questions about Cooper without getting pissed off, I decided to let Parker know, "It's no weirder than when Cindy brings over soup."

"She brings over soup?"

"Well, if we don't come by on Wednesdays, she knows Jessie or I must be sick, so she usually drops by soup if she can."

"Mill, the fact that you're on a first-name basis with all the fast food owners and waitresses in your area is incredibly strange."

"I'm loved."

"You're desperate," Parker laughed.

"Can we please get back to the fact that there is a known felon sitting with my niece in the other room?" Gray almost yelled, his fists clenched so tight his knuckles were turning white.

"It's nice to see you too, Grayson," Cooper greeted from the doorway. How he managed to still look menacing with his face and beard covered in lipstick failed me. All the pleasure I had witnessed in his face hours earlier as he declared Jessie the princess of the pillow castle, and the fear when she decided she wouldn't watch the movie we put on unless she sat in his lap, was gone.

Staring at Grayson was the exact guy Grayson didn't want to be around his niece.

The guy I was meant to stay away from.

An angry ex-inmate who was looking to punish someone for fucking up his life.

TWENTY-THREE

COOPER

"WE HAVE A problem here?" I asked.

I already knew I was the problem. I was waiting for this moment, when all the shit I had done for this guy, all the problems I was now facing, came back to bite me in the ass. I didn't get glory and happy moments—I got problems, one of which seemed to be holding pink balloons but clearly wished he had knives in his hands. The idea that we would work together to figure out a way to keep Flash safe was fucking ludicrous. I could already tell he was a goddamn prick to guys from the other side of the tracks. Got rid of his dirtbag dad, had a fancy college education, and he was suddenly better than other bastards with deadbeat dads.

"Just wondering what you were doing here. A little girl's birthday party just isn't a place I expected to see our resident team bad boy," Grayson stated. "Rumor has it the only party you like is at Poison."

I watched Flash flinch and wanted to punch the asshole. I knew she kept her late-night job a secret. I also knew she hated it, put on her costumes and, just like all those times she tried to push me away, pretended she was someone else. No one, not even some asshole I decided wasn't a big enough asshole to shatter, would make her feel less for putting in her time there.

"Wasn't aware this was a private party, but if that's the case, I'll just be on my way. But you should know, going to Poison isn't an insult. It's a good bar with good workers. You want to insult me, try and talk about something I'm actually ashamed of, like helping you win the last game." With those parting words, I looked Flash in the eye, nodded, and made my way to the door.

I felt her small hand grab my shoulder as I was opening the door.

"Thanks for today," she whispered. "I'm sorry about Gray. He's just protective of me and Jessie. I haven't really had a chance to talk to him since the game. Once I explain that we've agreed to help each other, he'll probably be nicer. He only needs to know that your criminal past isn't what he's used to. It's just his dad and his brother—"

"Babe, don't worry about it. Today was fun." I chuckled when she raised her eyebrow. "Okay, fun might be pushing it, but your kid is cute. You did good babe," I murmured softly.

"Thanks. I think so too." She smiled.

"You work tomorrow night?" I asked her, not letting the anxiety of leaving her enter my voice.

"Yeah," she said before looking behind her. "I'm a good four months away from having enough to quit. I usually work every night, unless I go to a game or need to watch Jessie."

"I'll be there, then," I told her before walking out and leaving the boy I was meant to hurt, the girl I was meant to forget, and the little girl I should never have even known existed behind.

Wondering how the fuck I was going to protect them all.

SHE WAS DRESSED like an angel, in white feathers and white lingerie. Her arms languidly moved from her body to her breasts with an intimacy that captivated and enticed. With one foot planted on the stage, the other slowly moved until it pointed to the sky with perfect precision. It was as if she wasn't human. On that stage, she was without flaws or imperfections.

She sparkled.

I was normally worried that the shouts from the audience might snap her concentration. That with one wrong step she would fall and hurt herself. I usually braced myself, ready to jump up and grab her stubborn ass before someone else could touch her.

But the music went on and on about seeing angels.

For the first time, I was fucking *transfixed*.

With her movements, the lyrics, and those goddamned feathers, I was starting to believe in something I'd always thought was full of shit—that God existed. I thought about all the things I'd seen and wondered if it'd all led to that moment. That there was a bigger plan and I needed to follow it so I could see this. Protect this. One of his angels.

The risk I was taking by not walking away was idiotic. And still I couldn't bring myself to do the right thing.

When she dropped her feathers and fully revealed those tiny silver tassels sparkling on her tits before she strutted off the stage, my pulse jumped and my cock twitched. I watched her walk toward me still in costume. She had only approached me once after a show to give me our damn art assignment; usually she headed straight off stage after the final reveal, to change, to leave, to pretend she was never there. I usually finished my drink, calmed my ass down, then followed her home on my bike before I headed back to my apartment, where I then texted her about class or her girl.

There was never talking at the club. No acknowledging that she was doing this for the money and that I was sitting there to safeguard her. If I had to arrive late because of work, she didn't even nod at my presence. She knew I would come, and I knew we would leave together. We didn't need words or gestures or explanations.

Her walking to me told me something was up. She wasn't doing any of our normal routine, and it was putting me on edge. When she got close enough, I reached out and stroked my finger along the thin white feathers she carried. Soft. Fragile. Tempting. "You still working?" I asked hopefully, keeping my eyes on hers. "This part of the routine?"

"No, I'm done," she said quietly as I heard a new girl start her routine on the stage and distract the audience. "I just wanted to come over before you leave. I've got this party I've been invited to tonight, and I thought I'd see if you wanted to come with me. I'm just going to change into jeans. Then I was hoping you wouldn't mind leaving your bike here and maybe we can take the truck over together."

"Babe, Gray gonna be there? Because he seemed pretty pissed to see me yesterday. Not sure if he'd be happy to see me again."

"Tonight's different. This party, it's at Marissa's other bar called Lucky. I wouldn't ask, but it's important. I'd feel better if I didn't have to go alone. Gray won't say anything to either of us. I'll make sure of it."

"You feeling okay?"

"Yeah, I just . . . I just need some company. Can we maybe just do this without a deep and meaningful discussion?"

"Done. Get changed. I'll meet you out by your truck after I cover my tab." I watched as she walked back behind the curtain and worried for a moment that maybe she knew more than she was letting on. If she was given a photograph of her own.

Maybe I didn't have time to sit at a fucking bar and watch her.

Maybe this fucking song and dance was so hypnotizing because it was the last time I would see her again.

MILLIE

IT WAS NATHAN'S birthday. The day after Jessie's.

The irony wasn't lost on any of us. And no matter how exhausted I was, how late I had to work, or the lies I would have to tell about where I'd been, I went to the party Marissa threw for him at Lucky's. I felt I owed it to him to smile, to cheers, to listen to the others reminisce and tell their stories. But it was too much. Last year I felt as if I was drowning, hearing about all the times they got to spend with him, the memories they got to share, the jokes they could tell. I stood around Lucky's nursing a single drink and each story hit me like a wave, reminding me about the person I'd missed out on. And with each crushing blow, I struggled to breathe and prayed that at some point I would be able to catch my breath.

I had one evening with Nate.

One.

We may have talked of the future, but we never had a chance to live it. And we never would.

The older Jessie got, the harder that fact was to swallow.

I forbid Tahnee from bringing Nate's birthday up around Jessie. It was my gift to her while she was young. I was suffocating, but I gave my little girl peace for as long as it would last before the truth eventually stripped the joy of the day away as she got older.

Just the thought of the night ahead was overwhelming. Coupled with the fact that I knew this evening made my desire to speak with a ghost worse. I would eventually go home after the party sad and alone. I would then spend my night talking to the Nate inside my head, wishing him a happy birthday. Building memories that didn't really exist.

I didn't talk about how hard this night was for me. I figured they knew, but I never asked for help, a night off, or company.

Until now.

I figured no one understood how I felt. But after watching Cooper let me help him to forget his pain on game night and focus on something other than his ghosts, I decided that maybe he could help me do the same. Maybe sharing this part of my life with someone else would bury the emotions that seemed to rise up and choke me when I had to witness the things Nate missed out on.

I swirled my key ring around my index finger until I saw Cooper walk out of Poison and make his way to my truck. He looked way too tempting in his worn black denim jeans and plaid T-shirt. I wasn't sure if he was the answer to my problems, but I also knew this night couldn't get any worse.

WHEN WE ARRIVED at Lucky's, I felt like I'd made a huge mistake.

I ignored everyone's confused faces as we crossed the room. We weren't even holding hands, walking in with about a foot between us, and yet I felt as if the bartenders, waitresses, and guests were all watching us make love. Analyzing how deep our connection was and struggling to decide if they thought my coming with someone was in some way spitting on Nate's memory.

I caught Marissa's eye in the crowd, watched as her eyebrows rose to the ceiling when she noticed the mountain of man shifting closer to me. Instead of passively watching like the rest, Marissa walked straight toward us. She always looked a bit of a rock star to me, the old Ramones T-shirt that hung off her shoulders, the ripped jeans and her strawberry blonde curls wildly framing her face always reminding me of modern-day Stevie Nicks.

I'd always wished to know what Nate thought of her. Gray adored her; she was basically his best friend. And even though I knew she was a pretty serious businesswoman and my boss, owning not only this bar but half of Poison, her age and violet eyes always made her seem approachable. Parker tended to keep her distance. They'd bonded after Nate's death, but I think Marissa's blunt manner and overprotective mama bear attitude toward Gray was something Parker found intimidating.

As for me, since Marissa and I seemed to be keeping a lot of each other's secrets these days, we'd gotten close. When I could hear her over the pulsating music, I suddenly wasn't sure if that friendship would change, going the way of our audience's facial expressions. It was clear the verdict was out and most in the room felt Cooper's presence this evening by my side was in fact the rudest thing I could've done.

Fuck.

"Is this the guy my mother keeps complaining about to me? The one she tells me is scaring customers away and acting like your bodyguard at Poison?" Marissa asked when she reached us.

"Yep," I replied, not breaking eye contact.

"Good. I'm glad you have someone looking out for you. Anyone gives you shit in here for this, you let me know and I'll toss their asses out. Tonight isn't about petty fucking people," she told me before catching the distressed gaze of her overwhelmed bartender. "Look, I've got to go deal with something, but I'm serious. Even if Gray is the one being petty, I'll toss his ass out. Find me at the end, yeah? Bring your boy. We'll all do shots together. Nate would've fucking loved that. Hell, you want the keys to the storeroom to bump uglies, he'd have gotten a laugh out of sticking it to all these people, so the room's yours. Don't run off tonight."

"I won't. Go run your club. We'll drink at the end."

"Flash, thinking maybe you need to tell me what we've walked into yeah?" Cooper mumbled from beside me as he took in our surrounding critics and Marissa's words. "Nate's your baby daddy, right?"

"That would be him."

"And from the angry looks people are throwing me, I'm guessing this party is about him?"

"Right again."

"Babe, you want me here, I'm here. But I can't promise that if one of these dickheads comes up to me and decides to voice their fucking opinion, I won't stop from punching them in the face."

"Not asking you to. I don't really know all these people. They were his friends, never mine. They only know me as the mother of his kid. Maybe they all assumed I would be his grieving widow forever. Maybe they think two years is too soon to bring a guy to his birthday party, imagining some sort of love triangle."

"Then I'm guessing you and I are going to need drinks to get through this party. You want to tell me what you want and wait here while I tackle the bar, or you want to come with?"

"I'll wait here, and if you could grab me a vodka and soda that would be great," I told him as I checked out the room. I barely noticed when he left me and maneuvered through the crowd. I was transfixed, staring at the small birdcages that hung from the ceiling. "Dracula's college experience" was what Parker used to call the place when she'd first started working there. I saw it differently.

With its waitresses in tight leather pants, the walls painted black, and silver counter tops and cages, it was a dominatrix's dream home.

Both scary dungeon and tempting play pen.

That, I wasn't sure if I was the one being whipped, or if I would finally be in control.

TWENTY-FOUR

COOPER

"SHE BROUGHT YOU here?"

I turned my head to the right to find Grayson Waters staring at me from a stool against the bar. He was nursing a beer and his eyes were sunken in. Instead of the hostility he'd projected the day before, he seemed exhausted. His stare seemed to be looking for something when it took in my shoes, my clothes, and my hair. Looking for someone. And instead of being angry, now he just appeared disappointed. Sad.

"Yeah," I answered, not giving him too much. I finally got how shit went down. I knew what had Grayson Waters, star quarterback of the Herons, a fucking mess at a college bar.

With the information Tony had tried to funnel to me, accompanied with Flash's stories, I had finally worked out the timeline and all the players in this drama. Flash got knocked up by Grayson's brother, Nate, their fucking father got his kid killed with his associations, and now I was fucked because I got myself messed up with not only a dangerous fucking con artist but his goddamn family.

Flash and I were both being dealt shitty hands.

I figured Gray here, once he snapped out of his grief, would eventually have his suspicions. Not too many prisons close to town. Wouldn't take a lot of research to track down the name of the one that his dad and I shared.

I just didn't want it to get back to Flash how fucking unlucky she was. I noticed how her body tensed and she started rocking a new mask of indifference as she walked in the club's doors. It was as if she was ready for a full-body assault. To be seeing the guy who shared a cell and was friends with the guy who'd put her daughter's father in the ground would probably have her fixing a mask that never came off.

I was shocked to hell when I heard Gray murmur, "Good. She usually finds this party pretty hard."

"No shit," I grumbled. I didn't want to be friends with this guy. I didn't want a bonding moment.

"We tell her she doesn't have to come every year. She didn't even know him that long," he continued while staring at his beer. "But she always does."

Before I had a chance to reply, one of the waitresses walked up and put her hand on Gray's shoulder. It wasn't until she asked him, "You behaving yourself?" that I realized the waitress was Flash's best friend. The little brunette who usually reminded me of a librarian. Except that night she was in leather pants, a tight black tank, and knee-high black boots. I almost laughed out loud. Surely if Gray was okay with his girl walking around in this getup, Flash would be able to talk about working at Poison. Her best friend might not be wearing pasties on her tits, but her outfit left nothing to the imagination. She also wasn't some angel able to throw stones at the devil in that outfit.

"Yeah, babe," Gray responded. "No need to worry. Go back to work. I'll still be here waiting for you when your shift is over. Still think it's silly you're working tonight."

"You know working always makes me think of Nate. I'm only on for another fifteen. Keep playing well with others," she replied softly before pressing her lips against Gray's cheek. When she turned toward me, I was still working out how I might convince Flash to tell them about her job at Poison. "I'm glad she brought you here, Cooper. I think I've seen her smile more these last few months since meeting you than she has in the last two years. If she hadn't showed up with you, I think I might've sent Gray here to find you. Our girl needs less pain in her life." With a final warning look directed at Gray, she headed toward the bartender to grab a tray of beers and disappeared into the crowd.

"Damn it," I muttered, humbled by the little librarian turned vixen. I knew after that angelic dance and now Parker's words pushed into the corners of my mind that I needed to make the hard choice.

Parker was right. Flash deserved peace.

She was also fucking *wrong*. I was only bound to bring pain into Flash's life.

When she walked away to serve some frat boys, I turned to Gray, decision made.

"We're going to need to talk." My no-nonsense tone snapped Gray out of his trance. "You want to wait until the end of this damn party, that's cool, but we need to talk tonight."

"This about the team?" he asked with the strength of a captain pushing through his grief to help a teammate.

"Wish it was about the game. Unfortunately, this shit has to do with your old man and the people we both need to protect."

"What the fuck?" Gray gritted out, his face changing from serious to pissed off. Before he could get out of his seat and drag me outside, I felt a light touch on my shoulder.

"They're not serving you?" Flash looked ashamed at the bartender and then Gray. I'd forgotten about our drinks. I had left her standing on her own for too long that she came looking for me. It wasn't until I took a look at the guys behind the counter that I realized she was right. They were watching me with hard eyes. They weren't overcrowded with customers. Some were even wiping down glasses behind the bench. However, with the way their eyes shifted from the main bartender to me, it was made clear that they had been ordered not to serve me at this bar.

"Maybe I made the wrong choice tonight. I can't control the fact that some people aren't very nice," Flash whispered, taking another look at the glances people were sending my way. The guilt I heard eating at her voice and destroying her mask had me put my plans on hold.

"Later," I muttered to Gray before grabbing Flash's hand and leading her onto the crowded dance floor.

"Count on it," I heard him reply before setting out to give Flash the peace she deserved right now.

Before I gave her the silence she needed from me to be peaceful forever.

—

MILLIE

THE OVERWHELMING PRESSURE to please everyone and talk to Nate dissipated.

I was too shocked.

Cooper Daniels, badass and the latest Heron superstar, was actually leading me to the dance floor while a slow love song drifted from the speakers.

When we began dancing, I nearly tripped over my own feet. Thankfully he didn't start leading me into anything complicated. We just swayed. I liked thinking that no one could see us among the couples crowding the dance floor. He pressed me tightly against his body and my mind went blank. My arms on his shoulders, his hands wrapped around my waist, I used the last of my remaining energy to keep my head up and stare into his beautiful irises.

I knew this was why I'd invited him, to be reminded that there could be beauty in my life.

I didn't need to focus on all the ways fate could be cruel and vicious.

"You don't need to worry about anything, babe," he whispered in my ear. "It's just you and me. Strangers who don't need to pretend with each other. And if that doesn't convince you, remember you promised that I get to protect you, so no one gets to make you feel like crap tonight without having to go through me."

My eyelids felt heavy, tears pooling. The act I'd been trying so hard to hold on to slipped away.

He gave my waist a slight squeeze and I let go, fell limp against his chest, head on his shoulder.

He was strong enough.

He held me up.

He held us both up and kept us dancing to Cat Power crooning about the sea of love.

"You tell me when you want me to stop, go back to the others," he said softly before brushing his lips across my hair. "You're calling the shots here."

I just nodded, then held on tighter, letting him rock me gently like the sea.

For the first time in two years, I was drifting instead of drowning. I was swaying with the current. I wasn't afraid of going home and getting dragged under.

I felt like parts of me had been split into pieces and by holding on, he kept me from falling apart. I thought it helped knowing that he felt as if pieces of himself were missing as well. We couldn't fix each other. It would be impossible. There had been too much damage. Yet by holding each other's pieces tightly enough together, it almost felt like we were whole again.

And *almost* was more than I'd had before.

It was everything.

COOPER

WHEN THE SONG ended, Flash lifted her head and smiled at me. I took a breath and felt it catch in my throat. *Damn, she's gorgeous.* The feeling I'd had since the first day I ever saw her, that she was the best thing I might ever aspire toward, fell like an anchor into the pit of my stomach. There wouldn't ever be enough dances with her to make up for what I was giving up, but I had to let her go and protect her the best way I knew how.

"I'm going to go find Marissa and Parker to say my goodbyes, and then I think I'm ready to call it a night," she murmured softly to me.

"Works for me," I muttered as if the words didn't sting leaving my mouth.

"Meet outside in fifteen?"

"Deal."

I watched as she threaded through the crowd before I headed back toward Gray. As soon as I caught the attention of the star quarterback, I noticed him get to his feet, clearly desperate to find out what the hell was going on. I gestured with my head to the front door. When I stepped outside into the cool air, the distant sounds of traffic almost made me feel like this could be any other day.

"Okay, what the fuck was that in there about my dad? And what the hell does that have to do with Millie?" Gray demanded the moment he exited the club.

I led us a few steps away from the doors before replying, "I was Tony's cellmate."

"Shit. And now you're hooking up with Millie, who might be the one person who has more reason to hate that guy than me. You don't want me to tell her, do you?"

"That's not it. I don't expect Millie to ever find out."

"Bad choice, dude, seeing as those sorts of secrets always fucking come out."

"I'm not going to be keeping the secret from her. I'm going to be staying away altogether. I promised your dad that I'd help him get a little retribution—"

"You did what?" Grunted Gray, clenching his fists as if he was about to take a swing at me. "You screwing with Flash for some sick retribution?"

"Fuck no. If you let me fucking finish, I was going to tell you that I had agreed to start a damn brawl when I finally got on the field. I was meant to ensure that you got hurt and lost your exciting future," I told him, keeping a close eye on the new stance of his body. "Dude, you want to take a swing at me, I'll let you get the first one in. I deserve it for being so damn stupid. But that won't fix the shit we're dealing with, and that isn't what I brought you out here to tell you."

He grunted at my words, letting me know he was following what I was saying but wasn't going to hug me anytime soon.

"Seeing as I didn't do jack to you the other day on the field, or anyone else, I think your old man worked out that I'd seen through his bullshit."

"Am I supposed to thank you for that?"

"Nah, man, what you need to realize is your dad's a conceited fuck, and before I even got back to my place, I had a duffel bag of photographs at my doorstep. A fucking warning about who might get hurt if I don't hurt you in our next game."

"Photos of Millie?"

"Yeah, she was one of them. I also have these girls I went through foster care with. Their photos filled the bag to the brim. At school, at work. Beth is only thirteen, and Lizzie's eighteen and just got approval to be her foster mom. I can't bring this crap to their door. But I won't attack you on the field and fuck with Millie's life either."

"So how the hell do you plan on dealing with the damn warning? My father's connections are dangerous."

"I'm going to leave town tomorrow morning, go protect Lizzie and Beth. I need you to stick close to Millie. Move in if you have to. I don't turn up to our game tomorrow, you and I both know I'm getting thrown off the team. Wouldn't be able to do shit to you even if I wanted to. Everyone will be pissed for a while, but the girls will be safe and we'll wait it out until the other crap blows over."

"That's your big plan? To leave town?"

"You know something better? I've gone through everything I could do. Fuck, I should've left already. Unless you've got a brighter idea, I need to get to Lizzie tomorrow."

"You've given me about five minutes to think this shit over."

"I got the package after last week's game. They didn't leave a due date, but I figure if I don't do shit tomorrow, then I might not be finding just photos on my doorstep"

"Fuck. Give me a few hours. Let me talk to Stars and get back to you."

"Stars?"

"Parker."

"Hell no. We aren't bringing any more people into this," I order. "I do not need your girlfriend's safety on my conscience as well."

"Brother, you think I'd tell my girl and put her in unnecessary danger? You've got me all wrong. My girl is the smartest person I fucking know.

Hell, she's the mastermind behind getting my dad behind bars in the first place. If we can work out how to fix this shit without costing the team a game, give Millie the only person who has made her smile in two years, and maybe put the screws to my dear old dad, then it's worth a shot. Also, she finds out we made some plan without her, I'm losing my balls in my sleep."

"I'm not too concerned about your balls. Millie just doesn't need anything more to worry about."

"Didn't this drama all start because you decided to not hurt me? Trust me, I'd give away my throwing arm before losing my balls. Also, you don't need to be concerned about Parker saying anything to Millie. If you staying away from Millie is the best plan, my girl won't say anything. She can keep a secret for years. Used to piss me off. Give me your number and I'll call you with her ideas."

"You have until tomorrow morning. I don't get a call before eight, I'm leaving town anyway."

TWENTY-FIVE

MILLIE

THE AIR OUTSIDE the club was ice cold, and I felt it pulling free the chains that had attached to my feet. Every year I knew this party would be hard to handle, but I often forgot the weight that I ended up carrying around the room.

Dancing with Cooper, catching Marissa's smile, and seeing Parker work the room were the only moments I cared to remember. Finally feeling able to go home, I looked down the street for Cooper.

I saw him leave the club as soon as we left the dance floor. I couldn't blame him for escaping at the earliest opportunity.

When I saw Cooper and Gray in a heated discussion near the road, I almost turned around and walked back inside. I was too tired for any more drama.

"Boys, if I have to walk over there and deal with any temper tantrums, the next time Jessie throws one, I'm calling you and you're getting her to calm down," I yelled from my spot near the doorway.

I watched them turn to me and noticed both their faces were white. Something was wrong. I felt it. They looked at me like I was about to be shot by a crazed gunman. The last time Gray looked at me like that was in the days following Nate's death.

I watched them nod at each other and then start walking toward me.

"You ready to go?" Cooper asked me when he got close.

"Yeah, everything okay?" I replied tentatively.

"Yeah, game tomorrow afternoon. Just worried about the other team's defensive line. They're meant to be a wrecking ball. Don't worry, no tantrums here," he said before pulling me in for a quick hug.

If I wasn't worried before, his casual touching put me on edge. Cooper didn't casually touch me. He was all about purpose. Intention. If he touched me, I knew he had thought about it before. Probably more than once. If his hands were on my skin, he knew exactly the response he was trying to elicit.

When we got into my pickup, I looked at him closely as he turned the ignition on. I examined the usual leather jacket, the way his hair fell over his forehead. I thought about all the things I knew about his past. I decided to let go of any problems I could imagine might be weighing on him. I didn't want to screw up my plans for the night. I needed a break from the constant worry.

"You taking me back to Poison?" I asked him softly.

"I figure you might need to get back to your girl straightaway. I can walk to the club from your house to grab my bike."

"If you want, we could go straight to yours. Tahnee offered to watch Jessie all night tonight. Guilt babysitting for leaving me to handle the party all by myself. I figured if you handled the party tonight, maybe we could spend the rest of the night together. We could get your bike in the morning?"

"All night, huh?" There was an edge to his voice that had me nervous.

"I was sort of hoping we could finally have some time together that didn't risk interruption. Unless that hasn't been circumstantial and you can only get off when you're afraid someone will see us," I asked him nervously, trying to hide my vulnerability in my light joke.

He looked deep in my eyes before he replied, "You're hilarious. You want to go to mine, we'll go to mine. But full disclosure, babe, my place is a pit."

"You've seen my house. It couldn't possibly be worse than that."

"My apartment makes your place seem like a resort."

"No way. Nothing beats my termite buffet."

"On the off chance there's a nail sticking up from the floor, tell me you're up to date with your tetanus shots," he muttered.

"I fell through our porch twice last year. Don't worry, I'm completely capable of handling anything your apartment wants to throw at me."

"You fell through twice? And it's only fixed now because of me? Really?"

"Well, what can I say? I was waiting to win the lottery."

COOPER NEEDED TO win the lottery twice in order to fix this place.

I was wrong. I was not prepared for his apartment.

It was worse than a pit. Calling it a total monstrosity would be too generous. The ceilings showed water damage, and the stench of mold and old meat filled the open-plan room, leaving no space untouched. The flooring was even slightly warped from faulty installation. I chuckled when I noticed the cheap pine air freshener sitting on a plastic crate he was using as a stool. A sad attempt at redeeming the unredeemable. It was as if he'd even tried to rescue this pathetic apartment.

"Pine?"

"Lemon was all sold out. Still want to spend time here?" Cooper inquired with a serious expression on his face. "We can leave. Go back to the park maybe. No one's going to be there at this time of night. Or I can also always take you home."

I stopped staring at the room, the damages, and took a hard look at Cooper. He stayed by the door when I'd walked inside the apartment. I hadn't realized until that moment that he remained unmoving as I ended up on the other side of the room, taking in every detail of each space. He was acting as if he were a doorman at an old established New York brownstone, completely stoic while waiting to reopen the door the moment I asked to leave. Even though his casual position leaning against the doorway was trying to communicate complete indifference, his terse gaze gave away his feelings.

He kept tracking my every move as if on edge. The anxiety pulsated from his body like a living, breathing organism. I remembered everything he had ever tried to keep safe, everything he had taken from him, and I wondered if he was concerned about bringing me here. If by agreeing to let me walk into his place, he was now braced for how I was going to leave.

"I want to stay. I think you don't understand the joy of a night off. You're forgetting I live in a dump as well. Besides your unique aroma, one dump at the end of the day is just like any another. Plus, I've yet to thank you," I said softly, looking him straight in the eyes across the room.

"Thank me for what?"

"For the porch. For coming with me tonight."

"Going to a party isn't really a hardship."

"That was not a party. It was like a wake with pitchfork-holding towns-people. I knew that was what we were walking into and didn't even warn you. You get a thank you."

Before he could respond or argue the fact—always the duty-bound bodyguard with no thought to himself—I slowly removed my clothes. Cooper didn't shift a muscle, just continued to lean against the doorjamb. We were far apart, but as each garment fell to the floor, I felt his eyes heat with every revealed body part. As I slipped out of my panties, I had a vision of that awkward scene in *The Notebook*, when they both removed their clothes slowly in front of each other. Except unlike innocent characters in a movie, I wasn't fearful about exposing myself to Cooper. I knew we weren't inexperienced partners unsure of where or when to touch each other. I was doing this to show him there wouldn't be any more masks from me. I wouldn't keep my guard up and fight him. Unlike nights at Poison, I was taking my clothes off without disgust, without an act, and with no regret.

He didn't even flinch as I stood before him completely naked.

"No clothes, tassels, or makeup to hide my scars," I muttered softly.

"You don't need to hide them," he replied.

I took a deep breath and waited for him to make his move.

He didn't shift an inch.

I could feel how we were on the cusp of something neither of us had before, but now I saw that it turned Cooper into stone. Maybe he knew we wouldn't be able to blame lust, passion, or alcohol tonight. We weren't living in the moment with no care to the future. This wasn't an impulsive decision we could claim we hadn't thought through or didn't understand the consequences of.

I thought he was seconds away from telling me to put my clothes back on. I decided I had run away from him so many times before that I was going to be brave enough for the both of us. "I'm going to step toward you. I'll make the first step. I'll make *all* the steps. But I'm going to need you to stand there and wait for me."

"I'm not going anywhere yet." His voice was thick with emotion.

"You ready to handle me?" I asked as he straightened.

"Fuck if I know. Never had anything like this before."

When we were standing a breath apart, I said quietly, "And I'd never had a tomorrow. But you gave me that. Maybe we'll both be surprised with what I might be able to give to you."

"I was wrong in that cafe. I thought you were a princess. You're a fuck-ing warrior." He ran a hand over the small scar I had from delivering Jessie.

"Does that mean I get to conquer you?" I replied cheekily, desperately trying to lighten the tension.

"If conquering means me on my back while you're on top, you won't hear me complaining, babe."

While he was still smirking at me, the nervous energy gone, I reached forward and ran my fingers through his hair. I felt his arms go around my waist and he hoisted me higher to meet his towering height. When our lips brushed, I let out a small whimper.

"I'm just going to hold on for a bit," he growled, his usual deep, grav-elly voice getting deeper.

"Fine by me," I said as I wrapped my arms around his neck.

"Hold tight," he ordered before grabbing hold of my ass and com-pletely lifting me from the ground until my legs automatically wrapped around his waist. In only three short steps, he had us maneuvered to the side of his makeshift bed, a sad mattress with even sadder blue sheets loosely tossed on top.

He turned us until his back was to the bed and carefully fell onto the mattress so I ended up on top.

"Tonight, I'm all yours." He looked so deep into my eyes that I almost stopped breathing at the intensity.

"Then I guess my first order of business is getting you out of these clothes." I helped him remove his pants first, laughing when I tried to pull his jeans off too fast and landed on my ass on the floor. When I finally climbed back up on the bed, I pulled at his T-shirt, lifting the fabric from his stomach, over his head, and past his arms. When he chuckled and laid back down, I caught sight of a small golden chain landing back on his chest. I leaned forward to get a better look at the tiny piece of jewelry. I never expected to find Cooper in a necklace, and a small smile played on my lips, ready to tease him about the small good luck talisman. That was until I moved close enough to recognize a little gold house. I froze, the smile vanishing from my face as shock settled across my features.

"What is that?" I whispered.

"Shit. I forgot about that. Don't make it a big deal," he started, avoiding my gaze. "I was going to give it back and kept forgetting about the damn thing. It weighs basically nothing."

"It's mine?" I stared at the small gold house charm hanging from his neck. "Why would you put it on a chain and wear it?"

"I thought we weren't going to make it a big deal," he groaned. "I found it in the student services building. Kept it in my pocket, but the damn thing kept falling out in the locker room. I had it on a shoelace at one point, and one of the guys had a spare chain in his locker. He thought it was some superstitious thing I carried for good luck and offered me the chain as like a welcome to the team thing. It's not like I went out and bought one."

"But you've been wearing it since the start of school. Since I lost—"

"Since I first saw you on campus. When I saw you drop it."

"So you picked it up and what, started wearing it?"

"Something like that," he mumbled.

"Babe, that's sort of creepy. Have you got a lock of my hair in one of your drawers too?" I laughed at the nerves that pulsated from Cooper's body. The guy who was always protecting me was suddenly uneasy of my reactions.

"Take the damn thing off me, remember to take it with you, and it won't be."

"Nope, it's always going to be creepy now. I think you should keep it. And I'm never forgetting." I smiled.

"Shit, it's just a house, not a heart or something lame and romantic."

"Actually, it's my dreams."

"Huh?"

"That's what the charm represents. I bought it myself with my first paycheck from Poison. A reminder every morning I put it on of what I was working for. When it went missing at the beginning of the year, I figured it was some karmic slap down. Another reminder that no matter how hard I worked, my dreams were always out of reach. At least that's what I thought. Until now," I told him softly as I ran my finger across the smooth surface of the charm and where it met his chest.

"What do you think now?" he asked carefully.

"That maybe my dreams aren't only mine to hold on to and work toward. Maybe it's okay if my dreams are in someone else's hands . . . or chest," I replied, looking into his eyes.

"Look at you talking about my chest. Now who's being creepy?" he teased, smiling at me.

I couldn't help but laugh and run my fingers across his hard body, leaving the charm resting at the base of his neck.

I began to lightly touch the scars hidden by ink and muscle as he'd done earlier to me.

"I wish I'd seen you that day," I admitted when I traced a scar that traveled from the bottom of his elbow all the way to his neck.

"In the student services building?"

"No, in the cafe, two years ago. I don't know if it would've changed anything, but I would've liked to have seen you."

"I'm glad you didn't," he whispered. "Losing Jake, leaving Lizzie and Beth, it killed me. Had there been even a glimmer of possibility between us, when the judge announced how long I was going to be put away for, I wouldn't be here now. It would've ended me."

"You don't think it would've helped? Imagining a future?"

"I struggled in prison," he told me quietly. "For a while there, I became pretty similar to my parents."

My breath caught. I knew what he was trying to tell me.

"No one was counting on me anymore. Nothing mattered. When someone explained that oxy could stop me from feeling anything, I took it."

"You don't have to explain—"

"You bared yourself to me. Tonight you deserve to know who you're climbing into bed with. The real scars aren't on my body, babe. They're deeper. I don't use now, haven't since I got out. It took me months to get clean. First it was so I could play. Now I'm finding other ways to get through the tougher days," he said gruffly, then raked a hand through his hair. "You don't need to worry about me around Jessie—"

"I know."

"I'm never going to act like my parents again. I've made some pretty fucked-up choices after Jake. I'm trying to fix them now." He took a long look into my eyes.

"I'm glad, but just so you know, as long as you're holding on to my dreams, I'll help heal your scars," I promised him. "If you need someone to drive you to meetings, if you want company when you're lonely—"

He reached up and took my mouth with his. With his left hand, he grabbed a rubber from the side of the bed. When he guided himself into me, we didn't move at first, taking the time instead to feel each other.

When I finally started moving, it was like a slow burn.

We weren't a sunrise, all yellows and golds filled with promise and excitement. We were a sunset. Just as hot, but sometimes easily missed. We were grays and blacks that you needed to closely examine before you could see the lines of pink and orange. If you turned on a light, looked away for a second, you wouldn't experience the magnetism.

It was there, you just needed to keep watching. Keep waiting.

TWENTY-SIX

MILLIE

IT WAS EARLY morning, the light drifting in through the fire escape window. The soft smell of pine and the cozy heat created from our bodies made me smile.

Wrapped in blankets and Cooper's arms, I decided that I was in love with this hideous apartment. Plastic crates and all.

The possibility that this love might *actually* belong to something or someone else in the room was quickly dismissed.

I was ready to lower the wall I had built around myself and start something with a man. I was *not* ready to admit that the joy I was feeling at that very moment might be because I had foolishly fallen in love with a troubled football player. It had to be this ramshackle place—a refuge from the world of pretenses and perfection—that was making my heart race and my eyes mist.

When I shifted closer to Cooper's body heat, he murmured, "You want to check your phone again or just want to go home? No hard feelings if you're desperate to get back to your girl."

I chuckled before softly replying, "Soon. I can probably wait a few more seconds before I make you move again." Since 5:00 a.m. I had checked my cell phone three times in fear that Tahnee had called with an emergency, each time knocking Cooper with my elbow. I doubted I'd be able to stay away from her much longer. I had a desperate need to check up on Jessie; however, I knew there was something special happening in this moment. I also feared that whatever solace we had found would be ruined the moment we opened the door.

It had been what happened with Nate. It was always how my luck worked. At night, it was easy to believe that our dreams and scars could be shared. We could forget the people we were pretending to be.

In the morning, I felt as if I needed to prepare for the future alone.

If this was the last time I got to speak with Cooper, what would the topic be? Unlike Nate, I wouldn't want a hypothetical future.

"I think you should invite them to a game," I said as I snuggled into the crook of his arm. "I've been thinking about it since we spoke at the park. The kids. Your family. They should come to one of your games. The stadium seats thousands, so there's no reason they can't come when hundreds of strangers will be there. They can see you. It will be different, maybe not what you want at first, but you make it to the NFL with a four-year college degree, no judge in the nation will prevent a single mother with her foster daughter from being around you. You'll be a role model, going from prison to pro ball. You'll be football's Iverson."

"Making it to the NFL is a pipe dream, babe. Not exactly a dreamer," he grunted while pulling me closer in his arms.

"Cooper, I'm not a recruiter or a coach. I know jack shit about the NFL and what it takes to get drafted, but I think I finally know you. If the NFL is what it takes for you to finally be with the closest thing you have to sisters and be able to help them, protect them, then I'd bet my money on you."

"If I tell you that they'll probably be better off if they never see me play—"

"I'll tell you that you're being a martyr, and that is less attractive than that face you made last night."

"What face?" he demanded as he rolled on top of me.

I giggled. "You know the one I'm talking about."

"Babe, you better take those words back," he growled as he bit my earlobe.

"Nope," I laughed.

"Then you'll never get to leave. I'll keep you trapped here. And babe, not sure if you noticed but it doesn't matter if you're a warrior or a princess. No one is staying alive in these four walls after twenty-four hours."

"Okay fine, I was teasing. Your face is always attractive."

"Not that I didn't know that already, but you're forgiven." He smirked.

"I wasn't kidding about your foster friends though."

"Babe, one day they'll see me play. On a field, in a park—it won't matter. It just matters that we're all safe."

I was about to tell him that they were all safe now. The drugs, his parents, prison, and everything else that haunted him could stay in the past. He could invite his friends to a game. He no longer had to be afraid. But as his hands traveled over my skin, all coherent thoughts in my head vanished.

It was just him, me, and a new morning of experiences.

COOPER

IT WAS A dick move, not telling her about the photos. About Tony. Keeping her in the dark about the shit I wanted to protect her from.

I had her to myself for an entire evening knowing that she might've left if she had known the truth. Telling myself that letting her come to me, holding her for one night, was the best goodbye for both of us.

I'd spent my whole morning knowing it was all bullshit. I knew what we needed from each other exceeded one night. Yet unless Gray or Parker had some genius idea about how we were going to move forward, I wouldn't say a word. There was no changing my mind; staying here and risking Millie's and Jessie's lives would never be an option. She would achieve her dreams without me. I would learn to deal with my scars alone if it prevented her from suffering.

When we went to pick up my bike from Poison, I replayed the previous night in my head. I recalled the soft sound of her nervous laughter each time she made a move toward me, the small smile she gave me every time I ran my fingers through her hair. I remembered evading every opportunity to tell her what was happening and where I was going—and being rewarded with kisses and smiles.

I couldn't think of never waking up like I did that morning. I was grateful . . . *happy*. It made even thinking about walking away feel like I was trying to climb out of quicksand. I was sinking further and further into the mess we'd stirred up inside one another. When I noticed at breakfast that she was anxious about asking me to go with her to Poison early and get my bike—convinced that she was disrupting my game day plans so she could head home early—I didn't correct her. I didn't tell her that I'd received a text message with Gray's address and instructions to get there as soon as I could.

As she smiled at me from the passenger seat in the car, she had no idea that her eagerness to see her girl and check that spending a night away hadn't left Jessie traumatized was perfect timing for my early morning meeting.

To ease her guilt, I listened to her tell me about a past emergency, about getting a call as she was about to grace Poison's stage when Jessie was eighteen months old. With hands gesturing wildly and eyes sparkling, she explained the shortest, most comical striptease she had ever done. Detailed the three red lights she ran to get to the hospital, the pasties attached to her nipples spinning in the wind, to find out that her daughter had decided to eat all the jewelry in the house to help her sparkle. When the doctors explained that the scans showed that nothing she had swallowed would in fact harm Jessie, Tahnee found her some scrubs and they both laughed out loud at the state of them. Of course, they stopped laughing when they were informed that, if they wanted any of their possessions back, they would need to scrutinize Jessie's poop constantly for the next month.

Her laughter reverberated around the truck as she described Gray's face when he couldn't find his championship ring a few days later. She snorted and scoffed as she let me know that no one bothered to correct his panicked state, allowing him instead to spend weeks with his hands in Jessie's poop. It even caused me to snicker.

"It was a stupid thought in the first place. Those rings are huge. No way my girl could've swallowed it without choking. Eventually Parker told him that she had put it in his side table drawer for safekeeping. But hot-shit Grayson Waters digging through poop is something I'll never forget. Even D started helping," she chuckled.

Watching her laugh, catching her checking me out from the corner of her eye, I knew she wasn't the same suspicious girl I'd first tried to befriend. No longer apprehensive about every protective act, she was carefree and weightless. I wondered if this was who she was before she got pregnant. Before Nate's passing.

It killed me.

In her eyes, I was going to be another mistake. Someone else who hurt her. A part of me worried that she would go back to the girl trying to handle everything by herself. This version of herself would be gone—again.

I hoped she knew deep down that if I had a choice, I wouldn't be going anywhere. When Gray gave her the golden charm back, when she found out that the light kiss I was about to give her before she stepped out of the car was actually goodbye, I hoped she knew that, wherever I was, I would be hurting as much as she would be.

I'd never had a tomorrow. But you gave me that. My mind played that soft statement on repeat.

I wanted to be the person who kept giving her tomorrows. Who made her believe in a future.

I just knew I couldn't be. I didn't have a tomorrow to offer.

I needed to protect Lizzie and Beth. Gray needed to protect Flash. And I would learn to live with the fact that everyone's safety was better than Flash and I sharing our dreams.

When we finally pulled up to my bike and she leaned over to brush her lips against mine, I kept my hands clasped tightly at my side. I didn't reach out.

I knew better than to try to hold on.

The night before I'd experienced the fairy tale. It wasn't in a castle. It didn't involve weird singing animals. But I did get to wake up with the princess.

Unfortunately, I was also the bad guy in the room, and no fairy-tale had the bad guy ending up with the princess.

TWENTY-SEVEN

COOPER

WHEN I PULLED into Gray's driveway, Millie's absence had already started eating a hole in my stomach. Rather than deal with the pain, I let the anger fester.

It fueled me. I embraced it and prepared for the shit storm ahead.

I was certain that walking into the star quarterback's fancy apartment, talking about their feelings and listening to them try to problem solve wasn't going to help. Discussing this crap for even a few minutes delayed the inevitable. It made each step I took toward the front door aggravating.

There was no way to clean up the dirt I had waded into. Not enough ways to apologize for how I'd dragged it through all their lives. *I should keep moving. Let Gray care for Millie. Accept my fate.*

I planned how my day would go. The conversation should take seconds, and then I'd give Gray the charm and head to my apartment. I'd fill my backpack with the limited stuff I kept close and go to Lizzie. I'd take the girls to Nevada. Al would help me sort my shit out, and together we'd plan how to ensure Anthony Waters regretted his decision to manipulate me.

I wouldn't let Al cut me out.

When I rapped my knuckles on the door, prepared to tell Gray that I wouldn't be there long. I was shocked to find Marissa opening the damn thing smiling.

"What the fuck are you doing here?" I snarled before pushing past her and locking eyes on Gray leaning against the banister of his stairs.

"Well hello to you too." Marissa grimaced as she gestured for me to enter.

"Don't get bent out of shape when we haven't even explained the plan yet," Gray started. "We've got some ideas, but it's going to take more than the three of us. Thought we'd save some time and bring people in now rather than wait a few hours."

"I never agreed to a fucking massive plan," I grunted as I noticed D walk into the room eating a sandwich. "I don't trust everyone I've ever met."

"Yeah well, we'll worry about who you choose to trust later. Right now you'll just have to accept that this shit is both our problems, and we've got to handle it fast," Gray replied before taking a seat at the kitchen table.

D just smiled wide at me before he stated, "Bro, I'm like family. No way shit was going down with Mr. Waters without people cluing me in." I watched as D took another massive bite of his food and leaned against the kitchen counter. I sneered at him before taking a seat opposite Gray at the table, ensuring the chair screeched across the kitchen tiles. D chuckled, letting me know he was completely unaffected by my hostility.

"He's also a part of my plan. We won't be able to fix this without him," Parker murmured softly as she entered the room and took a seat at the table. "And if you had trusted us earlier, maybe we wouldn't be in this mess."

"My girl's got a point," Gray chuckled as he leaned against the bench. "Plus, you have a problem with D, Parker, and Marissa being here, you're going to be pissed to know that in about fifteen, the whole team is going to be here."

"What the fuck! We were meant to discuss this shit together. This is not only about your family."

"Aware of that, bro. Also know we can't waste time, because I figure you've got people to visit after this conversation."

"Fuck it, just tell me what the hell you think will fix everyone's god-damn life."

"Maybe you should show Cooper around your place, Gray, before you all start talking?" Marissa suggested. "Let him settle in. Calm his shit before he hits someone."

"What is there to show? You can see the lounge from here, and unless you think he wants to see Gray's jocks on the floor, no point taking him upstairs. Or do you guys finally pay a cleaner now that I'm out of the house?" D asked Parker, smiling.

"Careful, Andrew, your privileged background is showing," Marissa interrupted. "Not all of us have always lived in nice apartments with clean-ers and drive fancy cars. And sometimes we like to look at new places. Not all of us have seen everything there is to see in the world."

"Rissie, you want me to show you around one of my family's vacation homes, all you got to do is ask." D chuckled.

Before Marissa could respond, Gray stood and placed a hand on her shoulder. The subtle reminder of sticking together stopped the venom from spitting off her tongue, but didn't prevent the snide looks Marissa and D continued to throw at each other.

As fucking delightful as it was watching them tease each other, I was so sick of being there already. "Can we just get down to business? Inform me of your phenomenal plan that will save the freaking day. I'd like to point out the flaws quickly and be on my way."

Before Gray could answer, a succession of rapid knocks sounded at the front door.

"Hold your discussions on the plan. I invited one more for the prelim-inary meeting." Marissa headed to the door. The confused expressions on both Parker and Gray's face suggested that they had no idea who the fuck she'd decided to invite. However, D's wide grin gave me a clue that even if he had no idea what was going on, he planned on enjoying every minute.

At least one of us was amused by this shit.

"OKAY, I'M HERE. You happy? I just got home and barely had a chance to kiss my little girl's head before you started blowing up my phone. If this shit isn't as important as you implied, I'm out of here. I don't feel right leaving Tahnee watching Jessie all night and now half the day," Millie seethed as she stepped into the house.

I saw shock coat her face when she noticed all of us in the kitchen.

The anger I was carrying around burst like a water balloon. I was standing in the kitchen, soaked in the remains of my pain and guilt. Unsure what to do with myself, I decided silence was the only reaction I could handle.

Millie looked straight into my eyes and I closed them. I wouldn't—couldn't—face her.

"What the fuck is this?" Her eyes moved from mine to Parker's, to Gray's, to D's, and to Marissa's. She noticed the guilt across Parker's face, the concern in Gray's. "Is this a bloody intervention?" she asked trying to come up with a reason as to why we all might be standing in the room together.

"Shit, you told them, didn't you?" She turned to face me. "That's why Marissa is here. Why everyone looks so sad and angry. You couldn't keep letting me work at Poison now that we've gotten together, could you?"

My eyes snapped open, moving to hers and then to the shocked expression on Parker's face.

"What the fuck?" Gray growled from the bench.

"You're wrong. That's not why we're here, and I never would've told them without your permission. You becoming mine wouldn't ever mean that I'd stop you from trying to help your girl," I stated clearly.

"She doesn't need to do that shit to help Jessie," Gray snarled.

"That *shit* is my second business, and if people in this town weren't so small-minded, they'd recognize burlesque routines as a damn art form," Marissa replied as she walked in front of Millie to stare everyone down. "But that's not what we're here to discuss, so can we all just table your ridiculous feelings about that shit now? We have more serious problems to deal with. Problems that should never have been discussed without all the key players in the room. Now I've rectified that, so we can start."

"This is bullshit," I muttered, looking at Gray, communicating with my eyes that I never would've agreed to this discussion with Millie in the room.

"Dude, I didn't invite Millie, but Marissa is right. We're all in this, so we might as well all be here. The way we have to play this for it to work, it's going to have to be big."

"If this *isn't* an intervention about Poison, then can someone please explain to me what's going on?" Millie looked ready to pull out her hair.

D moved in front of her, rested both hands on her shoulders, and with a wide grin, told her, "Okay, Millie, I'm gonna break it down for you. Your new golden boy here from the other side of the tracks bumped into the trash we kicked over the train line in a shared prison cell. Our always reliable con man Mr. Waters, who apparently hasn't lost his touch of being a completely full of shit son of a bitch even in prison, convinced this knucklehead here to help him dish out a little payback on Gray. Apparently, Mr. Waters has been crying that Gray orchestrated Nate's passing. Now your boy was an idiot in the slammer, but when he met you, your girl, and us totally upstanding citizens, he thankfully saw the light. Not to brag, but I think one of my tackles during training might've helped clear his head. Anyhow, Mr. Waters sent your boy a warning that if he doesn't enact some form of retribution, Coop's childhood friends plus you, my sweetheart, are in danger. Your boy's plan was for Gray to protect you and for him to leave town after grabbing his childhood friends. We were all to just lie in wait for Mr. Waters to make a move, while losing our best new running back and potential BFF. None of us think this is the best plan."

Once D let go of her shoulders and took a step back, Millie twisted her body to face me and asked quietly, "You were going to leave today even after last night?"

"Don't want my shit choices hurting yours," I responded dryly, ignoring the tears I saw briefly swirling in her eyes.

She exhaled, shook her head, and then turned to the group. "Okay, for everyone else who doesn't have the desperate need to be a martyr, what's the actual plan?"

"They fight," Parker said to the group. "Cooper and Gray."

The color draining from Millie's face must've encouraged Gray to quickly explain the details. "That's what Dad wants to see, so we're inclined to give it to him. It won't be the first time a fight has broken out during a college football game at halftime. Usually players start swinging at the other team, but I'm sure we can put on a hell of a show, even if it's just between us. You don't need to worry though, we'll take a page from my dad's book and make it complete pretense. From what Cooper has told us, Dad sounds just as full of himself—if not more so—than he was before he was locked up. We don't think he'd begin to believe we'd be able to pull off something so big and devious."

Parker continued, "We make it look like there's some in-team rivalry. A disagreement over a play, a fight for the spotlight. We have to make it fast and not let it touch our rivals. It goes on for too long, we're bound to get more than just a slap on the wrist from the coach and the NCAA. We also need everyone on the team in on it, make it look like this is boiling over from practice."

As Millie got a little color back into her cheeks, I acted as the devil's advocate, pointing out the major flaws in their plan. "What you're all talking about sounds like polishing the deck of the damn *Titanic*, because we'd go to all this trouble and Tony would still be able to take us down. You're suggesting we pretend to throw our fists at one another, like that'll be enough? He has fucking minions following my friends. And he'll be following us. If he knew Millie and I were together, someone has to be watching. Watching closely."

"Sorry to break it to you, Cooper, but someone is always watching us closely," Parker said. "Gray is one of the best college quarterbacks in the nation. Millie is the mother of his niece. People like to know about our lives. You're forgetting that Mr. Walters is in prison."

"Not to be insulting, but that doesn't mean shit to him," I replied.

"Maybe not, but he's wrong. It means something. Sure, in his head I bet he thinks that his ability to send you a single package and get information snuck to him proves that he's some top dog. He's not. He's reliant on others, most likely cheap hires because sitting in a cell, unable to con people out of their savings, doesn't help him build his fortune. And we aren't exactly surrounded by goons like when we were up against Mr. Simons. Mr. Waters doesn't have that many connections. He's a con man, not a local mob boss. He's likely paying petting criminals to do his bidding, lazy snitches who I would wager gather their information from the media and the closest family friend," Parker explained. "They probably don't bother following us when they see everything they need on ESPN, and more than a few people in this town like talking about Gray and his future. They probably spent a day following your friends and haven't been back since. I would bet my college degree on it. Mr. Waters is pretending he's not in a bubble, but he is. We don't plan on bursting it anytime soon. We just want to cover it with images and information that blocks him from seeing the truth."

"That's where I come in," Marissa informed me as she boosted herself onto the kitchen bench. "I take the photos, sell them to not one but all the local news outlets. Different angles, different poses. With the right lighting, I can make a slap fight between girls look like a McGregor UFC event."

"I can choreograph it," Flash chimed in. "The fight will be my best piece of dance yet. I planned enough angst-filled conceptual routines in high school to have it look real enough."

"I remember. I was always your victim. It's what gave me the idea." Parker looked at her friend with pain in her eyes. "Granted, we'll need you to do something else too. If you really want to help."

"What are you thinking?"

"The media know who I am, and my reactions will be recorded by Marissa, but we don't want just one media source reporting on this fight. We want all of them. You haven't been to a lot of games, but they know who you are. People talk about you. They've seen me scream over the most minuscule of tackles, and they usually take notice, but they'll quickly interpret it as just another game. But if you scream? Everyone notices that you don't cry often. Enough people know what Gray has done for Jessie. Marissa getting a photo of you breaking down on the sidelines—Gray's dead brother's girl worried about the only father figure her daughter has— would sell the story. No one would believe you were distraught over a small tussle. Everyone would automatically believe it to be real and serious. The media will eat it up. I think it'll go a long way to having everyone worried about Gray's condition and ending in Mr. Waters's information."

"No," I snarled. "We aren't putting her in front of the media to be picked apart."

"Of course I'll do it," Millie interrupted.

"Trick will play the rest of the game. He's ready. We'll keep him and a few select others who could run the game if we get suspended," Gray continued. "The way I see it, we've only got one issue."

"What's that?"

"Dad's got police informants. We need one of those to pass on this crap like it's real. We just need one. We know the other snitches will likely believe the news, but if one police officer sees that I've been carried off the field and there's talk of a career-ending injury, they'll expect me to press charges. When they go to their system and see that nothing came of it, they might tip my dad off—"

"I guess you figure that's where I come in?" I questioned. "Because that's my expertise? Finding the lowest of the low? Knowing someone dodgy enough to turn on one of their own on the inside?"

"Look, if you can't do it, we'll find another way."

"No, I can do it. If we're polishing the damn deck, I know where to find the oiliest son of a bitch," I said, raking my fingers through my hair. "And on the upside, the great thing about assholes is that they have no loyalty. They aren't even loyal to other assholes."

TWENTY-EIGHT

MILLIE

I LISTENED TO Cooper talk about his associations. I felt his self-disgust. It was tangible, like beads of sweat dripping down his back. It was obvious that he still thought running was the best option.

I had too many emotions coursing through my own body right then to remind him that his past associations weren't something he needed to feel ashamed of, let alone begin to explain how running away wouldn't clean any of this mess up.

"Okay, the plan's decided, then," D stated cheerfully before heading to the cupboard and pulling out a new loaf of bread. "I'll just fuel up and then be ready to get my groove on."

"Seriously? Another sandwich?" Marissa grimaced as she watched D place a jar of jelly on the counter.

"What can I say?" he replied, knocking her with his hip to have better access to the cutlery. "This body isn't created through eating that wheat grass shit you love."

"Don't knock into me."

"Don't stand in the way, then."

I took a deep breath as Marissa and D continued to throw taunting remarks at each other. Their bickering was a nice break from the heaviness weighing on the room. From the corner of my eye, I saw Parker move to the kitchen to boil water in the kettle, while Gray and Cooper threw pent-up aggressive stares each other's way. I reached for my cell phone to see if Tahnee had called me, hoping for a small moment of peace by focusing on my girl. When my hands patted my empty pocket, I realized I must have left my phone in the car. I backed away silently and headed for the front door. As I wrapped my fingers around the handle, I felt someone touch my shoulder.

When I turned around, Cooper was standing close, his thumbs hooked in his jean pockets and his green eyes filled with turmoil.

"Don't walk out," he growled.

"Huh?"

"I know you're pissed at me. You have every right to be. I was going to leave. I kept shit from you last night while I let you tell me all about your secrets. I never told you anything about Tony, the guy who helped make your life hard. The list of my fuckups is endless, but I want you to stay. Yell. Scream. I deserve it. I just don't want you to walk away—at least not until you've said your piece."

I took a hard look at Cooper's expression. Behind his beard, his tattoos, and the leather, I saw the scars.

The fact that he was standing before me like a dog ready to be whipped broke my heart. Beaten down by everything and everyone, he was just expecting more of the same. Someone who wouldn't understand him and the reasons that motivated him. Another person who thought he was an evil guy and was ready to hurt him.

The tears wanted to break free but I held them back.

"I'm not leaving," I said bluntly. "I'm going to get my cell phone out of my car, and then I plan on sticking around to help everyone put Mr. Waters back in his place. You're right that I hate that guy, and I'll do everything in my power to help shut his antics down. I also wasn't lying about being able to choreograph a kickass fight scene and break down in front of the cameras. But if you want to know my feelings about all the secrets you've kept and how that affects us, then here is it. I'm not angry. I'm sad."

When his eyes filled with disbelief, I continued with a deep breath. "Don't get me wrong. For a moment in there, I was furious. When I thought you had told them about Poison, I was ready to stomp on your largest toe with my sharpest stiletto. After D gave me the breakdown, I wanted to pull every hair from your beard as I replayed all of our conversations in my head. Conversations that never included your cellmate or your plans for revenge. We both shared some of our demons, but not once did you tell me that our lives intersected in more than just a cafe. Thinking about you sharing a cell with the man who basically murdered my child's father makes me sick to my stomach. But that's not why you're here. You're not here as his minion. As everyone got to talking, I realized that you're here to fix a stupid decision you made when you were locked away from your family. You've also told me about your parents. Your brother. The state you were in behind those bars. It doesn't take a genius to work out how you could believe the shit Mr. Waters was preaching." I tried to lock down my emotions, but felt my efforts fail as a single tear spilled onto my cheek. "I also know that you wanting to help someone you think has been victimized, even if it involves doing something stupid, is just who you are."

When he just continued to stare at me, I kept going with a shaky voice. "So I'm not angry. I don't need to yell at you. But the fact that you came here, that you didn't tell me to come with you, makes me sad. Because it means that I screwed up. Again. I confused our relationship with something it wasn't. I forgot that it was casual. A means to an end. We have sex in public places and after sad emotional events, for Christ's sake. We're lonely and emotional—we're trying to forget." I felt more tears begin to fall. "If what was going on between us was something more, you would've shared all about Tony with me last night. You would've known I could handle it. It's really not your fault. I'm fucked up. I've been daydreaming and having nightmares about a dead man for the past two years. Since the moment I met you, I stopped dreaming about Nate and started dreaming about you. As much as I've tried denying and ignoring it, my feelings for you have slowly taken root inside of me and have grown into something I never even wanted. I was meant to distract myself from my pain, and instead

I've opened myself up to more. Hell, since the night we made love in the park and followed that by spending the day together, I've been drifting to sleep with this stupid picture in my head. My hair is up in curls, a stunning white strapless dress hangs from my body, and I walk toward *you* in that damn park you told me you took Jake to. I've pictured this perfect life, built from the chaos we both had to endure." I felt the tears cascading down my face, hitting my shoulder and seeping into my clothes. Disappearing like my misguided dreams.

I finally told him softly, "I know it's crazy. And stupid. What can I say? I'm more dramatic and hopeless than I pretend to be. I'm just so sorry that I made you feel like you needed to be punished for not telling me. I'm aware that until a week ago I've tried to reject, ignore, and insult you. I should've realized my feelings were one-sided—"

"Don't. We're not just casual sex. You're not crazy. Or if you are, then so am I. Because I dreamed about us too. I dreamed about walking into that damn café with Jake, except it's this year and when we see you, we both walk straight over and start talking. I wrap my arm around your shoulder and Jake bugs Parker about his latest assignment. Because you and I are together, none of the events of that day have touched us, and we found a way to be happy with everyone in our lives."

"In your dream, the only way we can be together is if we live in a perfect world?"

"Babe, any situation where I get to wake up and wrap my arms around you after the shit I grew up with is a damn perfect world. But it's not as simple as wrapping my arms around you and living happily ever after— which is why I couldn't ask you to be a part of this last night or this morn- ing. Asking you to stay with me is like asking you to get in the car with a drunk driver, I wouldn't be inviting you to ride off into the sunset, I'd be inviting you to your death. I'm going to crash us straight into a ravine—"

"Then let's crash. Together. Stop trying to protect every damn thing in your life. That's what's going to kill you. Fuck, you're nineteen years old. And goddamn it, I'm older than you. If I'm not crazy, if this is more, I should get a choice. I can't give you any proof, but I'm pretty sure I have the skill and know-how to jump from a careening car if necessary. But just so you know, if I lock myself in, then you aren't inviting me anywhere. I'm attaching myself to you. And it's not your fault."

"Even if I was the idiot to believe in a con man?"

"Yeah well, we've all done stupid things before. Like forgetting my cell phone in the car."

He smiled at my attempt to lighten our mood, but then his face went somber again, "Look, before you get your phone and we join the others, I truly want you to know that I didn't want to leave. It was eating at me this morning not saying anything. Last night, all that we shared . . . I just couldn't work out how to keep you safe and let you stay with me."

"What do you want me to say, Cooper? That I forgive you? That you were bad for making a shit choice? I don't want to punish you or cause you more pain. Anything outside that, tell me and I'll do it. I'm yours," I told him, my voice cracking. "I gave you me the moment I gave you my name, so please tell me what it is you want me to do or say."

"I need you to promise me that you'll get through this shit and live." His voice broke on the last word. "That you won't risk you or your girl. I can't lose anyone else I love. You might be ready to sign up for a car accident, and you might not break, but I will. If my prison connections hurt Jessie—" He takes a deep breath. "I need to hear you tell me that if I'm about to crash, you'll jump. If not for you, then for me. For Jessie."

My breath caught as I heard each of his words. I took a step forward, wrapped my fingers around his neck, and brought him in for a soft kiss. When we broke apart for air, I whispered, "Okay. I promise if things are about to get too dangerous, I'll jump. For you and Jessie."

Staring into one another's eyes, my heart raced. I wished for just a moment that we could leave together and start comforting each other alone. Instead, I kissed him softly again with the intention of letting go. However, the moment our lips touched, I felt the heat that always built between us when we touched ignite, and our kisses became rougher—only to be quickly extinguished when the sound of exuberant clapping broke the silence.

We turned our heads and noticed that everyone in the kitchen was watching us, not even attempting to disguise the fact that they'd heard our entire exchange. Parker was wiping away tears. Gray was looking at the floor. Marissa winked at me. And D continued to clap.

When he finally stopped, he turned to Marissa. "You know, for the first time, you were right, Rissie. Daniels here definitely needed a tour of this place. He might've realized anything he said in that damn hallway can be heard around the whole apartment. I really wish I had popcorn instead of a sandwich during that exchange."

"If you've finished your sandwich, that means you're ready to get your groove on, right?" I asked D, not letting him continue teasing about our conversation. I knew we were both too raw, too exposed to have someone even joke about the things we'd just discussed.

"I'm all yours, dancing queen."

"Then let's get to it."

———

TWO HOURS LATER, I was in the lounge room instructing D and Gray to move furniture to make a mock dance studio. I was planning simple twists and turns in my head, hand movements that looked dangerous but were easily orchestrated. I researched poses on my phone that suggested pent-up frustration as Parker and Marissa removed all the breakables from the room.

I knew the authenticity of the fight would need to be sold by every football player's body and the way they interacted before anyone noticed their faces. Therefore, I had worked out a way for every action to be plotted and meticulously thought out.

With D beside me, letting me know who had to be kept out of it, I decided to assign each player to a group as they walked into the house. Those who would be involved in the fight, those who would look like they wanted to get involved, the ones who would hold back the wannabe fighters, and the guys who needed to get in the faces of the coaches.

Trick was the only one who complained about his allocation. "I want in on the action."

"We need you to win the game once we leave," Gray informed him.

"Been waiting to show everyone what I was made of all season, but now I don't want to," he whined. "I want to help Coop."

"Ah, cheer up, buttercup. You're going to have a front row seat to the show. Plus, maybe when you're captain, you'll get to stage your own fake fight with Cooper right beside you every year," D laughed.

"You think?"

"The team you'll become with Cooper next year, you're going to end up with jealous oppositions taking real swings at you," Gray told him.

With the vision of a real fight in his mind, Trick happily faded into the background and helped motivate the other players, appointing himself as the fight's mascot.

Unfortunately, I already knew building to the big fight moment wouldn't be the problem. The Heron football players found pushing each other around second nature. When Gray gave them a talk about why we were there and what we needed them to do, half of them were shoving each other and telling each other to shut the fuck up and listen. Asking them to hit one another? No problem. Asking them to *not* actually hit each other, To follow steps and control their punches, would be the hard part.

Working out how to make it only as big as we needed for Marissa's and the media photos, but have it die a natural death and get under control so fast that no one got benched or punished by the NCAA, was going to be close to impossible.

Each player watched with a little awe as I put on a demonstration. I threw Gray's high school helmet to the floor, started muttering obscenities, moved my body toward Parker, and with as much dramatics as I could without losing believability, took a right cross to her face. When Parker threw her head backward, I saw Gray and every football player in the room flinch.

Thankfully when Parker spun around and smiled at the group, everyone wanting to retaliate relaxed. If I wasn't so focused on the production quality of all of this, I would've thought it was sort of sweet that even the pretense of hitting the starting quarterback's girlfriend had everyone on the team queasy. Parker blushed and started moving backward, never one for the spotlight. However, if she thought she was fading in the background today, I was about to correct her. There was no way I would be able to manage this massive group of guys by myself if we were going to have everyone ready to perform during the game that day. Forcing Parker to practice my angst-filled high school conceptual dance routines in her bedroom years before wouldn't just inspire this whole activity—it would be the reason it might just work.

Before I sent them off in their groups to practice their individual roles, I reminded them of how serious they needed to take this rehearsal in my best teacher voice. "If you're going to be pretending to get hit, you need to stretch. Your neck, your shoulder, or whatever body part you think you'll be throwing around all day practicing. We don't want anyone here getting whiplash or not being able to go onto the field at any point. If you're the one throwing the hits and you aren't careful, you lose count, someone will get hurt. We're all going to make this look as real as possible for the reporters, but someone moves too quickly, turns too slowly, these hits will land. We need the least amount of air between punches and people's faces for things to look real. And with the amount of energy you'll have to use to make it look even slightly believable, things can get out of control. I repeat, you lose count, it won't be pretend anymore and the asshole that is Mr. Waters wins." While everyone looked ready, angry, and about to take all of this super serious, I let them know, "Also, before anyone goes out to the yard to practice fake hits, we need everyone to take off jewelry so no one clips each other."

I tried not to smile when this big group of guys started moaning and grumbling about taking their chains and championship rings off. When I felt heat at my back, I turned to find Gray anxiously staring at the door.

The moment we finished talking earlier, Cooper had snuck out the door to call Lizzie and visit his brother. "Do you know when he's getting back so I can walk through your routine?" I asked Gray.

"No clue. I figured it might be a couple of hours."

"Hours?"

"I'm hoping it's sooner, but I have no clue how long it'll take Cooper to convince his brother to do us a favor. Nate and I were pissed at each other for years. Just before the end, we'd made up. Parker was a big reason for that. But fuck, if Nate turned up at my house asking me for a favor like Cooper is trying to do, I'm not sure I would've listened. It might've taken me a while."

"Do you want to have a backup plan?"

"Can I hit myself and it look like a punishment? Have my dad get off our backs?"

"Not really. I mean, we could try and make you look like the victim of a stray hit. Though I don't know why Mr. Waters would stop bothering Cooper's friends if he wasn't the one—"

"If it's not going to solve all our problems, then we wait."

"Gray, Cooper hasn't told me everything, but I have a good idea about who his brother is to him. From his stories about protecting the other kids in the house and some actions that his brother put into motion, I know he isn't anything like you. You might've said no to Nate if he came asking for a favor, but that's because you base your decisions off loyalty, integrity, and foolish pride. What you would never do is sell your decision to the highest bidder without regard to the consequences. I get the feeling that in the family Cooper comes from, the highest bidder is all that matters."

TWENTY-NINE

COOPER

"THIS MEANS WE'VE got a deal," I repeated back to Eli.

The same six words I'd been restating every five seconds for the past ten minutes with uncertainty dripping heavily from every word.

My head was aching, while the suspicion in my eyes and body language grew when he rolls his eyes.

His unfazed actions were freaking me way the fuck out.

"Little bro, I have this covered. You signed the piece of paper I brought with me, the one the reporters told me I'll need. Now I visit your cell-mate. You play a dramatic football game. In a few years, we're both rich motherfuckers."

"The paper will be worth nothing if the douche I shared a cell with doesn't believe you. If I don't play another game because I'm too busy dealing with the destruction of Millie's, Lizzie's, and Beth's lives. We need you to tell him that Gray was seriously injured and pressed—"

"Bro, I heard you the first time. No point going through the whole story again. Fuck, dude, I did have to pass exams to join the police force. I'm not a complete idiot. I can remember a few fucking instructions."

I ran a hand through my hair and sighed. "You screw this up, you know Lizzie will feel this," I reminded him. "This isn't me begging you not to tell the Walters to send Jake back to the fucking group home. This isn't some hypothetical bad-case-scenario bullshit. He sent me photos, Eli. If I don't do something, they will get hurt. It's black and fucking white."

"You know I've done a lot of things that have led you to not trust me, little brother. I'll own that. But I never surprise you. I've been what I am for years. You knew I was going to call the Walters even if you didn't want to admit it to yourself. Get more kids in the home. That was always my instruction, and you knew it. I'm a guy who looks out for number one and works for a price. I'm a survivor. This arrangement isn't a favor you're asking me to do for you without compensation. It's something we both need to survive a little longer, and so I'll make it happen. You can stop carrying on and crying like a little bitch."

"If you try to make a better deal—"

"A better deal than you waiving your rights to interfere with any story or movie I try to sell about our childhood? You think this guy can offer me a deal that will involve more money than the amount reporters and fans will pay after I sell the shit out of our corrupt childhood? Fuck, bro, this con artist really did a number on you if you think he has more money than MGM and the people who love a damn NFL rags-to-riches story. I've already had three reporters hounding me since you made your ESPN debut. Now I get to profit off that shit without you stirring shit up. I'm going to win out over all this drama."

I took a deep breath. God, I hated it when he was right. It was just so much easier to put up with him when he was wrong.

"Then we're done here."

"Finally." Eli sauntered off toward his police vehicle, stuffing the waiver I'd signed into his back pocket.

As he gave me one last cocky smile, I couldn't help but feel grateful that we didn't look alike. Growing up, I'd always hoped I was secretly adopted or stolen during one of my dad's episodes. When I'd looked at Eli's tan skin and his rounded jaw line as a kid, I often dreamed about another family coming to collect me.

As an adult, I was glad I knew he was my brother. It showed me that blood didn't mean anything. Inside and out, we were completely different—I was my own man. No strings attached to my body. I didn't have to be like anyone in my family. I made my choices. I selected my path.

I didn't just have to survive.

I could choose to live.

And who I lived it with.

———

"WHEN YOU GET him on the ground and turn to punch, you need to extend your body. Leave your fist hanging out longer than you normally would. We want people to see. To scream. To worry and point. If you do this like a real fight, we won't be able to see anything and no one will know what's happening," Millie said nervously as we sat in her truck at the stadium.

Just outside our doors, we could hear people grilling burgers, drinking and laughing about the game. The typical tailgate party we usually ran into before entering the locker room. Everyone's joy and happiness behind our glass windows just heightened the serious atmosphere in our car; I felt like I was about to walk back into prison rather than a football stadium.

"Don't forget to instruct Gray in the locker room to make more noise. You guys were too quiet in practice. If the whistle isn't being blown by the refs, you need to make things look bigger," Millie continued.

I felt her pulse jumping as I grabbed her hand, bringing it close to my lips. Her eyes were filled with panic when she stared at our joined hands and then looked into my eyes. I knew her emotions were fueled by the fact that we couldn't run through our routine at the stadium, couldn't practice our jabs, defensive stances, or the left hook that would be the defining punch of the match. I could tell from the concentration on her face that Flash was playing over all the possible ways this could go wrong, rehearsing each step over and over in her head.

I gently brushed my lips over her knuckles.

"We've got this," I murmured. "We've practiced as much as we can. You were awesome. Everyone knows exactly what they're meant to be doing thanks to you."

"If it's not enough . . . if Mr. Waters doesn't believe it—"

"Then we work out a new plan. Together."

"That's how we're going to do things now?"

"Exactly."

HOURS LATER I was exhausted. Playing a shit game was more strenuous than playing a good one. Not that it was difficult to make the game look like a struggle; for the first two quarters, it was as simple as making each pass appear sloppy, acting as if we were treating this game like a scrimmage between friends at a park rather than a game against our rivals surrounded by 50,000 diehard Heron fans.

As soon as I got the ball, I ran straight toward the defensive linemen. I could hear Gray swearing like a sailor, his exaggerated hand gestures letting the hundreds of onlookers know the language he was using on the field. Our growing animosity was told through bad play after bad play. When Gray overthrew the ball, I made sure everyone in the stands felt my displeasure.

Coach Hardy started pacing on the sidelines after the first bungled interception during the first quarter. Seconds away from halftime, you could see his confusion and frustration at the forefront of his thoughts. Spectators looked on with concern and anger masking their features after the tackles came faster than ever before. Some in the stands could no longer remain in their seats—they started rising and pointing at the flaws in our playing.

We were damn lucky that no one was pulling us from the game.

Sure, we'd scored two touchdowns, but our offense looked like it had no rhythm. The hours of practice had paid off.

We were winning, but it wasn't in our usual style, and it wasn't a guarantee at this stage that after we finished this game we would still be thought of as the best team in the state. Thankfully due to Gray's superstar status, they were reacting exactly how we had predicted: waiting us out, hoping against hope that with a harsh talking to in the locker rooms that we would start communicating with one another. Start playing like we knew what the fuck we were doing.

They had no idea that we were more in-sync than during any other game.

However, as we reached halftime, the real game started. I almost wished Flash would get some credit for the show she had orchestrated for the audience.

We staggered our way off the field, giving the other team enough time to get to their bench so when we hit the 45-yard line and the pushing and shoving began, the likelihood of collateral damage was decreased.

"Get back," I yelled loudly when Gray knocked into me as he made his way off the field.

We heard the other offensive linemen move into position and mutter, "No he didn't" and "What's he gonna do, boy?"

I made a quick grab for Gray's helmet that he had yet to remove, just we'd we practiced. The move was slow, allowing enough time for pictures. Then we made it look like I'd thrown him to the ground. It was fast, with a few boys blocking the view of the tussle so no one could see the exact way Gray fell. Three of the offensive linemen immediately threw their helmets around and started pushing me from behind.

The action shot of a single helmet thrown in the air as everyone rushed toward the action was something Marissa worked on perfecting all afternoon.

A couple boys on the bench went to rise, and those who had rehearsed holding them back did so with loud outbursts to "Chill the fuck out."

I caught a glimpse of someone kicking the trash can over, trash flying into the air. I briefly noticed the cheerleaders frozen in shock, covering their mouths with their hands, eyes wide with each new comment made from the defensive linemen. The mess and their distress made me want to smile.

I thought if I were a spectator I would believe the story.

When the boys behind me caught sight of the refs and security guards running toward us, I felt their panic. Then it was as if I was watching everyone move in warp speed.

I knew we'd practiced this very moment, but I still barely had time to blink before the boys were coming in for Gray's defense and were hot on my back.

I briefly thought how they weren't giving me enough space for the fans to see the main punch, the big climactic moment that would end the fight. Until I realized it was my body moving in slow motion. I couldn't seem to get my balance. I tried turning around to catch my teammates' attention. With sweat dripping down their forehead, I could see that they looked as exhausted as I felt, yet they didn't appear to be struggling like I was.

As I turned to approach Gray, it was as if all control of my body was gone.

There was a sharp pain in my head. I felt myself fall forward.

Suddenly everything went black.

MILLIE

REFEREE WHISTLES SEEMED to be sounding from every corner of the stadium. Security was rushing onto the field. Trash was flying around the sidelines. Assistant coaches were pulling players off the field, while Coach Hardy and the offensive coordinator joined the drama.

I cried in the stands, big fat tears running down my face. I kept telling myself it was all part of the plan. My documented breakdown would pull at the heartstrings across the nation.

Except the longer I watched the mess on the field, the harder I was finding it to breathe. The action wasn't looking right. There were too many offensive linemen on the 45-yard line, and their expressions of distress were different from the looks we'd practiced at Gray's house. I noticed they were tired when they started leaving the field and worried that we didn't factor their energy levels into our plan. My anxiety was skyrocketing because a group of them had fallen into a pile, blocking what was happening on the ground.

When the boys on the sidelines dropped their act and grew completely still, I felt the ground beneath my feet begin to shake. My heart stopped.

I watched the referee and coach talking. They were no longer yelling at the players, instead lifting each one up and having them race off for help.

When paramedics ran toward the view being hidden from the spectators—more paramedics than we needed in our original plan—I started to shake.

When both Grayson and Cooper were put on stretchers, my crying stopped.

The act ended.

And the screaming began.

THIRTY

COOPER

MY VISION WAS what came back first.

Blurry colors swirled in front of me. Then the sharp pain of having a bright light shone in each eye. The noise quickly followed: the beeping of heart monitors, the constant chatter between doctors and nurses, the sound of doors opening and closing.

When I tried to raise my head to look at my body, I felt the neck brace. *Oh shit.*

"Sit back, nothing to worry about," the nurse told me from somewhere near my feet. "The brace was just a precaution while you were unconscious," she continued, as if reading my mind.

"What happened—" I tried to ask before the pain in my head exploded.

"You passed out during the game," D explained from the corner of the hospital room. I followed his voice with my eyes and found him alone, languidly spread out in a spare blue chair. Casually chewing on a protein bar, it looked as if he didn't have a care in the world. It was as if we hadn't just played a football game with more on the line than just winning or losing.

"How—" The pressure in my head prevented me from finishing my sentence.

"You were dehydrated," D said as he continued chewing. "Not enough water before or during the game apparently," he told me before winking.

"Water?"

"It might be best to wait a couple of hours before trying to engage the patient in conversation," the nurse scolded D as she finished checking my vitals and finally removed the neck brace. "At least until the IV has done its job and his body is fully recovered."

I saw D put on an apologetic facial expression for the pretty nurse, but I tried again to get answers.

"Was anyone else hur—" I managed before the pain had me giving up.

"Sir, if you like, we can get a doctor to come in. He just left to check on another patient. I can have him come back in a moment and explain to you what happens now that you're awake," the pretty nurse told me. I nodded, then heard her whisper to D. "Does he have family we should call?"

"A doctor would be good, babe, but no need to rush," D told her softly, sitting up properly and smiling at her. "And no family. We don't want to panic them. My boy's awake. I'm just gonna wait here with the fool and teach him shit I thought he already knew about H2O," D replied angelically, turning the charm on thick.

As soon as the girl left the room, smiling coyly at D, he closed the blinds and sat beside me, smiling.

"Dude, that was *epic*. Gray's totally fine, by the way. He's in a room down the hall. Everyone was going crazy when he got here, afraid the superstar had broken his arm or leg. He's got like a mountain of flowers already, but he's still pretending. He's all good. Mostly worried about you. We decided you needed my company more than he did."

"Yay me," I groaned.

"I jumped in the ambulance when you guys were carted off. No way was I missing this shit. After we all got out, Gray told me to listen to the doctor's instructions until Millie gets here. Dude, no one knew what put you on your ass. A few guys were afraid they'd pushed you too hard in the tussle and had actually hurt you."

"Did they accidentally—"

"Nah. Pretty much as soon as they ran your vitals, all the bigwigs in this joint have been bitching about the same shit. Players working out too hard before games, not enough water, yadda yadda yadda. Football's the worst for dehydration no matter the weather, we should all be better at taking care of ourselves or find another sport, bitch bitch bitch. Coach should've known with your history that you might not take the best care of yourself, moan moan moan. No matter what they say, dude, your play was genius. Passing out in front of everyone like that was total blockbuster shit. Although we probably should've practiced your fall. Even I thought you'd broken your neck."

"I didn't plan to pass out on the field," I growled, no longer sure if the pain was in my head or simply sitting beside me.

"Sure, whatever. Either way, we couldn't have planned it better. The medics were yelling about disorientation being a classic sign of dehydration. It's why everyone thinks you were playing like crap and starting fights. Gray said Rissie sent him a message that we got enough photos for people to think it looked like a serious fight. Your pulling Gray by the helmet is already being played on repeat by the media. Trick also texted and let us know that Coach was on a rampage after we left in the ambulance. Apparently the dean was in the stands, then in the locker room. He reamed Coach's ass for not realizing you were playing terrible because you were exhausted. Everyone thinks you were too busy trying to prove yourself to him still that you deserve to keep starting. All the assistant coaches are asking if we've seen you hydrate during practices. If you were tired after starting last game. On the upside, apparently you've now got a nickname: Machine. Totally unstoppable—unless you forget to give it fuel," D chuckled. "It's not as good as the D, but I guess it means they won't be kicking you off the team tomorrow."

When we heard a knock on my door, D hid his wide-ass smile. Expecting the doctor, he opened the door solemnly, his posture hunched and concerned.

Until he was pushed out of the way by a pixie on a warpath.

Lizzie's yellow sundress and combat boots brought both light and destruction into the small sterile room.

"Sorry, guys, fans aren't allowed—" D tried to tell them, mistaking the three people before him for zealous groupies.

Lizzie yelled over him. "Cooper Joseph Daniels, you better not be dead or I'm going to kill you."

"Shit," I muttered under my breath as I took in Lizzie, Beth, and Al standing before me, each with concern in their eyes—although in Lizzie's there was also a ton of anger. "I'm fine," I said gruffly.

"Do you have any fucking idea what you did to us?" Lizzie asked me angrily as she checked my vitals and began poking and prodding my body. "You told me you were just going to do some pushing. Dance moves, you said."

"It looks worse than it was. I'm only here because it turns out I forgot to drink enough water," I tried to explain. When she ignored my statement and instead elbowed my knee, I was no longer feeling the guilt. "Hey!"

"I'm checking that your legs still work. I've given up on your brain. Quit your complaining."

While Lizzie and I glared at each other, little Beth climbed onto the bed and wrapped her arms around my waist. At twelve, she was still tiny for her age. With long black hair and big brown eyes, she could easily be mistaken for a ten-year-old model. When I moved a strand of hair to take in the face I hadn't seen in years, she whispered, "You okay?"

"I'm all good, ladybug. I just forgot to do something pretty important. I was stupid today."

"You're never stupid." She smiled.

"Today I was," I said quietly.

"You can say that again," Lizzie growled as she slumped into the seat D had abandoned, her anger subsiding and a look of utter exhaustion etched into her forehead.

As she closed her eyes, mine moved to the monstrous man in the corner. Always larger than life, his more salt than pepper hair the only difference I could identify since our last meeting in the first weeks of my incarceration.

Al took a hard look at my coloring and ran his calloused hand over his pained face.

"Scared the shit out of us, watching you pass out on the field, boy," he muttered. "The girl drove like a bat out of Hell to get us here so quickly. Confessed to me that you'd called her before the game, told her some stupid plan you had to get your old cellmate off your back. He been taking photos of the girls?"

"Al, I was going to call you—"

"You think because you refuse to let me see you locked up and chose to go to college, I'm not there for you anymore? You better than everyone else now?"

"No. Shit, no. I just thought I could handle it all. Then I spoke with some of the guys from the team. We thought if we could make it look like I'd followed Tony's orders—"

"You got teammates now. Friends," he said as he took in D leaning against the doorjamb. "I'm glad. Been proud watching you run onto that field, even when all you did most of the time was warm the bench. I was worried what path you were going to take after you got out. Stopped worrying when I heard you'd been accepted onto the football team. I figured you'd gotten your priorities straight. The girls and I, we've watched every game since you put on that jersey. Never thought I'd see this though."

With my feelings caught in my throat, I tried to reply. "I'm sorry you guys had to watch—"

"Don't say sorry. I'm aware of what you were trying to do. Wasn't the stupidest idea I've ever heard. But from now on you call me first, before you get yourself in the damn hospital and we're an hour away."

"I didn't plan this shit," I groaned. "I was meant to be standing in the end. I guess with seeing Eli, calling Lizzie, and then practicing, I was a little preoccupied. Didn't think dancing took that much out of me. Didn't think playing like shit was taking that much of my energy until it hit halftime."

"God, you can be painful," Lizzie sighed. "Never taking care of yourself. Everyone else comes first. Almost throwing your life away, for what? Us? Because we would be okay without you? Did you not see what losing Jake did to all of us?"

"Girl's got a point. You're gonna have to get better at taking care of yourself," Al said quietly. "Think you're so indestructible. Stupid mistakes can be life-threatening. Your kidneys and shit can be at risk without water, the doctor told us. Boys from the club, the ones on the inside, they also mentioned you been screwing with your head."

"You don't need to worry. That's stopped. This was an accident," I explained. "I never make the same mistake twice."

"Don't be foolish, boy. Everyone makes the same mistake more than once," Al told me, rolling his eyes. "But the lesson is always different. Pay attention. Learn from the shit you're doing."

"And in case you haven't noticed, your lesson this time is," Lizzie whispered softly as a single tear fell down her cheek, "you matter."

"SHIT, DUDE, AND I thought my family was intense." D, whom I had forgotten was still there, whistled after Al, Lizzie, and Beth headed to the cafeteria.

"They aren't my family," I muttered, staring at the door.

"You got big sister and little sister doting all over you while trying not to cry. Angry dad telling you he's disappointed. Everyone sad about seeing you in a hospital bed and calling you stupid. That says family to me. Did I miss something?"

"They aren't my blood. I have a brother—"

"He on his way too? He gonna be angry that you nearly got yourself hurt? Make you feel like gum stuck on the bottom of his foot?"

"It's unlikely," I grunted.

D just raised an eyebrow, then shrugged.

"Look dude, it's just words. But you're feeling shitty right now because three people put you in your place. No one does that to me except family."

"Fuck, I can't do anymore lessons today," I groaned.

"Well, Machine, I'm gonna leave you to update your software and recharge your batteries," he said, chuckling. "Damn, I'm gonna love this nickname. In any case, I better go check on Gray. He's stuck with Parker and Rissie. All those women fussing over him, he might start to think he's actually hurt."

"I thought you weren't leaving until Millie got here?" I asked him, suddenly feeling that last lesson sink home.

"Yeah about that. Gray messaged while your fam bam were here yelling. She visited him and Parker, but—"

"She's not coming here, is she?"

"Like I said earlier, we totally should've practiced that fall."

THIRTY-ONE

MILLIE

AS SOON AS we arrived at the hospital, I felt unnaturally calm. The nurse at the information desk offered to walk us to the private room Gray was put in due to the media storm, but I let her know that we would take the elevator and follow the signs without a problem. We made our way across the polished concrete floors, and I tightened my grip on Jessie's little palm.

When I started following the ambulance to the hospital, I was just about to pass my street when I realized I couldn't keep going.

I needed to hold on to her.

I needed to feel her heartbeat.

I had to grasp tightly to the one tether I knew would keep me in the world of the sane. I had watched Cooper fall down in front of thousands, and it was like watching the curtains close on the movie I thought I'd been living in. Everything dawned on me then. I needed to go back to my original plan and protect myself. A relationship with Cooper was beautiful and scary and complicated. We were able to create dreams together that stopped us from living with our ghosts. I had become strong enough to deal with his problems and he with mine.

But some things were out of our control. And those things could be *catastrophic*.

If Cooper got hurt, it wouldn't be like Nate. I wasn't whole anymore. If the pieces of me that were already shattered got hammered even more, *there would be nothing left*.

I stared at Jessie's brown curls flying with every twist of her head and remembered how important it was that I didn't lose myself completely.

We exited the elevator on the second floor, passed hospital room doors and the cafeteria. Jessie tried to direct our steps toward the doors with the most noise and activity. This large building with so many hallways and doors to explore was like a carnival maze to her. It wasn't a place of sickness and pain, it was a labyrinth of white walls and red handles with the sound of unusual bells and whistles ringing in the distance. I lifted her and rested her weight on my left hip as I kept moving forward, counting the numbers above each door to find 205B.

When I paused in front of the right door, I was tempted to put Jessie back on her feet and allow her to pull me in another direction. I didn't want to face my fear, afraid I would see Nate sitting in that damn hospital bed. I wanted to be calm and collected. I hung my head, stared at my fancy ankle boots, and reminded myself that I was not in my pink Converse sketchers. I wasn't a kid anymore—I could and would handle this. I reached for the door, turned the handle and opened it to stare at Gray sitting in a hospital bed hugging Parker.

"I'm so sorry—" I began before being knocked to the side by a pushy pixie in a yellow sundress and black combat boots.

"What the fuck?" the stranger exclaimed as she stared at Gray and Parker snuggling on the hospital bed. "Where the hell is Cooper?"

"Liz, you sure we're in the right place?" a mountain man asked from behind. I turned to take in the bulky guy with a long salt-and-pepper beard and black leather vest holding the hand of a gorgeous little girl with long black hair.

"The guards downstairs said they brought the football player to room 205B, Al. They didn't stutter," the blonde replied offhandedly without taking her gaze off my friends.

"Well clearly the boy isn't here, so maybe we should leave these people in peace." He stepped into the room to grab her by the elbow.

"He's in 209B," Gray told them from the bed. "I'm the other football player."

"Okay then" she exclaimed, turning on her heels and leaving as abruptly as she'd entered. I don't think she saw me, or maybe she did and had no idea who I was.

Although I knew who they were from the stories. I took one last look at their fading backs before I turned to stare at Gray.

"Did you want to go with them?" Parker asked me.

"No. I think . . . I think it's best I give him some space," I muttered as I look down at Jessie.

"He's fine," Gray said. "D's with him. He's been texting and telling me that it was just dehydration. It was foolish and dangerous not to drink enough water with all shit considered, but it's almost a lucky break."

"Him passing out, possibly killing himself was a lucky break?" There was steel in my voice.

"Millie, you know what Gray is trying to say," Parker placated.

"Yeah I know. Look, I'm sorry. It's just been a rough day. I'm tired."

"How about you pass over my girl and go get a coffee?" Gray put his hands out for Jessie. "It's been a long-ass day. If you raced home and grabbed this one after all the drama, I doubt you've had a chance to sit down in silence."

"I came to be here with you. I don't really need a drink. I'm also sure after everything you've gone through today, the last thing you need is a two-year-old running wild—"

"Remember it was all an act. It only looks bad, but I'm fine. Parker's here if Jessie wants to get down and run around," Gray said before turning his attention to Jessie. "What do you think, Jessie my girl? Want to play with me, let your mom have a break?"

As soon as she noticed his outstretched hands, Jessie became desperate to get to him. I set the wiggling little girl onto the bed before she could jump out of my arms.

"You sure you're okay with her?" I repeated, staring at all the machines, flowers, and features in the hospital that a two-year-old could destroy in seconds.

"Millie, go get a drink, sit down for a second. We have her," Parker said. "Have a rest. We aren't going anywhere until the doctor clears Gray, Coach Hardy gets here to yell at us, and the media stops scrambling. It'll be awhile."

"Okay." I knew she was right, and if they wanted to have a moment with Jessie, I also understood that feeling. She was a pretty good reminder for why we'd worked so hard to be rid of Gray's dad.

THE COFFEE WASN'T good. The pastries were even worse. Everything tasted two days old, but I kept eating and drinking anyway. It was something to do other than think about going to Cooper. I realized that was Gray and Parker's ploy the moment they pushed me out of the room. Without Jessie to cling to, they knew all I would want to do was see that he was okay. They didn't know that the fear of talking to two ghosts was a big enough deterrent to keep me from room 209B and spend my time in the cafeteria.

The cafeteria wasn't too bad. It was somewhat peaceful because it was mostly empty. Besides a single table of old men playing cards and a woman who appeared to be in her late forties quietly crying into her coffee, the place was devoid of action or drama. I slipped in without notice and decided once I finished my coffee, I would slip out just as silently.

I had almost reached the bottom of my glass when I heard one of the spare chairs at my table move. I looked up from my mug, suddenly face-to-face with Cooper's childhood best friend. Her partially shaved, peroxide-blonde hair and gray eyes scared the shit out of me.

"You're Millie, right?" Lizzie asked abruptly.

"Yes—"

"Great," she exclaimed. "Watch this one, would you. I'm getting myself some of that crap you're drinking. Al's gone to find a bathroom. He'll likely be lost for a good hour. He sucks at directions. Why the man can't read a sign is beyond me. I also can't go another minute without caffeine. You need me, just yell. Beth, sit down."

"Sure," I said, feeling dazed and confused. When she walked away, no doubt to steamroll the coffeemaker into producing the finest quality drink in the entire state, I took a look at the little girl who sat silently beside me. She was stunning, making me think of what a young Cleopatra might've looked like with her long black hair and brown eyes that almost appeared black. She was also royally pissed off.

"I'm twelve," the pretty girl muttered under her breath when she sat down as instructed. "Not nine. I cannot wait until I'm older and taller so people stop bossing me around."

"Don't count on it," I told her between the final sips of my drink. "I was told to come here, and I'm not even sure I wanted to."

"You telling me I'm always going to have to do everything she says?" the little girl moaned.

"I won't lie," I laughed. "It's a strong possibility."

"Okay, I'm back. Sorry I didn't say anything in that other guy's room earlier. Your hair. The kid. Figured out who you were but was in a bit of a rush to see Coop," Lizzie said as she took the chair opposite me.

"Understandable."

"We saw him fall on the TV," Beth murmured. "Didn't look good."

"But we've seen him now. I poked and prodded, Beth cuddled, Al lectured. Al does a good lecture," Lizzie rambled with half a pastry in her mouth. "We all know he's okay if not stupid. I still can't quite believe how he forgot to drink during the game. He ends up in the hospital over water, are you freaking kidding me?" She was gesturing with her food, dropping little crumbs all over the table. "Annoyingly we all know he'll fuck up again. It's Cooper's nature to throw himself in front of buses and forget about the fact that he isn't indestructible. I blame the Batman and Superman comics the group home used to have in all the rooms. At least he's scrapped the shit that was still clinging to him from prison. Can you believe that psycho? And I thought the scum we met growing up were the worst. Who knew? Trust Cooper to find a pretty girl in all this drama though," she laughed.

"Look, I think you have the wrong idea about Cooper and me—" I tried to tell her.

"They filmed you crying," Beth whispered.

"Yes, I know it looked like—"

"You started screaming when Cooper was put on the stretcher," Lizzie pointed out.

"I'm aware of that, which is why I really need to take a step back—"

"Good luck," Al said from behind me. I turned to take in the giant outlaw and watched as he took a seat beside me. "I was gonna take a step back. Found a troubled kid sleeping in my car, gave him to social services. I wasn't good for no one back then. I definitely wasn't father material. I did the right thing, but that boy gets under your skin. There's no shaking it."

"I remember when I first met him at the home and he told me he planned on protecting me," Lizzie laughed. "I tried to get rid of him for months until he punched a kid who tried to slap me on the ass when I was eleven."

"I didn't talk for a month when I met him," Beth whispered. "He didn't leave though. He read me stories about princesses."

When all of them nodded, I tried to pretend their words didn't apply to me. I was more determined than they could obviously imagine, more single-minded than soft-hearted.

"Look, it was really nice meeting you all. You seem like great people. I'm glad Cooper has more than one person to yell at him for not taking care of himself. But I have a daughter I should be getting back to her."

When I left the cafeteria, it was lucky that I didn't see Lizzie's, Beth's, and Al's wide smiles or hear their conversation.

My dramatic exit wouldn't have been the same had I realized they were discussing Thanksgiving and where they were going to find a booster seat for Jessie.

THIRTY-TWO

ANTHONY

I LIKED THE boy. He had vision. Not something that could usually be said about cops. I usually preferred to only deal with the police officers I paid to keep my company, but for Eli, I would make an exception.

I saw something in the boy that reminded me of myself.

Imagination.

"My brother was hurt trying to hurt your boy. It was masterful," the boy praised. "The way you convinced him to attack the captain of the football team on national TV, genius. They'll bounce back, of course. I don't know if you saw the replay, but neither were very good at throwing punches worth a damn. Your son might try and press charges, but I doubt they'll stick. That school cares too much about winning championships to suspend both of them from the team, let alone throw my brother back behind bars. Those boys might be stupider than a fly close to a blue light, but they can run a ball up a field."

"Son, I don't know what you're talking about. I had nothing to do with your brother's actions today. I was shocked by the sight I saw on the television," I feigned ignorance. It didn't matter that Eli had arranged his visit after hours. As far as I was concerned, Eli could pay every guard in the entire prison to leave and I still wouldn't admit to shit.

Confessing to one's actions was for amateurs. The glory was always in the awareness of the victim, never the attention of the audience.

"I'm a cop. I get it. Don't tell me shit. Respect, dude," Eli told me, smiling. "I wasn't here for your confession anyway. I came to discuss the future."

"The future?"

"Whatever you were planning to do next. To my brother. To your son or their families. I want you to kill it. Shut it down."

"Boy, rest assured, I have no such plan," I murmured softly. Too softly.

"Don't bullshit a bullshitter," Eli chuckled. "I'm not trying to deny you your revenge or your comeuppance. I'm here to offer you a different idea. My idea. You don't want in, that's cool, dude, but you'll screw up a good thing for both of us if you play shit differently."

"I'm listening," I replied coolly. I didn't enjoy being made to feel like the student in any arrangement. I taught others lessons, not the other way around.

"Reporters. Talk show hosts. They'll come to the prison and pay your ass to talk. Your son and your ex-cellmate make it to the NFL, they'll give you whatever you want to reveal the secrets you have to the public. If you want them to believe that your mere presence creates athletic superstars, or your dangerous past inspired them to be greater they'll listen. People will read the memoir of Grayson Waters's imprisoned father even if it is complete fiction. Fuck, the interviews, book deals, and television movie deals will set your ass up for life. It'll buy a defense attorney worth a damn," Eli rambled. "I've already been contacted by some eager reporters wanting to sell my brother's rags-to-riches story. I can give you his number. You just need to make a choice. You want to see them punished, or you want to see your ass sitting in a diner outside these goddamn walls?"

"I sit on my ass while my ungrateful boy becomes famous?" My tone was part annoyance and part intrigue.

"You sit on your ass and start writing. Get ready to tell your story. Trust me, if you let your son and my brother make it into the NFL, people will want to listen to everything you say."

It wasn't the future I'd pictured. I preferred a little more drama, a little more suspense and action. However, I could see the benefits of Eli's words, and I did get to see my boy on the ground knowing it was me who put him there. That could be enough for act two. I would have to wait years, no doubt, before my stories would be worth the money I would want to demand, but I'd never had a problem in encouraging suspense.

For act three, I would be outside these walls, my pockets full of cash and sitting in a front row seat.

I liked the sound of that.

As the idea was planted and took root, I nodded Eli. "You're a smart kid."

"You're leaving my brother and his friends alone," he said, smiling. "I'm just repaying the favor."

—

I WAS STILL thinking about my pockets filling with cash when I was led out into the yard the next day.

After Eli had me returned to my cell, I came up with a rough draft of sorts. I decided I would make Nate the villain. Every good story needed a villain. The drug-dealing bartender who entered a world of chaos. I would simply leave out my part in the tragedy. The drugs in Cooper's story would also be absent, deciding the boy's background and anger issues were enough for some interesting side notes.

As I plotted the climactic moment of imparting my wisdom to my cellmate that inspired the boy to become a walk-on and future star, I didn't notice the men from Nevada's biggest MC moving across the yard. My mind was on the outfit I would wear in my first live interview, so I didn't catch on to the circle that had formed around me, blocking my body from prying eyes.

I had decided on an opening line when I felt the knife slice into my kidney.

"This is for Al's boy," the guy holding the knife to my back growled.

I heard the song I would've requested be in my Lifetime movie when

I felt the knife go into my gut.

"This is for Al's girls," the inmate pressed against my belly hissed.

When I felt the knife go into the side of my neck, I no longer thought of my bright future.

As I felt the blood gush from my body, I could only wonder who'd orchestrated this third act.

COOPER

I WAS SITTING in a damn wheelchair because of the hospital's protocol. Apparently they didn't let you walk out the doors even if there was nothing wrong with you anymore.

I grumbled and fussed, but when Lizzie and the nurse clearly weren't budging on the stupid rule, I stayed seated. It didn't hurt that Beth climbed into my lap and started pretending it was a race car when Lizzie began pushing us to the exit.

When we got outside, Lizzie started moving toward the parking lot. I placed my palm on hers and squeezed it to get her to stop, then gestured to the long black limousine parked against the curb. Its sleek paint was a stark contrast beside the cement pavement.

"I'm taking that," I told her. "And you guys are going home without me."

"You're leaving the hospital in a limousine?" Lizzie questioned. "You enter the NFL when I wasn't looking?"

"Funny. No, I'm going to Flash's. Going to pull out the big guns to win her back to me."

"She might need a little more time, Coop. She seemed a little shaken when we ran into her in the cafeteria yesterday. Maybe give the girl a break for a bit, focus on the game and apologizing to your Coach. You can use my car to drive back and forth. Wait until it's been at least twenty-four hours since you sat in a wheelchair to tell your girl you're not in danger anymore." She looked concerned.

"I wouldn't be in the damn wheelchair if you and the nurse hadn't insisted. I'm fine," I hissed. "Liz, I'm serious. I'm not going back with you guys. I'm staying here."

"You're going to keep living in the apartment your asshat cellmate set up?"

"Fuck no. I'm going to live with my girl."

"God, you're cocky," she replied, rolling her eyes. "You think you can go from her not returning your phone calls to living with her, her daughter, and the daughter's grandmother?"

"Yep." I smirked. "I finally have a plan for my future, the plan *I* want, and it's about me getting the girl, fixing a house, and playing ball."

"God, you and your damn plans. Please at least tell me Tom's in the driver seat?" Tom was a limo driver that Al did free maintenance for in exchange for the occasional free ride.

"Yep."

"Fuck. Okay, at least your plans won't send you broke. But before we leave and you go humiliate yourself, I want you to promise me something. Promise me that you won't make up an excuse to avoid Thanksgiving at ours. It's been years, and we all deserve a nice day together. No one from social services will be knocking on our door that day giving us shit about an ex-con being there because no one does that shit on Thanksgiving."

"Done," I replied. "But we'll need a booster seat for Jessie, and a spare spot for her grandmother, Tahnee."

"Al is already on it."

"You never thought I was coming home with you, did you?" I asked.

"I told you I saw the redhead yesterday."

"Yeah. So?"

"She looks like Ariel."

"Who?"

"The mermaid princess," Beth explained. "From the book we used to read."

"Ah. Yeah."

"I knew we didn't have a chance in hell," Lizzie chuckled. "Not when we were competing with a princess."

"So you sent Al to get a booster seat the day after you met her?"

"He said he was sorting out your shit today. For all I know, he's finding you a lifetime supply of water bottles."

"Funny," I muttered.

"Seriously, Coop, we're just excited that you're smiling. Just like you would for us, we're ready to do anything to keep you happy."

"Thanks."

"Wish Jake was here to mock you for how whipped you are right now." Lizzie looked at Beth and me siting in the wheelchair, then at the car I planned to use to get my future back.

"Me too."

THIRTY-THREE

MILLIE

I WAS SITTING on the porch swing, trying to forget about the last twenty-four hours, when I saw the limousine turn around the corner. *Criminals in this neighborhood really need to be a little more covert if people aren't meant to know their occupation. No one living here can afford to ride around in a limousine unless they're obtaining it illegally.*

When it stopped in front of my house and Cooper climbed out of the back seat, all my internal snarky comments vanished.

"What are you doing here in a limo?" I asked, shocked.

"I just want to take you on a ride around the block. Celebrate everyone being safe."

"Yeah right. Look, Cooper, I'm glad you're well and that everyone is all right, but this really isn't a great time for me. You showing up on my doorstep in a fancy car doesn't change that. It just makes things weird."

"Weird," he repeated, laughing. "Babe, have you forgotten all the crazy shit we've been through over the last couple of months? The false starts and insecurities? The con man? The fact that just yesterday, we decided we were going to make plans together to only have you ignore my phone calls today? Flash, me showing up in a limo trying to celebrate the good in life isn't weird. It's a fucking break from the weird."

"You keep feeding and giving water to the driver," I replied, looking quizzically at the man sitting in the front seat eating his lunch during our discussion. "You're pulling sandwiches from a cooler."

"Tom's a family friend, and since I figured it would take you an hour to come out and talk to me, I sweet-talked the nurses to put together a little something for him. I figured it was a good idea to fuel him up before I asked him to take us around town. Turns out you can't have too much water." He winked.

"That's not funny. And that's part of the reason I can't do this any-more. You don't take care of yourself, and while I thought I was ready to sign up to help you figure your shit out because you were helping me work through mine, that game made me realize I can't. It hurts too much to watch you fall, Cooper. I need to be there for my daughter, and I won't be there if I'm breaking down over you getting hurt. If I'm grieving over another man. You made me promise yesterday that I would jump if we were about to crash—for Jessie. This is me keeping my promise."

I saw pain and acceptance settle on his features.

We stood in silence outside my house for what felt like an eternity. "I should be going back inside," I told him. "To my family."

"When I picked up your dreams in the student services building," Cooper stated quietly.

"I'm sorry what?"

"You once told me you became mine when you gave me your name. I wanted you to know that I became yours the moment I held your dreams in my hand."

"Cooper, don't—"

"I wasn't saying that to convince you to get into the car. I've heard you. I get it," he muttered, the pain in his voice slicing me open. "You're right that I made you promise me that you'd be safe, and at the end of the day, babe, if you think that means staying away from me, I want you to. I can't promise you that I won't get hurt. That I won't do something stupid or an accident won't happen. One day you might have to grieve over me.

So I'll let you go, if that's what you want. My life seems chaos free at this moment, but I don't know how long that'll last."

"Thank you," I whispered.

He nodded and I walked inside before I could change my mind.

I FOUND TAHNEE leaning against the wall.

"You're going to teach your daughter to run?" she asked with one eyebrow raised.

"I'm sorry, what?" I asked.

"Your daughter will feel the loss you do. She'll have the same experiences you had. Stories will be told about her dad that she won't be able to relate to. I don't talk about his birthday, but one day she'll find out. It's only natural. She'll picture a life that might've existed without him and it'll hurt her. But she'll look to you. She'll know you went through the same pain and she'll try to follow your example. Are you going to show her that running away and insisting you do it all on your own is the only way to handle the pain of losing someone?"

"That's low," I murmured, my eyes filled with tears.

"I love you. I want what's best for you. And I have watched you grieve for my son and protect my granddaughter above all else for too long. I've let you work at the place to help you feel in control, and I have loved you like the daughter I wish you could've been, hoping that you'd be happier. But you only started being happy the day that boy outside pushed his way into your life and you stopped talking out loud to my dead son whenever you thought I wasn't in the room. I'm going to say this and say this quickly before he drives away. If you think you're helping your daughter by closing yourself off from loving that boy, you're a damned fool."

Mom's right, Pamela. I don't want to come back to you. I want you to be happy.

"I don't know if I could handle this all again," I told both Tahnee and the ghost I saw standing beside her. "The good moments sometimes don't feel like they can compete with how bad I feel when things go wrong."

"Millie, you are the strongest person I know. You can handle anything,"

Tahnee stated. "I won't tell you what to do, even if I wished that boy out there did. I will encourage you to stop talking though. Stop worrying. Get out of your head. Feel, live, and deal with whatever comes at you later because the good can't compete if you don't give it a fighting chance." With those piercing words, she turned her back on me and walked over to where Jessie was playing with her dolls.

With Tahnee's and Nate's words ringing in my ear, I ran back outside to see Cooper's limousine turning around the corner.

I had a good guess as to where he might've been going, so instead of feeling defeated, I ran back inside.

And grabbed my keys.

I WENT TO the park. It was the only place I thought Cooper might go to, to seek refuge following my verbal thrashing.

When I saw Tom eating another sandwich in his car, I exhaled the breath I was holding. I scanned the park, looking for Cooper, when I saw him sitting on our bench.

I started running.

"I screwed up just then," I puffed out when I finally stood before him. "I was wrong. I can't get out of the car. It's too late. I'm in love with you. I want you to help my dreams come true, and I want to help yours. I probably won't stop worrying or freaking out on you. I might change my mind twelve times a day about how I'm going to be able to handle this, but I want to try. I'm shit at making choices, but I really want to choose us."

"What if something happens to me? If I get hurt? You aren't wrong. I can be careless."

"If I can't help prevent it, if I have to deal with something happening to you, then I show my daughter that tragedy happens every day. I teach her that no matter what, you can get through it, and to be grateful for the time you had and make new dreams."

"Flash, you fucking slay me," Cooper murmured, looking into my eyes.

"And you drive me insane on a daily basis."

"How about for the rest of your life?"

"What?"

"Tom's not just a limo driver. He's also an officiant, and I love you. Marry me. Here. Now. Tick off one of your dreams."

"I'm not ready for that dream just yet," I laughed. God, I wanted to be foolish and say yes though. "How about we try for a week without drama and some more family time with my daughter? You need to try living with a two-year-old before you marry into this family. She might not look like me, but my girl is possibly more dramatic than I am and possibly bossier than you are. Simon Says you're going to meet your match."

"Deal. Al already helped put my stuff in the car."

"What?" I asked, my eyes narrowing on his cocky smile.

"I had to give up my fucking apartment due to its connection to Tony anyway. I would love to live with you."

"And you figured I would just invite you to live with me?"

"Babe, it's going to be great. I've already decided to let Jessie decorate my beard every morning, and I'll help Tahnee fix the gutters. I'm free labor, and I think she already loves me."

"You're going to win them both over with bribery?"

"That's the plan. Plus, when I ask you again"—he grabbed my hand and pulled me into his lap—"to marry me in this park, you're going to say yes. And you'll need them to help you do your hair in those curls and find that strapless dress you wanted."

"You remembered what dress I mentioned?" I asked him, leaning closer.

"If I'm going to make your new dreams come true, I have to listen," he murmured softly before kissing me. "And I'm ready to prove to you that I'm the best choice you've ever made."

I said nothing, just grabbed either side of his leather jacket and held on tight.

EPILOGUE

MILLIE

THERE WERE TOO many people in Al's small apartment. It was so lovely that they made room for all of us, but this was lunacy.

"I feel like I should apologize," I said to Cooper as I watched Jessie put her entire hand in a jar of cranberry sauce and start licking it off her palm.

"Babe, they know she's two. We didn't expect perfect table manners at Thanksgiving from her."

"Oh, I'm not talking about Jessie. I'm talking about those two idiots trying to carve the turkey." I gestured to D and Gray, dressed in identical "Kiss the cook" aprons and making a mess of the bird Parker had just pulled out of the oven.

"Al was happy to have everyone who considered themselves your family. Lizzie and Beth almost fainted when they realized you came with seven people."

"I would've gladly left them behind," I muttered.

"They wouldn't have let you," Cooper replied as he noticed Beth and Parker huddled over Beth's science project. "With the team playing tomorrow night, it's actually nice that we can all be together. You're loved by a lot of people, Flash, no escaping it."

"It might be a few less in a moment," I said quietly. "Especially when one of mine takes out one of yours."

"Huh?"

"Lizzie is flirting with danger."

Cooper looked around the room until he spotted Lizzie walking toward D with a soft smile on her lips. "Babe, she could do more damage to him than he could to her. Trust me."

"I'm not worried about D," I told him as my eyes shifted to where Marissa was sitting with Tahnee on the couch, but watching D's and Lizzie's interactions like a hawk.

"I thought they hated each other," Cooper stated, confused.

"Are you serious?" I groaned. "I thought Grayson and Parker were the only ones with their heads buried in the sand. Please not you too. I need an ally, and they clearly need to get their shit sorted."

"Are you going to start rescuing people now?" Cooper laughed. "Did I abdicate my throne when I moved in?"

"You're hilarious." I reached for his hand and squeezed. God, I loved my guy.

"Pwetty man! Pwetty man help me!" Jessie yelled from her booster seat at the table as she tried to reach the barbecue chicken wings that were out of her reach. "Help me."

"My new princess calls," Cooper chuckled as he left to follow the instructions of his new dictator. "I'll be back."

"Pushover," I called after him, laughing when he gave me the finger behind his back.

"Do you think she'll ever call him by his actual name?" Parker asked when she made her way over to me and took in the sight of Cooper following Jessie's every command. Her eyes filled with warmth. "Or do you think that's also something she inherited from her father?"

"I hope it is," I replied. "Do you see how Cooper lights up when she calls him 'pwetty'? It's his favorite thing." I rolled my eyes.

"Look, I know it's not time for presents yet, but Gray and I are going back home to see my dad during the Christmas break, and I wanted to give you something before I left."

"You brought me a gift?" I inquired.

"Well actually, I'm returning something I stole." She blushed, then led me to the front door and reached for a bag she'd left near the coat and umbrella pile. As she pulled out my old pink Converses, I nearly started crying. "I was waiting to give these back to you when I knew you were back to smiling."

"Parker—"

"You don't need to say anything, especially if you're gonna yell at me for pulling these out of your trash. I did get them cleaned, so you don't need to worry about their smell. I just love every part of you, Camille Monroe, and I was waiting for you to work out how strong you were. To realize that you could be your carefree self and a kickass mother. I'm so grateful to Cooper for helping you stop worrying all the time."

"It wasn't only him. All of you have helped me so much."

I stepped forward and hugged her hard, tears flooding my eyes. As we laughed and rocked back and forth, we didn't notice D feeding Lizzie and her thanking him with a quick kiss. We definitely didn't see Marissa get up from the couch, grab her jacket, and storm out the front door.

When we parted, Gray and Cooper—with Jessie on his hip—were both looking at us with concern in their eyes.

Parker and I laughed.

"You okay?" Cooper asked when I walked over to him and kissed my girl's cheek, tasting cranberry sauce. I knew he didn't like seeing me cry.

"I'm more than okay," I replied as I watched everyone slowly make their way toward the dining table to start eating Thanksgiving dinner.

"You sure?" he repeated, always acting as my protector.

"Is my girl happy? I replied as I stared at Jessie smiling up at Cooper.

"Yeah."

"You making it your mission to make me happy?" I queried.

"Definitely. . . ." he responded staring into my eyes. .

"You also ensuring *you're* happy?"

"Flash, I'm living the fairy tale, I can't be anything else."

"Well then I've never been better," I whispered before kissing him and reaching for Jessie.

PLAYLIST

"How to Save a Life"—The Fray
"Congratulations"—Rachel Platten
"No Church in the Wild (feat. Frank Ocean)"—Jay-Z & Kanye West
"Never Forget You"—Mariah Carey
"Bad Blood"—Taylor Swift
"River Lea"—Adele
"Retrograde"—James Blake
"Sea of Love"—Cat Power
"Have a Little Faith in Me"—John Hiatt
"Home"–Gabrielle Aplin
"Words"—Birdy
"Latch (Acoustic)"—Sam Smith
"Hotter Than Hell"—Dra Lipa
"Stranger"—Katie Costello
"Many Rivers to Cross"—Jimmy Cliff
"Don't Let Me Be Misunderstood"—Nina Simone
"I'm with You"—Avril Lavigne
"Medicine"—The Wild Youth
"Even If It Breaks Your Heart"—Eli Young Band
"Too Good at Goodbyes"—Sam Smith
"Stay with Me"—Sam Smith
"Arsonist's Lullaby"—Hozier
"Talking to the Moon"—Bruno Mars

CONNECT WITH MALORIE

If you would like to keep up-to-date with all things #Penmore please
follow me on:
Facebook Author Page:
www.facebook.com/malorieverdant.author/
Instagram:
www.instagram.com/malorieverdant.author/
Goodreads:
www.goodreads.com/author/show/14819550.Malorie_Verdant

ACKNOWLEDGEMENTS

THIS IS AS close to an Oscar acceptance speech as I will ever get and there is no music forcing me to stop typing, so here it is, the long list of people who continue to help my dreams come true.

First and foremost: My family. If they weren't supportive and encouraging, there is no way I would be confident enough to leave my never-ending day job and think it would be a great idea to spend my entire evening writing.

Chantal Fernando, your work ethic, your enthusiasm for romance writing, your encouragement, our sprinting sessions and your words of wisdom are things I'm constantly grateful for.

Stephanie Knowles, you're so busy, states away, and yet you make time to help me. I will never regret taking my clothes off in front of a complete stranger at a romance convention ever again.

Lauren Bille, countless drafts, countless condoms and countless Facebook messages. Thank you so much for being with me from the beginning of this story.

Teneale Zamarini, thank you for not stabbing me every time I told you to "Don't keep reading that version, I've got a new one."

Claire Hielscher, I've always tried to make my family proud of me, not once thinking about how it would feel if my friends were proud of me. Thank you so much for giving me that experience and for supporting me through every step of my writing journey.

Maxime Saltmarsh, I can only hope to be as helpful to you as you have been to me. I absolutely adore you.

Amy, Lorna, Christine and Leeann, thank you for giving up some of your holiday time to help me and my characters.

Rose Tawil your belief in me has humbled and awed me on so many occasions.

Regina Wamba, thank you for my wonderful cover and Yuli! Thank you for putting up with all of my emails.

The team at Hot Tree Editing! It was exciting the first time you helped me, but going into this process knowing how reliable, helpful and enthusiastic you all are to all your authors was a pure blessing.

The amazing girls at Give Me Books Promotions! Thank you for everything you have done to promote Flash!

And Jake, I might have written this book a year earlier if it weren't for you, but my understanding of a man with a plan who would bend over backward for others would not have been nearly as accurate.

Xoxox

www.ingramcontent.com/pod-product-compliance
Lightning Source LLC
Chambersburg PA
CBHW031107260626
47172CB00001B/252